Lost Feather

by

Richard James Dussart Regnier

Cover Design by

Chris Hieb

**Authors' Publishing House
Midland, Texas**

Copyright (©) 2007 by Richard James Dussart Regnier. All rights reserved. Printed in the United States of America. No part of this book may be used or reproduced in any manner, whatsoever, without written permission from the author or publisher, except in the case of brief quotations embodied in critical articles and reviews.

ISBN: 0-9788843-7-X (ISBN – 10)
ISBN: 978-0-9788843-7-6 (ISBN – 13)

For more information, contact:

>Authors' Publishing House
>2908 Shanks Drive
>Midland, Texas 79705

Or visit our website at:

www.authorspublishinghouse.com

Dedication

With a grateful heart, I dedicate this book to my

son, Richard James Regnier, Jr.

Without his help, the printing of this book would

not have been possible.

About The Author

Richard James Dussart Regnier is a coal miner's son and was raised in a small town in Colorado. He is a veteran of World War II and Vietnam, with fifteen years of military service.

He has a bachelor's degree from Southwest Texas State University, and a master's degree from Sul Ross State University, both in Education.

Mr. Regnier has been a teacher, as well as a probation officer, and is retired from both professions. He spends his retirement time as an artist, poet and author.

Lost Feather

CHAPTER I

Jimmy Warrior held his arm up against his body and tightened his right hand around his upper left arm. He needed to stop the flow of blood from a half dozen puncture wounds. His shirt had holes and tears in it, made from the claws of the hawk. Slowly the blood stopped dripping off the ends of his fingers. He made his way around the outside of an old run down building that was once a one-room bunk house for farm laborers. He looked around, then hurried down the gravel lane towards the main road.

His eyes darted back and forth looking for a place to hide. He saw a culvert that ran under the road. His satisfaction quickly faded because he knew he would never make it there without being seen. He left the lane and made his way into the field and over a hill. He stopped at the bottom and looked around.

To his left he saw some tall grass and weeds. He hurried over to them, parting the grass as he moved. His arm movement reopened the wound. He quickly raised his arm to stop the blood flow. The blood loss caused him to grow weaker. He staggered and almost fell. He wouldn't be able to go much farther.

He dropped down in the weeds, exhausted. His breathing was hard and fast. Jimmy put his head down into the dirt when he heard a noise to his left. Fortunately, the weeds where he was lying gave him cover so no one saw him. Shivers ran up his spine when he heard the man he knew as Mr. Lucas, talking to the two teenage boys Jimmy had problems with earlier. They were mad.

"Which way did he go, Brad?" Mr. Lucas asked.

"I thought I saw him head this way, Mr. Lucas," Brad answered.

Lost Feather

"Yeah," Joe replied. "It was easier to trail him when we could follow the drops of blood, but I guess he quit bleeding."

"This is a fine fix you two got me into," Mr. Lucas said. "We've lost the hawk and the boy, and it's all your fault, Joe. Can't you ever do anything right?"

"It's not my fault he's a slippery Indian," Joe replied, getting mad. "I had him locked in that old shed. No one could have gotten out of that place unless he was slippery, and that's what that kid is, slippery. That's what he is, ain't he, Brad? We've tried to get him before, but he always manages to get away. The first day he arrived in town, we tried to chase him out of town. I even hit him in the back with a big rock, but he didn't get the message. Indians never do."

"Aw, shut up, Joe," Brad said, as he hit him on the side of his face, sending him sprawling on the ground. He turned and looked at Mr. Lucas. "Let's find him and finish the job. He'll never show his face around here again after I get through with him today."

Joe got up, slowly rubbing his cheek where he'd been hit. "You're always hitting me, Brad," Joe whined. "What's the matter with you?"

"Shut up, punk," he said, and grabbed him by the shirt and shook him.

"Will you two quit!" Mr. Lucas yelled angrily. "Find that Indian and take it out on him, not each other."

As they talked, they walked past Jimmy and headed toward the road. Jimmy didn't move as long as he heard their voices. Then there was silence. He was about to look around and see where they were when something told him not to move. The minutes passed slowly, almost like hours, as he lay still. Then he heard the man's voice so close to him that he jumped in his skin.

Lost Feather

"He must have made it to the road by now," Mr. Lucas said, looking around. "There's a large storm drain over there that runs under that road. I'd say he's probably in it right now, scared stiff. Spread out and let's go get him."

Gravel crunched under their feet as all three ran down the lane toward the road, leaving Jimmy behind in the tall grass. He breathed easier but knew they wouldn't give up. Slowly he crawled through the grass before he raised his head and looked around. He saw them as they came close to the road. He stood up and ran back in the direction he came from.

"Where can I hide?" he thought as he neared the bunkhouse and slowed down to a walk. His strength was leaving him again. "It has to be a place they'd never think of looking, and I have to find it quick." He kept looking but could not see a good place to hide except in the tall grass, and they would eventually find him there. Then he hurried towards the old bunkhouse. He knew the exact place where they'd never think to look for him.

He moved quickly and was soon back to the place where he was tied up. Painfully he pulled the door open, stepped inside and closed the door. The rope he was tied up with was on the floor behind the chair. He walked over behind the chair, knelt down on the floor, and brushed the rope away with his good hand. He felt around on the floor, and soon his fingers found the metal ring imbedded in the floor. He lifted the ring and pulled the trap door up. That was how he got out of the room after he untied the rope. He remembered one of the legs of the chair got stuck in the metal ring when he tried to get loose.

He made his way down the steps and into the cellar. He reached up with his good hand and closed the trap door. He felt his way around the cellar, remembering there was a

Lost Feather

shelf-like area that was dug out to store canned goods. He found it and sat down. It felt good to sit down and rest, knowing there was no one around. He suddenly felt dizzy. Slowly he lay down on the shelf, rested his head on his hand, and closed his eyes. He thought of what happened to him months earlier. The dampness caused him to start to shiver all over. He finally stopped and relaxed.

It hadn't been long since he was in a damp place just like this one. His mind recalled the jail cell in Newark, New Jersey. It was so clear that he blinked his eyes and sat up to see if it was real. Realizing where he was, he lay back down. He saw nothing in the blackness, so he closed his eyes again. His overnight stay in jail left a picture in his mind he would never forget. He was caught stealing apples one day and was taken to the large police station downtown. It was his first time there, but he already earned a reputation around that town of getting in trouble.

The policeman taught him a lesson by putting him in jail two floors under the police station for 24 hours. There were others in the cells around him and he broke down and cried himself to sleep. He also remembered that his mother came by the next day, and to his disbelief, she refused to have anything to do with him. She told the police to send him to a reform school. His father was in World War II and was now somewhere in a veteran's hospital in Texas, suffering from alcoholism. He needed his father's help but there was no way he could help him. Jimmy was given the option to go live with his grandparents in Mercer, Colorado, or be sent to a reform school.

He didn't want to make any adjustments in his life, but he decided to try the Colorado deal. Jimmy was told he could leave any time he wanted after a six-month trial period, if his mother would agree to let him come back and live with her.

Lost Feather

His grandparents sent the money for his bus ticket and soon he was on a bus heading for Colorado. In Illinois, he let the bus leave without him and he started hitch hiking. He wanted to go and see his dad who was in the Veteran's Hospital in Big Spring, Texas. A highway patrolman picked him up and took him to the next town and put him back on the bus.

So he came from the big city to this small hick town with nothing to do. Life in this small town was a big zero. He did not care for the town or the people. He ran away a couple of times. The second time, he really got in a lot of trouble when he was locked up in a boxcar. If a railroad yard policeman hadn't checked the car, he could have died. That really shook him up, and he gave up trying to run away.

It wasn't long after that that he captured a hawk. He got some books and read how to train hawks. As the days passed, he was drawn closer and closer to the hawk as they worked together. The hawk soon became the center of his life, and unknown to him, it began to fulfill a need he had deep inside to have something of his own to care for.

The hawk turned out to be a trained hunter, and it wasn't long until it was helping supply needed food for the Warrior household and others in town. Jimmy was so proud of his hawk that he started showing her and winning prizes at the falcon shows. This gave him some spending money, plus he could now help with the bills. He named his hawk Lady Samson, because she was big and strong. When the newspapers printed the story of her winning contests, it wasn't long until her previous owner learned he had her and came by and took her away from him. He told Jimmy that her name was Strong Feather. Later, Jimmy combined both names and came up with Strong Feather Lady Samson.

Lost Feather

Red Ross, her previous owner, mistreated her and when she got a chance she got loose and came back to Jimmy and her three babies. His friend Mary helped him catch two of her babies and train them. The three of them became well known at all of the hawk contests around Colorado.

As he lay in that damp, cold cellar he thought about her fondly. In his mind he saw her soaring high above him. Round and round she went until she found the right air currents and then became motionless, riding the gentle wind currents. She watched him to see what he wanted her to do. She was ready to hunt.

He smiled and rolled over on his side, and then quickly bit his tongue to keep from yelling. A sharp pain from the puncture wounds in his left arm ran up into his neck, bringing him back to reality. He realized where he was, and was scared. His body shook as he wondered what would happen next. Again the shaking stopped. He swallowed hard and took a deep breath.

It wasn't long until he realized that he was getting colder. His strength and his body heat were being depleted as he lay there. His shivering returned. He sat up and stared into the darkness. He needed to do something to get warm. He climbed down off the shelf and felt around the cellar with his right hand. He moved his hand back and forth and touched lots of empty jars. Then he touched something, but didn't know what it was. He picked it up, examined it the best he could. It was an empty potato sack.

This find spurred him on. Shortly, he found four more. He worked at putting one inside the other, then pulled them up over his feet and up around his waist. He placed another one on the ledge where he was lying earlier and lay down on it. He picked up the last two and placed one inside the other, then snuggled around under them until

Lost Feather

he was sure he was covered. It took a while but his body slowly stopped shaking and he felt a little better. "The sacks were not much," he thought, "but they helped keep some of the cold out." He would have been in trouble if they hadn't been there.

He tried to remember how he got into such a mess. His mind would not work right, so he put his hands against his head and took a deep breath. His thoughts returned to early that morning when he went out to feed his hawk, Lady Samson.

It was a beautiful day as he stopped in front of the hawk pens. He smiled at the sight before him. The majestic Continental Divide mountains reached high into the deep blue sky. White clouds floated over the tops of their high snow-covered peaks like white fluffy sheep jumping over them in slow motion.

A noise to his left caused him to turn to see what it was. It was Lady Samson moving back and forth from one foot to another. She wanted his attention and she got it. She stopped, stood still and looked at him.

"Well?" he said, smiling, "You wouldn't be jealous of a couple of hundred mountains and clouds would you?"

His talking to her was what she wanted. She moved her head up and down as though she was saying yes. The love of a young lad and his hawk was a sight to behold.

He was so glad to see her sit there and look at him. It was a bright sunny morning, and everything went great for the young fourteen-year-old boy. Pride rose within him as he looked at her. She won another falcon championship the day before at Greeley, Colorado. He watched her move her head back and forth, greeting him. She cocked it to one side, then sat and watched him. People around the small town of Mercer praised him for the way he trained her. It

Lost Feather

wasn't long until she was known as the number one show hawk in the state of Colorado.

He heard the sound of a car coming up their gravel driveway in front of the house. He turned and hurried around the side of the house to see who it was. An old pickup truck with a funny looking camper shell slowly made its way around their circle driveway. The camper shell was made of old plywood that swayed back and forth as the truck moved along towards him. It finally stopped within a few feet of their front porch.

A short, stout man opened the truck door, crawled out and closed the door. He made his way around the truck, stretching as he walked along. Then he saw Jimmy standing by the side of the house and walked over to him, "Hi, Jimmy," he said.

"How does this man know my name?" Jimmy wondered, as he stared at him.

"I'm Emmett Lucas, Jimmy," the man said, sticking out his hand. "I'm a good friend of your dad."

Jimmy's face lit up when he mentioned his dad. "Hello, Mr. Lucas," he replied, taking his hand and shaking it. "What can I do for you?"

"Well, Jimmy," he said, looking at the front door to see if anyone was going to come out. He seemed to be relieved when he realized there might not be anyone there but Jimmy. "I came to see you and your hawk. I've been in the Veteran's Hospital in Texas with your dad, Tommy, for about a year. He got over the shell shock and alcoholism and is working part-time for a local air-conditioning and heating business.

'We were roommates until they let me out last week. You know what? All Tommy did was talk about you and your hawk, and his parents, Jimmy. He asked me to

Lost Feather

stop by and let you know he'll be coming out here to see you as soon as they feel he's ready."

"That's great," Jimmy said, wanting to hear more. "Do you know when that will be?"

"No, I don't, Jimmy," he answered. "But it shouldn't be too much longer. He's doing great and looks good." He frowned and looked at the front door again. "Are Tommy's parents home?"

"No, sir," Jimmy said. "They went to Longmont to do some shopping this morning. They should be back about noon."

"Oh," Mr. Lucas said, smiling. "Sorry I missed them. Maybe I can see them next time. But I would like to see that hawk your dad said you and he hunted with when he came home last month."

"Follow me," Jimmy replied as he turned and headed for the back yard. Mr. Lucas followed, but he was a little heavy and he had short legs, so he almost ran to keep up with Jimmy.

"My dad and I had a good time hunting together last month," Jimmy said. "Dad learned real quick how to hunt with Lady Samson, Mr. Lucas. She's so easy to work with and so smart. She teaches me new things almost every time I go out with her."

They rounded the corner of the house and walked out to the hawk pens in the back yard. Mr. Lucas stood and looked at the three hawks inside the pen. Jimmy didn't say a word. He wanted to see the man's reaction.

Mr. Lucas walked slowly back and forth in front of the two pens. "This has to be Strong Feather Lady Samson," he said, stopping in front of her pen. "She does look a little like a bald eagle, like your dad told me. The other two are fine looking hawks, too, but she's the best I've

Lost Feather

ever seen. I can see why you win so many contests with her, Jimmy"

Jimmy beamed. "That's her, Mr. Lucas," he replied.

"How much did you win with her yesterday at the county fair in Greeley?" Mr. Lucas asked.

"How did he know about that?" Jimmy wondered. "Maybe it was in the morning papers."

"She won the hunting contest, the best in class and the best in show," Jimmy replied, walking up next to Mr. Lucas.

"How much?" he asked again.

"$150.00 total, Mr. Lucas," Jimmy answered with pride. "That's the most she ever won, but it was the largest contest she ever entered.

Mr. Lucas stood and looked at the hawk for some time without saying a word. Then he said, "Are you going to hunt with her today, Jimmy?"

"I was only going to feed her today, Mr. Lucas," he said, looking at her. "She put in a long, hard day yesterday and she deserves a rest."

"Oh, that's too bad," Mr. Lucas replied. "Your dad told me that you would be glad to show me how she hunts if I just came by and asked you. I came out of my way just to see her hunt. But I can see why you wouldn't want her to work today. I'll tell your dad that she was too tired to hunt."

Mr. Lucas let Jimmy think about what he said. Jimmy didn't want to work Lady Samson today, but he didn't want his dad's friend to tell him he wouldn't show him how good she was. He didn't know what to do as he stood there and looked at Lady Samson.

He could take one of the other hawks out and show Mr. Lucas how they worked. "How would it be if I show you how Lady Joan or Lady Gwen hunt?" Jimmy asked, looking at Mr. Lucas. "They're both Lady Samson's babies.

Lost Feather

My friend Mary Wilson and I captured them and taught them to hunt. They're very good."

Mr. Lucas thought about it for a while then said, "I don't think so, Jimmy. I just came by to see Strong Feather Lady Samson hunt. I've been thinking about it all morning long. Your dad painted such a beautiful picture of her hunting that I could hardly wait to see her. Now that I've seen her it really doesn't matter if I see her hunt."

Again, he let Jimmy think about what he said.

It was a tough decision for Jimmy to make. He didn't want to let his dad down, and it seemed he was by not letting Mr. Lucas see Lady Samson hunt.

"Well, Mr. Lucas," Jimmy said. "Lady Samson likes to hunt. I took her out every day last month when we needed meat for food. I'm sure she wouldn't mind hunting for us today and resting tomorrow."

"That would be great, Jimmy," Mr. Lucas said. His face registered the excitement of winning his little game. "I tell you what I'd like to do, Jimmy," he said.

"What's that?" Jimmy asked, getting excited.

"I stopped and talked to a Mr. John Brown when I was coming over here," Mr. Lucas said. "He has a farm a couple miles out of town and he said he has a lot of quail on his farm. Can Lady Samson catch quail?"

"She can catch anything, Mr. Lucas," Jimmy answered proudly.

"Great," he replied.

They walked around to the gate of Lady Samson's pen. "Have you ever hunted with a hawk?" Jimmy asked Mr. Lucas.

"No, Jimmy," he answered. "I've just watched."

Jimmy laughed. "Maybe you'll want to do more than watch after you see her work." He stepped into the pen and put a heavy, leather glove on his left hand, and Lady

Lost Feather

Samson came to his fist at once. He took a hood off a nail on a post near by, placed it over her head, and carried her out of the pen. She sat on his fist like a beautiful falcon stone statue.

"Is it all right with you if we take my truck?" Mr. Lucas asked. "I'm not too good at walking anymore. Lady Samson can ride in the back of my camper shell. I built it myself."

Jimmy remembered how the camper shell looked when he drove up the driveway. "I don't know," he said slowly.

"Oh, it's plenty safe, Jimmy," he replied. "I've got a makeshift perch in the back she can ride on."

"You do?" Jimmy asked.

Mr. Lucas let the question go without answering it. "This is exciting, Jimmy," he said, and headed for the front of the house. "Come on. I can hardly wait to see your hawk hunt for us. This will be a day we'll never forget. You'll see. Come on, Jimmy. We'll need to be back before your grandparents get home from their shopping trip."

Jimmy followed Mr. Lucas around the house and up to the back of his camper shell. Mr. Lucas opened the door of the camper shell and Jimmy looked inside. Sure enough, there was a make shift perch for Lady Samson to stand on. As he placed her on the perch, he took off the leather glove. He placed it next to Lady Samson on the perch and closed the door. Somewhere in the back of Jimmy's mind a question lingered, "Why does Mr. Lucas have a perch in the back of his truck?"

When Jimmy walked around the truck he saw Mr. Lucas coming back from the house. Before he could ask him about the perch, Mr. Lucas said, "I just left Alice and Tom a note, Jimmy. Don't want them to worry about your not being here when they get home. I told them we'd be

Lost Feather

back in a couple hours. That should give us plenty of time to do some hunting if we leave right now."

"How long it takes will depend on how many quail we find," Jimmy replied, and they both laughed.

They got into the truck and Mr. Lucas drove around the driveway, out to the street. He turned at the end of the street onto the highway and headed south away from town. Mr. Lucas talked about everything that he and Jimmy's dad did together. He told him a lot about life in the Veteran's Hospital. Jimmy was so interested in the stories that he didn't pay any attention to how far they went. Mr. Lucas finally turned off the highway and drove down a narrow dirt road that Jimmy never saw before.

It was late summer but the tall grass and weeds were still green and late wildflowers adorned the side of the road. Jimmy barely noticed as Mr. Lucas kept the stories coming as they drove along, turning here and there, not letting on to Jimmy what he was doing. Finally he slowed down and turned off the dirt road. Jimmy turned and frowned as he looked out the windshield of the truck. He never saw this place before.

The truck moved slowly down the narrow dirt lane with lots of weeds on both sides and a shallow irrigation ditch on the right side. An old fallen-apart farmhouse, lay at the end of the lane they drove down. To the left side, he saw a run-down old building still standing. He looked all around to see if there was anything familiar.

"This is the place where Mr. Brown said we can get all the quail we want, Jimmy." He smiled, then looked around. He stopped the truck in front of the fairly large shed and they got out. He opened the door on the camper shell, and Jimmy picked up his glove. He reached in to where Lady Samson was perched and touched the back of her feet. She stepped backwards and upwards onto his fist.

Lost Feather

He talked to her to calm her down. He took out his comb and rubbed her neck feathers. She always got a little nervous when she rode in the back of a truck. But with a few kind words from him and a few strokes of his hand on her head, her fears left and she no longer showed any sign of being nervous. Jimmy looked around to see where Mr. Lucas was. He walked over and stood near the long shed.

Jimmy walked up to him with Lady Samson on his fist. He stopped, then looked at the shed and frowned.

"It used to be the bunk house for the field laborers that worked the fields around here," Mr. Lucas said. Then he smiled as he looked at the hawk. "She sure is a beauty sitting there on your fist, Jimmy."

Jimmy smiled. "She's ready to hunt, Mr. Lucas," he said.

"Let's go get those quail," Mr. Lucas said, making a motion for Jimmy to go in front of him. As he walked by, Mr. Lucas grabbed Lady Samson with both hands. She had never been grabbed while sitting on Jimmy's fist. She held onto the leather glove with her left talon, but the other one pulled free. With her free talon she grabbed at whatever she could so she could stay upright. Her right talon sunk deep into the upper part of Jimmy's left arm.

Jimmy screamed with pain as it tore into his flesh. Mr. Lucas kept trying to pull the hawk free. He pulled with all of his might and pulled the talons loose. Having a hawk that big in his hands startled him. Before he could take advantage of it being loose, she grabbed Jimmy's arm again.

Jimmy screamed as Mr. Lucas started yelling at both Jimmy and the hawk. "Quit yelling and let go of her. She's a dumb bird, Jimmy. Don't she know I won't hurt her?" The more he pulled, the more it tore into Jimmy's arm. Blood now ran down his arm from the holes her talons

Lost Feather

made. Jimmy screamed and fell to the ground. Lady Samson flapped her wings as she held on, and Jimmy yelled louder.

The door to the old building flew open and two young boys ran out, yelling. Jimmy squinted and moaned from the pain. He saw that they were the two guys that he ran into the first day he arrived in Mercer. They were bad news.

"Let me at that punk Indian," Brad Bradley said. He jerked Jimmy up by his shirt and hit him on the side of the head with his fist. Jimmy's moaning turned to deep sobbing, as he rolled back and forth trying to get away from the fist that hit him.

"Let me have my turn," Joe Crow yelled at Brad. He tried to kick Jimmy in the face as Brad raised him up to hit him again.

"Stop that, you two," Mr. Lucas said. "Help me get this hawk off his arm. Then you can do what you want with him. I want this hawk."

Brad stopped his fist in mid air and looked at Mr. Lucas.

Joe reached over and grabbed both of Lady Samson's legs and pulled. The claw that was in Jimmy's arm came loose at the same time the one in his glove did. Surprised at what he did, and having a live hawk in his hands, he held onto the legs of the large flapping hawk. Its wings flapped back and forth hitting him in the face. He turned loose of one of her legs and grabbed at her head. Her head kept moving back and forth, but he finally grabbed her head. The hood that was over her head came off in his hands. Surprised again, his eyes got big, and he just looked at it and let go of her leg. He never saw anything like it before.

Lost Feather

Lady Samson fell to the ground and flapped all over the place. She got up on her feet and hopped along the ground. She flapped her wings and took off. Brad dropped Jimmy and stood with the other two and watched as the hawk flew higher and higher. It wasn't long until she was high above their heads, perfectly still on the wind currents. She was where her master always wanted her to be. Only this time she watched to see what happened to her master, Jimmy.

"You clumsy fool," Mr. Lucas yelled at Joe. "Look what you've done. I ought to knock your head off." He reached for Joe, but Brad pushed him backwards. He lost his balance, stumbled, and fell to the ground. He was sprawled on the ground looking up at Brad.

"I'm the only one that knocks Joe around, Bub," Brad said, looking down at Mr. Lucas. "We've still got this jerk of an Indian. That hawk's not going anywhere without him."

Mr. Lucas started to get up and show Brad who was boss, but stopped short when Brad stepped on his chest and pushed him back to the ground. "Let me up," he yelled. "I'm not going to hurt you."

"I know you're not, Bub," Brad replied. "I've whipped bigger guys than you before breakfast. As long as you know I'm boss around here, we'll get along fine."

Mr. Lucas realized that he fell into their trap and not they into his. Quickly he formed a new plan in his mind for getting the hawk.

"I know that," he said. "You can have the Indian kid, Brad. All I want is that hawk. I'll give you the $50.00 like I told you I would when I have her in the back of my camper shell. Then I'll be on my way."

"You give us the money now," Brad said. "We gave you the plan to get them out here, so pay off."

Lost Feather

"No!" Mr. Lucas said. "Joe let the hawk go. No hawk, no money."

Brad reached down and grabbed him by the shirt and pulled him off the ground. "You want to bet on that, Bub?" he said.

"I'll tell you what I'll do," Mr. Lucas said, with Brad's face next to his. "I'll give you half now and the rest when we catch the hawk. That's the only way I'll do it."

Brad smiled and looked at Joe, then dropped him back on the ground. Mr. Lucas reached into his back pocket and pulled out his billfold. He took out a twenty and a five and held it out to Brad, who grabbed it. He looked over at Joe and saw a smile on his face.

"OK," Brad said. "Get up, old man. Joe, you pick up that kid and take him into the old bunk house and tie him up."

Joe ran over and grabbed Jimmy by the shirt collar and dragged him into the building with Brad right behind him. Mr. Lucas got up and slowly followed along, shaking his head. Joe had Jimmy sitting on a chair when he walked in and was tying him to it with the rope he gave them. Jimmy sat there sobbing most of the time, except when he yelled from pain when Joe tied the rope tight against his punctured left arm.

Brad raised his hand to hit Jimmy again to shut him up, but Mr. Lucas grabbed his arm. "No more of that, kid," he said. "I need to know how he gets that hawk down. Let me talk to him."

Brad shook Lucas' hand off his arm and stepped back. Joe looked at Brad to see what to do. Brad motioned him back and Mr. Lucas knelt down beside Jimmy.

"Jimmy," he said. "Will Strong Feather Lady Samson come down for me?"

Lost Feather

Jimmy sat there sobbing. Mr. Lucas got mad. "If you don't tell me I'll let these two do what they've been wanting to do---beat you up real good. Come on. You tell me right now!"

Jimmy realized he must say something, anything to keep them from hurting him again. "Yes, sir, she will" Jimmy said, between sobs.

"Good," Mr. Lucas said. "I thought she would. Your dad said she hunted for him, but you were with him when she did."

He got up off his knees and motioned for the two boys to follow him outside. When they got outside he closed the door and walked over to his truck. "All we have to do is scare up some of the quail the farmer said were all over this place, and that hawk will come down and we'll have her. Let's go."

"Wait a minute," Brad said. "Joe, you go inside and get that glove laying on the floor by that Indian. I'm not going to go get the hawk without it. Maybe you two are nuts, but I'm not."

Joe ran back inside the shed and they heard Jimmy yell a couple of times. Joe came out laughing. "I had to grab his arm to pull the glove off, didn't I?" he asked, not expecting an answer. Brad laughed at him when he walked up and handed him the leather glove. They got their kicks out of torturing the Indian boy.

Mr. Lucas shook his head again and walked away, looking for quail in the bushes alongside the small dirt lane. He turned around and looked back down the lane that ran up to the old farmhouse that fell down years ago. There were a few piles of old wood and adobe blocks. There wouldn't be any quail in them. He turned around looked across the field and said, "Come on you two. There should be something over there in those bushes."

Lost Feather

The three of them walked up and down the dirt lane trying to flush something out of the bushes and tall grasses, but they couldn't find anything. They looked up and saw that Lady Samson was following them, expecting something to happen.

"It's hard to scare anything up this time of year without a dog," Brad said. "You should have brought that mutt of yours, Joe. She's not much good for anything, but she might have scared up something."

"Yeah," Mr. Lucas said. "It's getting late. It'll start getting dark in another hour. We've got to find something fast. He looked up at the hawk again and saw she drifted off to his left. "She's headed off to the left. Maybe she sees something. Come on. Let's go."

They ran along, trying to stay with the hawk, but soon she was way ahead of them. They stopped, out of wind, as Lady Samson disappeared over a hill. Brad and Joe looked at each other and sat down to catch their breath.

"I sure can't run like I used to, Joe," Brad said, looking at him.

Joe shrugged his shoulders. "My mamma thinks it's the cigarettes that cause it."

"Yeah, I know, my mamma says the same thing, but I think that's silly. How could a cigarette do that?" Brad said.

"Yeah, right," Joe said. "Your mamma is like mine, she has some crazy ideas."

"Shut up about my mamma," Brad said angrily.

Joe leaned back and put up his hands.

Brad smiled and stood up. "Let's have some fun," he said, moving toward the bunkhouse.

Joe grinned, got up and was right behind him.

Mr. Lucas waited a bit, then followed. "I want my money back, Brad," he said.

Lost Feather

"No way, old man," Brad said. "You stay out here and wait for that hawk to come back. We have something we've been waiting to do for a long time. Come on Joe. Let's go have some fun." They ran toward the bunkhouse, laughing. They were tired, but not that tired.

Joe got to the shed first and opened the door. Brad pushed him aside and ran inside. He had it all planned out. He'd grab Jimmy while he was tied in the chair and give him a good beating. For a long time it was something he saw happening in his mind. To his surprise, Jimmy was gone. There was blood all over the place, but the ropes lay on the floor, next to the chair. Brad stood there not believing his eyes as Mr. Lucas came through the door and looked around.

"He's gone. We left him right here!" Brad said, almost crying. He sat there shaking his head and breathing hard.

They looked at each other in disbelief. How could he have gotten away? Joe started walking around the cabin hitting the palm of his hand with his fist. He stopped and listened. "What was that?" he wondered. He didn't hear it again so he peeked out the windows of the shed. Then he looked through the cracks between the boards on the walls. They stopped, looked at each other again, and shook their heads.

Joe thought about the noise he thought he heard and went to the door. He stepped outside just in time to see something disappear over a small hill out in the field. He looked again but saw nothing. He yelled, "I saw something go over that hill. It's probably him!"

Joe ran towards the hill. Brad and Mr. Lucas rushed out and followed Joe. By the time Joe got near the top of the hill he was breathing so hard he couldn't run any more. He slowly walked up to the top and looked around but there

Lost Feather

was nobody in sight. He turned around and saw that Brad and Mr. Lucas also stopped before they got to the top of the small hill. Running took its toll on the three of them.

This was not what Mr. Lucas expected to be doing. His weight and his short legs made it especially hard for him to run uphill. Also, he was flatfooted, so his feet hurt. His dream of having the prize hawk all to himself faded. Even its owner was gone. He had to find Jimmy.

Brad staggered up to where Joe stood. They looked all around.

Mr. Lucas walked up beside them.

Joe bent over and looked all around below but saw no sign of Jimmy.

"I don't see him, Joe," Brad said.

"Me either," Mr. Lucas agreed.

"Are you sure you saw him come this way, Joe?" Brad said, getting mad and starting towards him.

Joe ducked and moved off a ways. He looked around again, then, smiled. "Yeah," he replied. "I saw something." He took a few steps backwards and was glad when he saw Brad stop. He lowered his eyes and looked down at the ground and smiled. "See right there. There's some blood on those weeds over there. That Indian came this way and he's leaving us a trail to follow."

"How about that, Buddy," Brad said, now grinning. He walked over and patted him on the back. "We got him now."

They were excited as they walked through the weeds and looked for more weeds with blood drops on them. There was only one problem--the sun started to set. It would soon be dark.

Lost Feather

CHAPTER II

Jimmy awoke with a start. He first heard someone walking around above him. Then he heard someone talking. He lay there and tried to remember where he was; then it came back to him. The dampness of the cellar filled his nose as he lay there. He hoped it wasn't who he thought it was. Then he heard Mr. Lucas yell at Joe. He froze as he listened to every word.

"I think that slippery Indian came back here," Joe said. "I just feel it in my bones. He found a way out of here that we don't know about. Let's look around and see."

"You're crazy, Joe," Brad said. "I've always said you were crazy and now I know it. Let's go back to town. He's probably home by now, telling everyone what happened. We need to let people know we didn't have anything to do with it. They'll believe us before they'd believe that punk Indian kid."

Joe paid no attention to him as he kept looking at everything in the room. He checked all the boards on the wall plus the two windows. He lowered his head and stuck out his lower lip. That Indian did it again. Then he saw something on the floor. "There it is, Brad," Joe said, and walked over to the table. "Look at that. There's a trap door here in the floor right behind the chair we tied him to. He went down into the cellar and got out that way. I just know he did." He reached down and pulled up the trap door in the floor.

They smiled as they stood there looking down into the dark cellar.

Jimmy slowly got up when he heard Joe say he was going to look around the room. He made his way through the darkness towards the place where he dug out earlier. He

Lost Feather

found the hole in the dark and pulled himself through the opening. When he was halfway through, his left arm scraped along the side of the opening. He put his hand over his mouth to keep from yelling.

He closed his eyes tight and lay still for a couple of seconds. He fought back the pain and tears, shook his head, and quickly pulled on through. He raised himself to his knees and felt better, knowing he made it safely outside. He got to his feet, holding his left arm up against his chest. Slowly, he made his way down the dirt lane he and Mr. Lucas drove up earlier that day. He had to make it to the road and get help. That thought gave him the strength to go on.

Back in the shed, Joe stepped down onto the first step and waited "I need a flashlight, Brad."

I've got one in the truck," Mr. Lucas said, and hurried out to get a flashlight out of his truck glove box. He hurried back in and handed it to Brad, who handed it to Joe.

Joe directed the light into the cellar and carefully went down the steps. He shined it all over the cellar, then stopped. "He's been here, all right," he said, excitement rising in his voice.

He walked over to the dirt shelf. "There's some sacks down here he wrapped himself up in. One of them has blood all over it."

Mr. Lucas and Brad ran out the door and looked around. It was almost dark now and they couldn't see anything. Mr. Lucas hurried out the door over to his truck, and got a large lantern from behind the seat.

Joe ran out and shined his flashlight all around. He ran around to the back of the house, looked in all directions, then ran around to the front of the house.

Lost Feather

Mr. Lucas turned on his lantern and walked around checking out the bushes. Back and forth the light beams went, but there was no sign of Jimmy.

"He's got away again," Joe said, throwing the flashlight on the ground. "I told you he's a slippery one."

"I give up," Mr. Lucas said, turning off his light. He walked over and picked up his flashlight, looked all around, then, went back to his truck. He put the flashlight behind the seat, got in and looked out the windshield as the moon rose in the east. Brad and Joe came over, crawled in beside him, as he started the truck. The three tired troublemakers didn't say a word. Nothing worked out the way they planned. Mr. Lucas turned on the headlights, put the truck in low gear, and gave it the gas. The truck spun around and headed back down the lane toward the main road.

As they sped by, they didn't see Jimmy lying in the irrigation ditch next to the lane, with water covering all of him but his nose. They were mad at the world, especially the two bullies, for not getting their way. All of their grand plans fizzled out, and they felt sorry for themselves.

After the truck lights passed, Jimmy got up and stepped out of the irrigation ditch. He stood with water dripping off his face and watched the truck reach the end of the lane and turn onto the main road. It turned right and was soon nothing but two red taillights growing smaller and smaller. They were gone. He was finally rid of them, he thought, and he gave a big sigh. He stood there in his wet clothes and felt his arm start to bleed again. He decided to try to find a farmhouse and get help. He tried to run down the lane toward the road but stumbled and almost fell. He slowed down, but kept going.

He stopped and looked both ways as he reached the road. There were no lights in sight. He wondered which way he should go. He decided he would head down the

Lost Feather

road in the same direction Mr. Lucas and his pals went. It was a warm day, so it wasn't too cool yet. The moon came up, which helped him to see. But his clothes were wet and he got a chill again. As he made his way along the road, the moonlight got brighter. "Too bad it's not the sun," he thought, "because I need something to get me warm."

He looked out into the field he walked past, and saw some kind of a large mound. He stopped. It was a big haystack. He slowly made his way over to the fence and climbed through.

He walked over and gathered some of the dry hay from the edge of the haystack into a pile. He soon had enough for a bed. Next he gathered some more so he could cover himself. When he had enough, he lay down and pulled the big pile on top of himself. It wasn't long until he was nice and cozy. With his body warming up, he relaxed. Soon the soft sounds of one asleep came from inside the pile of hay.

It started to get light in the east when the pile of hay moved. He sat up and tried to look around. He felt a little dizzy and shook his head. His eyes were almost shut from the beating Brad gave him. He stood up and brushed some hay off his clothes. A sinking feeling came over him. He'd been gone all night and his grandpa and grandma would be worried about him. "Maybe they have a search party out looking for me right now," he thought. Then he realized they didn't know where he was.

He walked over to the fence and climbed through. Up on the road he went in the direction the truck went. He held his arm as he walked. His clothes were now nice and dry and his arm was not bleeding, but he started shivering again. The sleep restored some of his strength, but walking quickly drained it out of him. Up ahead he saw a car appear

Lost Feather

as if from nowhere. He ducked into some weeds beside the road as it got closer and closer. He barely saw what came towards him. When it got close enough for him to see what it was, he breathed a sight of relief. It was a car and not Mr. Lucas' truck.

Jimmy stepped out onto the road as the car got closer. He heard the tires start to skid on the road as the car came to a quick stop. "What are you doing way out here this early in the morning, Jimmy?" a familiar voice asked.

He squinted to see who it was. It was the voice of his friend, Mr. Miller. "At last, someone has found me," Jimmy thought.

"I'm headed over to Mr. Fisher's place, Jimmy, to check on a horse he wants to sell me." He stopped and took a good look at Jimmy. "What happened to you, Jimmy?"

Jimmy could hardly hold back the tears as he told him, "A man named Lucas, that said he was a friend of my dad, brought me out here to an old shack not far from here for Lady Samson to hunt. We came in his old truck with an old plywood camper shell on it. When we got here Brad Bradley and Joe Crow were here waiting for me. They tried to capture Lady Samson, but she got away. They beat me up and then tied me up. When they were trying to catch her, I got away. It's a long story but finally it got dark and they gave up and left."

"That sounds like the truck that almost ran into me as I left town a while ago, "Mr. Miller said. "Get in the car and we'll see if we can catch them."

He turned his car around as fast as he could, and off they went back down the road heading back to town. The car slid around a few corners with Jimmy hanging on with his good hand. Soon they were back on the highway headed

Lost Feather

toward Mercer. They didn't see Lucas' old truck anywhere in sight.

They pulled up in front of Mr. Wilson's garage. Chuck Miller got out and looked inside the office window to see if Mr. Wilson had come to work yet. The place was empty and he walked back and got into his car.

The sun was just coming up, so they sat in the car and watched the shadows slowly move along the ground all around them. They rolled their windows down and enjoyed the cool morning air. No one was around and it was quiet. Then off in the distance they heard the sound of a truck coming. It wasn't long until it came around the corner. It was Mr. Wilson heading for work.

They got out and watched as he drove up and parked his truck beside the garage. He walked over to where they were. He started to smile, then stopped. He stared at Jimmy's face, all black and blue with swollen eyes, and his shirt all bloody and torn. He walked over and took a better look at Jimmy as he held his left arm. He didn't say a word, but turned, hurried over and opened the door to his station. Jimmy and Chuck followed him.

"Mr. Wilson, did you see an old truck this morning with a man driving it and Brad and Joe riding with him?" Jimmy asked.

"No, I didn't," he answered. "I haven't seen Brad and Joe for over a week. What in the world happened to you, Jimmy?" he asked. He didn't wait for an answer as he guided him into the office and pointed at a chair. "Sit down in that chair," he said. He disappeared behind the counter and came up with a first aid kit. He grabbed a pair of scissors off the counter and returned to where Jimmy sat.

He started cutting the sleeve off Jimmy's shirt, but that wasn't fast enough, so he grabbed the sleeve in his hands and tore it up to his shoulder. "Those are bad

Lost Feather

looking, deep wounds, Jimmy, and bad looking scratches," Mr. Wilson said. "I never would have thought that Lady Samson would have ever done anything like that to you."

Jimmy told him how it all happened. When he finished, both men were mad. Mr. Wilson fixed the wounds the best he could, then said, "Chuck, you take Jimmy home. His grandparents will be worried sick about him. Alice can fix Jimmy up a lot better than I can. I want to find out why those two boys and that man did this."

"Are you going to call in the county sheriff, Bill?" Mr. Miller asked.

"No, Chuck," he said. "Being the town marshal, I should be able to handle this."

"OK," Mr. Miller replied. "I'll be back as soon as I take Jimmy home and tell them what happened."

Jimmy was surprised to learn that Mr. Wilson was the town marshal. It would have scared him if he'd known it before, but now he was kind of glad.

When they pulled up in front of the Warrior house, Jimmy's grandma, Alice, came out to meet them. "Did you have a good time over at Mr. Miller's last night?" she asked.

"What?" Chuck said looking at her.

Alice then saw Jimmy's swollen face and bandaged arm. She opened the car door and helped him out of the truck and up the porch steps and into the house. She was too busy taking care of Jimmy's arm to listen to Mr. Miller asking what she meant by what she said. It was as if she couldn't hear a word he said.

Jimmy tried to tell her what happened, but she kept on cleaning out the wounds in his arm, and he did more yelling than talking.

It took her some time to get the deep wounds cleaned out. When she finished bandaging Jimmy's arm,

Lost Feather

she looked at Mr. Miller and said," Calm down, Chuck. I'll tell you what I meant, if you'll tell me what happened."

Chuck nodded and waited for her to start. "Well," she said, yesterday when we got back from shopping I read the note you left on the door saying you and Jimmy were going hunting. You said for us to not worry. So I thought that you two probably came in late last night from hunting and Jimmy spent the night at your place. Don't you remember what you wrote?"

"What?" Chuck and Jimmy said together.

Alice walked over and opened a cabinet drawer and took out a piece of paper. She brought it back and showed it to Mr. Miller. "Here's the note, Chuck," she said. "It has your signature at the bottom."

"That's not my writing, Alice," Chuck said.

"Well, it has Mr. M, signed at the bottom," she said. "You're the only Mr. M I know around here."

Jimmy took the note and looked at it. "I think that's a funny looking "L" Grandma."

She looked at it and said, "Oh, I guess it could be."

Jimmy told her what happened. When he finished, Alice shook her head and looked at Chuck.

He nodded his head. "Bill is going out to talk to those two kids and their parents, Alice. He'll also try and find that Mr. Lucas, but I'd say he has left the area by now. I'll be back later and let you know."

"Thank you, Chuck," Alice said, as she walked him to the door.

Mr. Miller left and she came back to where Jimmy sat. "You need to have something to eat to get your strength back," she said. She hurried around the kitchen and got a big bowl of vegetable soup out of the refrigerator. She put it on the stove to warm, then came over and helped Jimmy

Lost Feather

take his shirt off. She looked at it and folded it up. It would soon be dust rags. Nothing went to waste around her house.

Jimmy forgot all about food; now he realized how hungry he was. He sure felt a lot better when he pushed the empty bowl back and put the spoon inside the bowl.

"You need to go to bed and get some rest, Jimmy," Alice said softly. "Come with me."

Jimmy got up and followed her down the hall to his bedroom. His grandma turned back the covers while he got undressed. He slid in between the soft sheets. It felt good to lie in his bed. Gently, he placed his bandaged arm on top of the covers. Then he remembered. "Grandma," he said, sitting up. "Has Lady Samson come home?"

"She wasn't there a while ago, Jimmy," she said. "I was out back right before you came home and she wasn't there. I thought she was with you."

"She's gone!" Jimmy cried, trying to get up. "I've lost her again, Grandma!"

"No, you haven't, Jimmy," she replied. "She'll never leave you. Lie back down and get some rest. I'll wake you when she returns to her pen."

With those gentle, soothing words, Jimmy felt better. He lay down and his grandma tucked him in. He smiled up at her as his eyes slowly closed, and he soon fell fast asleep.

Alice sat down in the chair next to Jimmy's bed and watched her grandson as she thought about all that happened to him. Yes, his face was puffed up from the beating he'd taken, but he was alive. She breathed a sigh of relief, got up and hurried out of the room and out the back door. She gazed up into the sky and looked in every direction for the hawk. It was nowhere in sight. "Oh Great One, Creator of everything," she said, as if He was standing there beside her, "that grandson of mine needs that hawk.

Lost Feather

This is no time for him to lose the one thing that means so much to him. Have it come home where it belongs. Thank you. Amen."

She went back inside and found her husband in the kitchen. Tom was up and he heard all the commotion in the kitchen, but by the time he got himself dressed, everyone was gone. He sat at the table and looked at her when she came into the room. He wondered what was going on around there this early in the morning.

Alice sat down beside him and told him what happened. He shook his head, got up and headed for the door. "I'll be back later, Alice," he said. "No one can treat that grandson of mine like that and get away with it."

Alice stood up and Tom stopped. "Tom," she said, "it has taken us a long time to gain the friends we have here in Mercer. You know it hasn't been easy. Please don't ruin that in one day. Everything will work out for the best. Let those who can work it out take care of it for us."

Tom knew she was right. "Yes, dear," he said. "I'll just go see what's being done. I won't cause any trouble, but I've got to know. You know that."

Alice nodded her head as Tom went out the door. She sat down at the table and smiled. She also would like to know, but she knew she'd find out later. The two boys that caused the trouble were known troublemakers. They got away with so much because their parents didn't seem to care what they did. They let them do what they wanted, and would cause trouble for anyone who tried to stop them. Maybe Bill Wilson could do something about it this time.

She got up, went back into Jimmy's room and sat back down in the chair next to his bed. She sat there until her grandson woke up. She wanted to be near in case he needed her. Tom brought her a plate of food.

Lost Feather

The day passed slowly and the evening shadows stretched themselves across the yard outside his bedroom window. Alice still stayed by Jimmy's side. Tom looked in again, smiled but said nothing, then gently closed the door.

She got up and turned the desk light on, then went back and sat down next to the bed and waited. In the middle of the night she saw some movement. Jimmy turned over but didn't wake. "His body is starting to fight off the infection. The salve I put on his wounds should take care of that. He'll be fine in the morning," she thought as she closed her eyes. A tear ran down her cheek.

When the morning sunlight crept into the small bedroom, with its soft beams coming through the window of Jimmy's room, Alice was in the chair next to the bed watching her grandson. She would be there when he woke up. They both needed that.

The sun was up a couple hours when Alice saw Jimmy move again. His eyelids fluttered a couple of times; then he opened his eyes and looked around. Alice saw true fear on his face at first. Then, he saw his grandma sitting there beside him. His fear was washed away in an instant when he saw the love in her eyes. Her hand gently brushed some hair out of his eyes and he smiled up at her.

"Good morning, Jimmy," she said. "It's time to get up."

Jimmy sat up and threw the covers back. He got out of bed and started looking around the bedroom for his clothes. He saw them in the corner, and walked over and started to pick them up.

"Not those," Alice said. "Put clean clothes on after you've taken a bath."

"A bath," Jimmy said. "Do I have to?" Then he remembered his arm was hurt and he looked at it. "My arm doesn't hurt, Grandma."

Lost Feather

"I'm glad to hear that," she said. "I put some salve on it last night that will help it heal and should keep it from hurting."

Jimmy moved his arm back and forth until he moved it the wrong way. "Ouch!" he said, putting it back at his side and looking up at her. "It still hurts a little, Grandma."

Alice shook her head at him. "Boys will be boys," she thought to herself. "You still have to take care of it and not hurt it," she scolded him.

"Yes, ma'am," he replied. Then came the usual question again. "Do I have to take a bath?"

"You do," she said, "if you want to stay around here, especially, if you want to eat. You don't want to be dirty when I fix pancakes for your breakfast do you?"

Jimmy rushed out of the room and into the bathroom. She soon heard the water running in the bathtub. "Boys will be boys," she said out loud as she walked down the hall past the bathroom. She wouldn't have it any other way.

Lost Feather

CHAPTER III

After breakfast Jimmy thanked his grandma, got up and went out to the back porch. He sat down on the steps and looked at Lady Samson's empty pen. His heart ached as he remembered Mr. Ross, the tall, lanky man who showed up one morning and claimed the hawk was his. Jimmy told his grandma, "It's not fair." Mr. Ross answered, "She's my hawk, kid." Lady Samson screeched at Mr. Ross until he put the hood over her head. He said, "You've spoiled her rotten, kid. What she needs is a lot of discipline and that's what she's going to get from now on." Jimmy knew that Mr. Ross was mean to her earlier.

After Mr. Ross left, Mary came over and cried when Jimmy told her what happened. Tom and Alice tried to comfort them. Tom reminded him, "You have two of Lady Samson's babies and now you can teach them all you learned from working with her." Actually, they were no longer babies. They sat on their perches and looked at him. They, too, were Grand Hawks. His friend, Mary, trained one of them, Lady Joan, and he trained the other, Lady Gwen. He was happy they were there, but his eyes returned to the empty perch in the other pen.

Jimmy looked up at the majestic Colorado Rocky Mountains. The sky was blue, with a puffy white cloud here and there. As he lowered his eyes, the hill across the small creek behind his grandparents' house caught his eye. Memories flooded his mind.

He was again in his favorite place, on his favorite hill. He loved to lie there with the tall grass all about him. It closed out the world and brought peace like no other place he ever knew. He felt the cool Colorado air as it moved so softly, causing the grass to gently sway back and

Lost Feather

forth like a fan. The gentle breeze flowed over and about him as it moved towards its unknown destination.

That was all it took. He got up from the steps and walked past the hawk pens and headed towards his favorite place. He needed some peace of mind after what he'd been through with Mr. Lucas, Brad and Joe. He smiled as he made his way towards the creek. He walked up next to an old dead tree near the creek bank. It looked like a large white marble post standing there. It was about twelve feet tall. All of its branches were gone and it was a beautiful sight among all of the green trees around it. Reaching out, he touched it as he remembered it was right here that he first saw his hawk, Lady Samson. She caught a large rabbit and was taking flight when another hawk dived at her, trying to take it from her. This attack caused her to fly into the dead tree. She dropped the rabbit and fell to the ground.

Jimmy ran over to where she flapped around on the ground and watched. She hurt her left wing and couldn't fly. Quickly, he took off his shirt and threw it over her. "I caught my own hawk," he thought. He started to pick her up and heard a noise coming from the top of the old dead tree. He walked over next to the dead tree and put his ear up against it. He heard the noises clearer and was sure that it was baby hawk noises.

A couple days later he told his friend Mr. Wilson about his hawk and the babies. Mr. Wilson's daughter, Mary, was there and she got excited and asked if she could go with him to see if there really were babies in the old dead tree. They went to the tree and climbed up into a tree close by. They saw that there were three. They got a ladder and Jimmy climbed up and got two of the largest of the three baby hawks. That gave both of them a hawk of their own to train.

Lost Feather

As he thought about them, he wondered what happened to the other baby and its daddy. He saw them sitting on top of the old dead tree a few times. He walked over and put his ear up against the dead tree and listened. There was no sound. They were gone.

He looked up and searched the sky. Off to the west he saw two hawks circling way up high. One of them dived and went out of sight behind a hill. He smiled, knowing what happened. The other hawk continued circling round and round as it got lower and lower. Then the first hawk came into sight, flew over the hill, and headed in Jimmy's direction. The other joined it. They were headed home.

As they flew closer, he could tell they saw him. They suddenly veered off to the left and headed for some other trees up the creek. As they flew out of sight, Jimmy wondered where they were. It had to be somewhere like this.

He had only been in Mercer, Colorado a few months. As he tried to remember a place where they might have gone, he thought about a large dead tree near the railroad tracks where he hopped the freight train one of the times he tried to run away. The tree was beside a creek.

Jimmy felt good knowing that they had a place to stay. Anyway, this old dead tree belonged to Lady Samson and her two babies.

He patted the tree, then turned and walked towards the creek.

It was late summer as Jimmy walked along heading towards his favorite hillside once again. It was there on this gently rolling hill that he first saw a large falcon hawk circling high above him.

That sight was burned into his memory when he was in the cold, damp jail cell in Newark, New Jersey a

Lost Feather

few months earlier. He cried himself to sleep a couple of times, but the cold woke him each time.

"To be like that great bird," he thought, "would be wonderful." There would be so many places he would go if he could fly. He would love to leave all of his worldly cares below and soar so high that he could hardly be seen. He loved to lie there and daydream about so many things, but now it was not the same. Now he lay and searched the sky like before when Lady Samson's first owner came and took her away. Again he searched the sky for just a glimpse of his hawk.

Deep inside, his heart hurt over the loss of his hawk. The scratches and punctures her claws made on his arm were almost healed. The scabs started to itch and soon would fall off. Scratching them probably helped them to come off quicker. But the wounds in his heart were much deeper. They were not healed, and it seemed nothing helped.

His eyes became heavy and he slowly drifted off. With a slight jerk of his head he opened his eyes and sat halfway up and looked around. He was almost asleep, but he couldn't sleep now. "Not now," he thought. He lay back down and looked up at the beautiful Colorado blue sky. There was no hawk anywhere in sight. Off in the distance he heard a strange roaring sound. It was a sound he never heard before. The strange noise got louder and he could tell it came from behind him. He rolled over and parted the grass in front of him and looked off in the direction the sound came from. It was a flock of birds. As they flew, they suddenly veered off in one direction, then in another. When they did, they made the strange whirring sound he heard. "What a beautiful sight," he thought. Nearer and nearer they came. He turned over as they flew directly over where he lay. They were blackbirds.

Lost Feather

He was amazed at how quickly they all turned together. Then, there was that loud whirring sound again as they turned. They were headed toward the trees that grew along the banks of the Mercer creek at the bottom of the hill. Then, as if someone waved a magic wand, they all seemed to land in the trees at the same time. One moment the trees in front of him were empty and the next they were literally alive with birds everywhere. There, of course, were those that were not satisfied with the branch they were on, so they flew to another branch, or to another tree.

As Jimmy watched the trees quivering with life, the birds started chattering. Some of them flew down to the banks of the creek to get a drink. Then a few more, and then it seemed they all decided to join them. He watched the trees now turn from black back to green. There were always a few in the trees though, keeping a lookout for the others on the ground. Many of those that drank soon returned to the trees and the lookouts then flew down to get their drink. Jimmy noticed that some of the birds had a red mark on both wings. "They're redwing blackbirds," he thought, as he remembered seeing pictures that looked like them in one of the books his dad left for him to read.

Then, there was a great fluttering sound as the blackbirds took off. Again they made the whirring sound as they all turned in unison, flying back over where he lay. This time he quickly turned around to see them better, which caused them to veer off and fly away from him. They were now headed towards the nearest hill. Jimmy jumped to his feet and watched until the last of the birds disappeared. They were gone like they came. Now and then he heard off in the distance the faint whirring sound, then silence.

The silence somehow seemed almost as loud as the chattering of the blackbirds. Jimmy sat down and broke off

Lost Feather

a piece of long stem grass. He put it into his mouth. As he bit into the tender end of the grass, a sweet nectar filled his mouth. It surprised him and he took it out and looked at it. He smiled and put it back in his mouth and continued biting on it. His mind once more raced along as he thought of what happened.

A change in the wind suddenly interrupted his daydreams. It was a cold gust of wind against his face. Summer was not over, but now and then a cool breeze came down off the mountains and across the foothills. People who lived in the area told him they knew that when this happened it wouldn't be long until there would be a change in the weather.

School would soon start in the small town of Mercer, Colorado. He didn't know why, but he started to look forward to school. He found that some of his days were lonely. "Maybe school will help me forget the loss of my hawk," he thought.

He took a deep breath and slowly let it out. The cool breeze that passed by a minute ago changed to a warm gentle breeze. The tall grass gently swayed back and forth about him. He saw how the breeze moved over the tops of the grass in front of him. It then moved down to the creek where the short grass seemed to shiver as the breeze passed by.

He looked at the cottonwood trees along the banks of Mercer creek. Their leaves moved back and forth like they were beckoning him to come and be by their side. He looked closer and saw that a few of the previously dark green leaves were now golden yellow. Soon fall would come and all of the leaves would be a golden yellow. He wondered what the future would bring. He didn't like changes. Changes in his life usually brought sorrow. Sighing, he walked down the hill towards the creek.

Lost Feather

As he reached the creek, a big rabbit jumped out of a clump of bushes on the other side. Jimmy stopped and watched it run off into the field. He smiled as he remembered when he and his hawk, Lady Samson, went hunting. If a rabbit jumped out of the bushes like that one did, she dove down and grabbed it for him. He looked up in the sky from habit, and to his surprise he saw a hawk diving at the rabbit. "Could it be Lady Samson?" he thought. He stood there with his mouth wide open watching in disbelief. Then he knew. There was no doubt in his mind. He yelled as loud as he could. "Lady Samson! Lady Samson! You've come back! You're not lost. You've come home!"

Down the creek bank he ran and across the creek getting his shoes and clothes wet from the water splashing all around him. Then up the other bank he went. He stopped abruptly at the top and watched.

The hawk's dive ended directly above the rabbit as it swooped upward, then downward, catching the rabbit. She hopped along on the ground. She stopped when Jimmy ran up to her. He stopped, then slowly walked up to her and reached down to get the rabbit. Lady Samson released it.

They looked at each other as if to say, "It's good to see you again." Jimmy laid the rabbit down on the ground. He took his handkerchief out of his back pocket and placed it over Lady Samson's eyes. Gently he tied a knot so it wouldn't fall off.

He took his shirt off and wrapped it around his right hand. She stepped onto his hand and he felt her talons come through his shirt and into his fist a little, but nothing like they had into his arm the last time they were together. His left arm was healed, but was still weak, so he didn't want to take a chance on spraining it by lifting her. Inside, he jumped up and down with joy as he looked at her. She was

Lost Feather

so beautiful that it was hard for him to take his eyes off of her.

He picked up the rabbit with his left hand and held it up. It was a good-sized rabbit. They would have rabbit at the Warrior house tonight. He walked as fast as he could back to his grandparents' house. He quickly crossed the creek and made his way through the field until he stood next to the hawk pens. He opened the gate, carried Lady Samson inside, and placed her on her perch.

He put the rabbit down and took the shirt from around his right hand and put it on. He gently rubbed the newly healed wounds on his left arm. "It feels good to have her off my fist," he thought, as he smiled at her. Having her home where she belonged gave him a nice warm feeling inside. He looked down at the new scratches she made in his hand. He knew she did not intentionally scratch him. She loved him too much to want to hurt him.

Lady Joan and Lady Gwen in the next pen flapped their wings to get his attention. There was excitement in the air as he removed the handkerchief from Lady Samson's eyes. When she saw where she was she spread her wings out to their fullest and looked at Jimmy. She was glad to be home, and had a grand way of showing it.

Jimmy hurried out the gate, closed it, latched it, and ran into the house. His grandma was in the kitchen fixing something to eat for dinner when he came running in. "She's back, Grandma!" he yelled, running over to her and giving her a big hug. "She's back! Lady Samson's back!"

Alice dropped the knife she was holding and hugged him. "I knew she would come back, Jimmy," she said. "I told you she wouldn't stay away too long. No matter what happens, that hawk will find its way back to you. She loves you, I think, just about as much as you love her."

Lost Feather

"Where's Grandpa?" he asked.

"He's over at Mr. Wilson's garage, Jimmy," she replied. "He's watching the filling station while the Wilson's go to Denver to get Mary. I was going to tell you when you came in for lunch that Mary would be home today. That makes two good things that happened to you today."

That was good news. Mary was away for two weeks. He sure missed her going hunting with him. When Lady Samson didn't return he quit taking the two younger hawks out to hunt. Now that Mary was back, they all would get some hunting time in. Jimmy could hardly wait to see her.

"Do you know when they'll be back, Grandma?" he asked.

"You eat your dinner, Jimmy," she said, "and then go down and sit on the bridge on the Denver highway. You won't have to wait too long."

He sat down at the table and ate two sandwiches and drank a glass of milk. Then out the door he ran, yelling, "See you later, Grandma," over his shoulder.

Down their driveway he ran, and up the street to the highway. He stopped and looked down the road into town. Mr. Wilson's garage was up the street on the corner. He could see his truck parked next to the garage, but their car was not there. Turning right, Jimmy walked down the highway to the bridge that crossed Mercer Creek. He walked onto the bridge, stopped in the center, and leaned over the railing. There wasn't much water in the creek this time of year. He stepped back, then picked up some rocks off the ground. He climbed up onto the bridge railing, sat down and began throwing one rock at a time into the creek. The water made a good splash as the rocks hit, making a thumping kind of sound.

Lost Feather

The sound caused a small frog to jump into the water up the creek a few feet. The splashing water caused all kinds of water spiders to scurry along the top of the water trying to find a new hiding place.

Then a dragonfly came skimming along the top of the water, darting here and there looking for something to eat. Jimmy now had a target to throw at, but try as he might, he didn't even come close to hitting the dragonfly. A little put out at his bad aim, he jumped off the bridge railing and walked back along the side of the road, looking back at the small town of Mercer. A horn sounded behind him. It startled him, and he jumped off the road into the bar ditch. He whirled around and looked up the road. It was Mr. Wilson with his family, headed his way. He looked at the back seat to see if Mary was with them. She was.

The car slowed down and stopped next to where he stood. "Didn't mean to scare you like that, Jimmy," Mr. Wilson said, laughing. Mary and her mother, Helen, were also laughing. Jimmy found a grin creeping across his face. He realized what he must have looked like to them when he jumped off the road. "Just wanted to say hello and let you know Mary is back."

"That's great," Jimmy said, smiling at Mary. "Lady Samson is back. She showed up while I was out on the hill behind our place about an hour ago."

"That is good news, Jimmy," Mr. Wilson said. "Hop in and we'll drive up to the garage. Your grandpa is there and I've got something good to tell both of you."

Jimmy climbed into the back with Mary. Mr. Wilson put the car in gear and drove into Mercer. He pulled up in front of his garage and parked. He got out and met Tom coming out of the filling station office.

Lost Feather

"Hello there," Tom said. Then looking surprised he said, "Well, look who's here. Hello, Jimmy. Didn't know you'd gone to Denver, too."

"I didn't, Grandpa," he said. "They picked me up by the bridge."

"I know," Tom said laughing. "I saw you walking down the road toward the bridge a while ago. I figured you just couldn't wait to see Mary." They all laughed. Jimmy's face turned red. "Well-l-l, I couldn't wait to tell Mary my good news," he said.

They all smiled as they walked into the office. Mr. Wilson took a piece of paper out of his pocket and opened it up. "Got a telegram here from Big Spring, Texas, Tom," he said, looking at Tom, then Jimmy. "Jimmy just told me that his hawk, Lady Samson, returned."

Tom looked at Jimmy to see if it was true. Jimmy nodded as a big smile spread across his face. Tom turned and looked at Bill.

"That's a lot of good news at one time, Bill," Tom said.

"It sure is," he replied. "I stopped at the Denver police department on my way to pick up Mary this morning. They had this telegram they received this morning from the Veterans Administration. It is about that Mr. Lucas that Jimmy had trouble with. It seems he left without permission and they were looking for him.

"Seems that he went back to Texas from here and was picked up near Lubbock. They took him back to the hospital in Big Spring.

"I then found out that he had also been in the Korean War like your dad, Jimmy. He was sent to the hospital because of what they call shell shock. He has problems. Thinking he could make a lot of money from stealing your hawk was not normal thinking. Everyone

Lost Feather

around here, of course, knows her, and even your dad saw you and Lady Samson in a sports magazine."

Bill stopped and thought a minute, then continued. "I found out yesterday morning that Brad and Joe are working up in Wyoming. It seems they left town the morning I went over to check on them. Their parents told me they left the day before, which we know was not true. Anyway, it looks like everything is working itself out. Mr. Lucas is back where he belongs. Brad and Joe will walk real lightly around here from now on. We can't prove anything, but they know that I know. It's Jimmy's word against theirs, Tom, and you know what that means."

Tom thought about what Bill said. "Yes, I know," he said sadly. "But it looks like everything is working out fine, Bill. Jimmy has his hawk back. What more could we ask?"

Bill put the paper back in his shirt pocket and said no more about it. "How about a Nesbitt orange, Jimmy?" he asked.

"Yes, sir," Jimmy replied. "I sure would like one right now."

Bill went over and opened up the pop cooler and took out two Nesbitt Orange drinks. "The rest of you can get what you want," he said. "Jimmy and I are going to enjoy our favorite bottle of pop, Nesbitt Orange."

After they enjoyed their favorite bottle of pop, Mary nodded at Jimmy and walked out the door. He placed his empty bottle in the bottle rack and followed her outside.

"Tell me everything that happened to you, Jimmy," she said excitedly. "My daddy told me you had an exciting adventure right after I left. I sure wish I'd been here to help you. Tell me all about it."

Her excitement rubbed off on him and he started telling her how everything happened, as if it was one big

Lost Feather

adventure. It felt good to be able to tell someone everything that happened, in detail, and how he felt about it now.

When he finished she grabbed his arm and hugged it. Jimmy let out an "ouch" and she let go.

"I'm sorry," she said.

"That's O.K.," he said. "It's still a little tender."

He opened his shirt and pulled it down so she could see where the claws had gone in. "The scabs from the scratches are all gone, and the holes where her claws went in are almost healed now. It feels a lot better, and they don't bother me unless I hit them, or someone grabs hold of my arm."

"I'm really sorry, Jimmy," she said. She really did feel bad about what she did.

"That's O.K., Mary," he replied. "You didn't know." He pulled his shirt back on and buttoned it up.

"That will be something you'll always remember." Mary said. "I still wish I'd been here to help."

"Mary," Helen called.

"Yes, Mother," she replied. She walked back inside the office.

"We have to go on home and put your things up," she said. "We'll go on by ourselves and leave the men here. They don't need us hanging around in their way." Mary really wasn't ready to leave, but she said nothing.

They went out and got into the car. As they drove off, Mary waved at Jimmy. "I'll see you later," she said.

"O.K.," Jimmy yelled, as he waved back.

"I'm going home, Grandpa," Jimmy said. Then he looked at Mr. Wilson. "Thanks, Mr. Wilson, for telling me about Mr. Lucas being back in the hospital in Texas. I'm going to write my dad and tell him what happened."

Lost Feather

"You're welcome, Jimmy," he replied. "I'm glad it worked out like it did. I think it's a good idea to write your dad."

"I'll see you at home later, Jimmy," Tom said. Jimmy nodded at his grandpa and walked out of the office.

A slight part of that breeze he felt earlier on the hill behind the house, met him as he walked down the road towards his grandparents' house. He looked up at the nearby hills that lay off in the distance. Rolling foothills stretched up to the massive mountains above. The majesty of the Rocky Mountain range stretched across the western horizon. Their high peaks were covered with snow. During the summer most of the snow melted and left many of the peaks bare. But these cool winds were letting everyone know what could not be seen. It was letting all know that snow was in the higher parts of the mountains. Even though it could not be seen, it was saying, "Ready or not, I'm here."

Jimmy's good friend, Mr. Miller, told him some great stories about the mountains when he first came to Mercer. Chuck Miller owned a farm just outside of town. He let Jimmy and Mary Wilson train Lady Samson to catch the pigeons in the loft of his barn. Jimmy loved to sit and listen to him tell story after story of the great hunts he was on during his lifetime.

Jimmy sauntered along and thought how he came to love his grandparents and their friends. His eyes wandered back and forth over the mountain peaks. He then realized he was standing still. He looked around and was glad no one saw him standing in the middle of the road. He didn't want people to think he was losing his mind.

He felt the cool breeze again and his eyes traveled once again to the top of the mountains that lay beyond his grandparents' house. He smiled, then walked toward the

Lost Feather

house. His grandma was right when she told him that something else good would happen to him today. Knowing that Mr. Lucas, Brad, and Joe were not around Mercer did make him feel a lot better.

"What will be the next good thing to happen to me?" Jimmy wondered, as he went up the steps to the porch and into the house.

"Hello, Grandma," he said, as he walked into the kitchen. "Got any of those good oatmeal cookies with raisins in them, Grandma?"

"You know I do," Alice said, laughing at her grandson.

"Great!" he said. He smiled real big and headed for the table. Something else good just happened.

After four cookies and a glass of milk Jimmy thanked his grandma for them. "I think I'll go to my room and rest, Grandma," he said.

"That's a good idea," she said. "You go on and I'll call you when supper is ready."

He went to his room, took his shoes off and lay down. It sure felt good. He was tired. As he lay there, his mind traveled over the events of the last couple of days. He closed his eyes and started to drift off to sleep when there was a tapping on his door.

The door opened and his grandpa looked in. "Are you asleep, Jimmy?" he asked.

"No, Grandpa. I was close though," Jimmy said, opening his eyes wide.

"Good. I want to talk to you and I think this is a good time to do that."

"OK," he said rolling over and sitting up on the edge of the bed. "I'd like that."

Tom came in with one arm behind his back. He walked over to Jimmy, looked down at him and smiled.

Lost Feather

"I've been thinking about this for some time and I believe this is the right time. There is a custom in our tribe that young men who do certain things that show bravery, compassion, kindness, certain honorable skills, love for others, stamina, and other good things in his life are rewarded. These awards are not to make one feel they are better than others, they are just a way that the tribe says thanks."

Jimmy's grandpa had his attention.

Tom brought out from behind him a piece of wood that he had carved the words 'Jimmy Warrior' on, and had stained it brown. It was about two inches wide, twelve inches long, and flat on the bottom. It was carved like a half circle where the sides were three inches tall with the center four inches. In the top there were ten small holes.

He handed it to Jimmy, and said, "I carved this out of a 2 X 4 piece of wood while I was taking care of Mr. Wilson's garage. I also used his drill press out in his shop to drill the holes."

Jimmy looked at it and smiled. "Thanks, Grandpa," he said looking up at him. Tom knew what he was thinking.

"Let me show you how it is used, Jimmy." He took it and placed it on his desk and turned it so they could see it. He reached into his shirt pocket and brought out a beautiful white feather. It was about eight inches long. He stuck the quill of the feather into the center hole of the piece of wood.

He turned it so that the width faced them, and then sat down next to his grandson. "I've been looking for that feather all day. Chuck Miller came by the station and I asked him if he knew where I could find one. He said he had some nice ones and I could have one. So there it is, your first feather. I told you that you earned the tribal name of Strong Feather. That is now your Indian name."

Lost Feather

"This feather is just an award for showing your love for those about you. Even though there have been many dark days, you have come through them well. You have changed and I'm proud of you."

"I couldn't have done it without you and Grandma," Jimmy said, and hugged him.

Tom didn't say a word for a while as he enjoyed the love that flowed between him and his grandson. He hugged him and then pulled back and gave him a real serious look. "Oh, yes," he said, "your grandma said to come eat."

They both laughed as they got up. Fun was fun, but eating was the best. Especially Alice's cooking.

# Lost Feather

CHAPTER IV

Slowly, Jimmy rolled over in bed the next morning and opened one eye. He saw a dimly lit wall, so he rolled back over and looked toward the window to see if the sun was up. To his surprise, it was still dark outside. He lay there and listened, trying to determine if some noise awakened him. There was nothing but silence all about him. There was usually a bird singing or his grandmother making noise in the kitchen. But all he heard was his heart beating slowly in his inner ears.

He rolled back over again, and pulled the covers up over his head. The covers were nice and warm to his touch. The satin along the top edge of the cover was his favorite part of the blanket. He lay there rubbing his cheek against it as he drifted off to sleep. Then he heard a noise. This time he knew it wasn't his imagination. He got out of bed and went over to his door. He put his ear up against the door and listened. There it was again. He heard someone talking softly. Then he heard noises in the hall, and before he could step back from the door there was a loud knock. He grabbed hold of his ear. It sounded like someone beating a drum next to his ear.

He kept his hand over his ear as he ran back to the bed. Again, someone knocked. He quickly climbed back in bed and said, "Yes," as if he just woke up.

The door opened and his grandpa came into the room. He walked over to the bed and sat down. "Good morning, Jimmy," he said, shaking him gently. "I need you to help me today. I need to haul a couple loads of railroad ties. Mr. Wilson told me he saw some yesterday when he came back from Denver. I have a feeling that they won't be there very long. Winter is coming early this year and it will be here before we know it. We'll need to store up as much

Lost Feather

firewood as we can before it gets real cold. I'm sorry I didn't say anything to you about this yesterday. But I talked it over with your grandma last night, and we decided we'd better go get them while they're there. I'd like for you to help me. Can you do that?"

Jimmy's ear stopped ringing. "Yes sir," he said.

"Good," his grandpa said, and he stood up. "Your grandma is fixing us a lunch to take with us. Wear your old shoes and clothes. Breakfast will be ready in a few minutes." He walked over to the door and opened it. He then looked back at Jimmy. "Sure am glad you're here to give me a hand, Jimmy," he said, and gently closed the door as he went out.

Jimmy quickly got dressed, then hurried into the bathroom and cleaned up for breakfast. He walked into the kitchen and found a plate of biscuits and eggs waiting for him. Honey was being poured over some butter and beaten together until it was nice and creamy. His grandmother poured his milk as he sat down. Tom said the blessing for the food. The food seemed to taste better when his grandparents asked the blessing. Jimmy looked around the table and remembered when it wasn't too long ago that there wasn't much food on the table. There was always enough, but that was all. He picked up his glass of milk and took a big swallow. It tasted so good.

Next he tried the biscuits. He opened one around the middle and placed the bottom half on his plate. Scooping up some of the butter and honey with his spoon he poured it onto the biscuit. Some ran down his fingers and dripped on his plate. He licked off the excess from his fingers and then ate the biscuit. Smiling at his grandpa, he picked up another biscuit, repeated the previous process, and it too disappeared. Next came the eggs and they tasted just as good.

Lost Feather

When the food was all gone he sat back in his chair and drank the rest of his milk. It tasted so good. He thought about his mom's cooking. "She was the best cook in the world," he thought. He caught himself as he drifted off in a daydream about her and smiled as he looked across the table at his grandparents.

The three of them looked at each other. "Grandma," Tom said, looking at his wife, Alice, "that was some fine eating. Jimmy and I would like to thank you for it."

He walked over to the counter beside the refrigerator and picked up the two sack lunches Alice fixed for them. "If our lunches are close to being as good as this breakfast, we'll probably eat the sack along with all that's in it."

Alice smiled, knowing her husband kidded with her. She didn't answer him but got up and poured a half glass of milk for Jimmy. "I'm giving you a little more than you usually get, Jimmy," she said, and sat back down. "You'll be working hard today, so you'll need extra food and drinks."

"Thanks, Grandma," he said.

Tom got up and looked at his grandson. Jimmy finished his milk and put the glass on the table. "Let's go get those railroad ties, Jimmy." He looked at Alice. "I don't know exactly when we'll be back, but with Jimmy helping me it should be early this afternoon."

He walked over to Alice and kissed her on the cheek. They loved each other and it showed. Jimmy got up and hugged his grandma, then headed for the front door. Tom smiled and winked at Alice, then turned and followed his grandson.

The pickup was parked in the garage. Jimmy waited beside the garage as his grandpa went inside and got into the truck. It started with a slight touch of the starter button.

53

Lost Feather

Mr. Wilson saw to it that their truck engine was always in good shape.

Tom turned on the lights, backed the truck out of the garage, and stopped. Jimmy got in and they waved at Alice. They drove off, headed down their lane, and out onto the road. They came to the highway a block away, turned right, and headed up the road in the direction of Denver. Daylight was beginning to show in the eastern sky. They were happy it was going to be a beautiful day.

The bridge Jimmy played on the day before came into view. The headlights of the truck and the light from the new dawning day gave it a strange glow as they passed over it. Jimmy tried to see the water in the creek, but it was still a little too dark.

As they drove along, Jimmy suddenly realized the right rear fender that always made a lot of noise was now quiet. "What's the matter with the right rear fender, Grandpa?" Jimmy asked.

"Nothing, Jimmy," he said, looking in the rear view mirror on Jimmy's side of the truck. Then, he realized what Jimmy was talking about. "Oh, you mean the rattling noise it used to make. Mr. Wilson and I worked on it a couple of days ago. We welded a piece of round steel behind the crack in the fender. It seems to be working just fine, doesn't it? Just think, we could have done that a long time ago and not had to put up with all that noise," he said. Jimmy agreed and they both laughed.

As they rode along, Jimmy laughed at some of the stories his grandfather told him about his childhood on an Indian reservation. They enjoyed just being together. Some stories were sad. Growing up Indian was not always a good experience.

The light in the east grew brighter as they drove along. Everything outside took on a nice rosy glow. He saw

Lost Feather

a few sunrises since he'd been here but this one was different. There was a nice warm feeling deep inside of him. Nothing was said as he watched the tip of the sun come up over the horizon.

Rays of different kinds of light now filled the sky. Larger and larger the sun grew as he watched. A slight haze on the ground caused the brilliance of the sun to look like a big orange. Then in an instant the haze was gone and the light became too bright for him to look at.

"Don't look directly at the sun, Jimmy," his grandfather said, looking over at him. "It can damage your eyes, and once they're damaged they seldom ever get well again."

Tom reached down on the dashboard and turned the truck lights off. Morning was there. Up ahead, Jimmy saw the railroad crossing. He remembered the train that parked there the night he ran away. He recalled how he crawled aboard one of the boxcars and went to sleep. When he woke up the next morning he found himself locked in the boxcar.

It wasn't until two days later that a railroad officer in Colorado Springs, Colorado, found him when he checked all the boxcars. The officer looked at him in disbelief. He asked Jimmy over and over what in the world he was doing in a locked boxcar. Later the railroad officer called his grandparents and told them one of the local police officers would take him to Denver, where they could find him. When they picked him up, he told them he made a vow that if he ever got out of that boxcar he would never run away again.

They drove over the crossing and down the road. Jimmy looked at his grandfather and asked, "Where are these railroad ties located, Grandpa?"

Lost Feather

"They're a little farther down the road, Jimmy," he said. "The railroad tracks run along the side of this road for a couple of miles. All we have to do is keep our eyes open now. The ties have been taken out of the railroad bed and laid alongside the tracks."

"How come they take them out?" Jimmy asked, as he started looking for the railroad ties.

Tom was looking, too. He slowed the truck down to a lower speed. "They have to take out the ties when they get old. If they didn't, the train might have an accident. They hire men who go up and down the tracks on a little railroad car called a putt-putt."

Tom slowed down even more. "They're always going up and down the tracks looking for bad ties. Men that work on what's called the extra gang do the work. They go out and remove the bad railroad ties that the man on the putt-putt marked. Then they replace the bad ties with good ones, putting new spikes in the tie to hold it in place under the iron tracks. When that's done, the men smooth out the gravel along both sides of the tracks so it will look nice and neat. That's their job."

"You can tell by the ties you sawed up for firewood that some of the ties are in fair shape, while others are in real bad shape. I've worked the extra gang a few times, Jimmy. They don't mind if someone gets the old ties to use for firewood. In fact, it keeps them from having to pay someone to come pick them up and haul them off."

Jimmy looked down the tracks and saw a railroad tie lying beside the tracks.

"There's one, Grandpa," he said, pointing.

"You have sharp eyes, Jimmy," Tom replied. "Just like your hawks."

They both laughed. Hawks were known for having sharp eyes. Tom pulled off the road and stopped the truck.

Lost Feather

They got out and walked across a grassy area between the road and the railroad tracks. His grandpa stopped and kicked the ground now and then. He then stopped and stomped on it. "I want to make sure I can drive the truck on it, Jimmy. It hasn't rained for some time and the ground is good and hard."

They walked across the field and came to the barbed wire fence that ran along-side the tracks. They walked up to it and stopped. Jimmy looked at it and frowned.

"What kind of a fence is this, Grandpa?" Jimmy asked. "It only has three wires nailed to each wood post with sharp things on them."

"This is a barbed wire fence, Jimmy. This one here marks the boundary line of what's called the railroad's right of away. That means the Railroad Company owns all the land on this side of the tracks and also on the other side, even though there is no fence over there," Tom said, pointing.

"In the early days, when the railroads were being built across this country out here in the west, there were lots of animals that roamed this area. There were large herds of buffalo, and later on when the farmers came out here there were lots of cattle. The trains were stopped a lot of times due to large herds being on the tracks. So fences were put up to keep them off the tracks. There's one thing that can stop most animals from going where they want to, and that's barbed wire. In fact, it stops most humans, too. But some are like us and we go through them anyway. Very carefully though."

He lifted up on one of the strands of barbed wire, making a hole large enough for Jimmy to go through. After he crawled through, Jimmy held the wire up for his grandpa. He found it to be easier than he thought it would

Lost Feather

be, as the wire was old. His grandpa quickly crawled through without getting caught by any of the barbs.

They walked up the slope and stepped over the first rail of the two tracks and stopped. "You know Jimmy, it's amazing," his grandpa said, looking down at the tracks. The railroad companies sure own a lot of land. The government gave it to them. Of course, they had to lay down tracks like these two, all over this country that they called the west. With ownership comes the responsibility of keeping it in good shape. See how nice and neat the area on both sides of the tracks looks. It doesn't just happen, Jimmy. It takes a lot of work.

"It's the same with anything else we have, whether it's given to us, or we work for it. It all comes with a price. I've found that when you take care of what you have, you take pride in it, just like you have done with the hawk. Even though you got her free, it takes a lot of work to keep her looking good for the shows you take her to."

"It sure does, Grandpa," he said, thinking about what he said. "It sure does."

"Let's look at all these railroad ties they gave us, Jimmy. It's free. Do you think there's any work involved in it?" Tom said.

They both laughed as they continued looking at all the ties. "You stay here, Jimmy, and I'll go get the truck. I'll back it up in the middle of all of the ties. First, we'll carry the ones that are the furthest away from the truck. Then, when we start getting tired, we won't have to carry the rest of them as far. That's using the old head," Tom said, laughing as they went back to the fence. Jimmy held the wire so his grandpa could climb through. He watched him hurry over to the truck and get in.

Tom drove the truck across the field to where Jimmy waited, turned around, and slowly backed the truck

Lost Feather

up against the fence where Jimmy stood. He got out and climbed up into the back of the truck like a young man. Jimmy smiled as he saw how agile his grandpa was. Tom walked to the back of the truck, jumped over the tailgate and the fence at the same time, and landed next to Jimmy.

He reached over the fence and unhooked the chains on the sides of the tailgate of the truck. It fell on top of the barbed wire fence. The wire bowed down a little but held it up, which kept it from hanging straight down.

"After we put a half dozen ties on the truck it will start to flatten out," Tom said to Jimmy, as if he knew what Jimmy thought.

He was right. After they put a few ties into the back of the pickup bed, the truck's springs bent enough that the tailgate lay flat. The more ties they put on, the lower the truck went. Jimmy wondered if the barbed wire would snap, but his grandpa assured him that it wouldn't. Later, Jimmy wondered if maybe his back would snap instead of the wire. The railroad ties, that were light when they started, somehow gained a lot of weight. Short breaks were taken at first, but soon they got longer and longer. They worked for a long time when his grandpa looked at Jimmy and then at the sun.

"It's dinner time," he said, smiling.

Tom looked up and down the railroad tracks. "Not a tree in sight," he said. "I guess we'll have to eat in the cab of the truck. That's the only shade there is for miles. They crawled over the top of the ties on the tailgate and got down on the other side of the fence. When they opened the doors on the truck, they felt the heat come out. They climbed in and picked up their sack lunches and looked inside.

"Let's dig in!" Tom said.

Lost Feather

They enjoyed their meal of fried chicken and biscuits, and especially enjoyed the big slice of cherry pie. There was not a word spoken for some time. By the time they finished, the truck cooled off a little.

After a short nap, Jimmy's grandpa woke him up. "Come on, Jimmy," he said, as he got out of the truck and closed the door. He climbed up onto the ties, and jumped to the ground on the other side of the fence. "A couple more hours work and we'll be done." Jimmy nodded as he followed his grandpa and jumped to the ground on the other side of the fence.

They worked pretty fast at first but got tired a lot quicker than they had in the morning. They had to take more rest periods. "Only four more to go, Jimmy," his grandpa said with a grin, as they loaded a tie on top of the others in the back of the truck bed.

He rolled the tie over against another tie and pushed it up against the back of the truck cab.

"I'll be glad when we're done," Jimmy replied as he looked at all of the ties on the truck.

"Me, too," Tom replied as they walked back to where the four remaining ties lay. Tom started to bend over to pick one of them up. He straightened up and looked at Jimmy. "Let's take another breather, Jimmy," he said, taking his handkerchief and wiping his face.

Jimmy stood up and nodded his head in agreement. He placed his hands on his waist and bent forward, then backwards a couple of times. He sat down on the railroad tie they were going to pick up.

His grandpa went over and sat down on the end of the tie next to it. He slowly lay back on it and took off his hat so his head could rest on the tie. He covered his face with his hat so the sun wasn't in his eyes, and gave a big sigh. He took a couple good breaths as he lay there

Lost Feather

enjoying this time of rest. All of a sudden he sat up and slapped his neck hard. Something fell off his neck and onto the collar of his shirt. He then pinched the collar of his shirt together as hard as he could.

"Come here, Jimmy," he said, beckoning Jimmy to his side. "What was it that bit me? Can you see it? Did I get it?"

Jimmy jumped up and moved around so he could see his grandpa's shirt collar. "It's some kind of spider, Grandpa," he said. "It's black, but you got him. It's dead."

"Find a small stick and take him off, Jimmy. Be careful. I need to see what kind it is. I need to know," his grandpa said, twisting his neck, trying to see the spider.

Jimmy quickly found a small stick and scraped the spider off his collar. He removed it slowly, and brought the stick around until his grandpa could see it.

"I was afraid of that," his grandpa said. "It's a black widow spider. You'll have to get me home as fast as you can so your grandmother can doctor me. Help me over to the fence, Jimmy. Quick, we have no time to lose. I'm starting to get dizzy. I'll be passing out soon."

Jimmy put his arm around his grandpa to help him up. Tom started grasping the air with his hands trying to get up. Jimmy pulled him all the way up and helped him across the tracks, down the embankment, and up to the barbed wire fence. He knew he couldn't pick him up high enough to put him over the fence. He'd have to put him through the barbed wire. He placed one foot on the strand next to the bottom and bent his grandpa down close to the wire. With his free hand he lifted up on the strand above his grandpa's body. He then slid him through the opening, and Tom helped as much as he could. When he was through he fell on the ground on the other side. Jimmy jumped onto the back of the ties on the truck, took a couple of quick steps,

Lost Feather

then jumped off where his grandpa lay. Tom tried to get up but couldn't. Jimmy helped him up and over to the door of the truck. He opened the door and helped his grandpa get inside.

"No, Jimmy," he said slowly. "You're going to have to drive. Help me move over and you get behind the steering wheel."

Jimmy had never driven before, but he was so worried about his grandpa's condition he didn't think about that. He jumped onto the running board of the truck, and helped his grandpa over to the passenger's side. He sat down behind the steering wheel, closed the door and sat and looked at everything in front of him. Everything looked awesome. "Now what?" he thought.

He reached for the keys and turned on the switch. He'd seen his grandpa do that. He pushed the starter button on the dashboard. The truck jumped back and then sprung forward. The barbed wire kept it from going backwards. "Push the clutch in, Jimmy," his grandpa said, pointing at it.

He pushed the clutch in and his grandpa reached up and put the gearshift into neutral. He tried again and the truck started. His grandpa pulled the gearshift down into low gear.

"Let the clutch out slowly," he said, as he sat back and closed his eyes.

Jimmy let the clutch out, and the truck jumped forward a few feet, and the motor died.

"Try it again, only this time slower," his grandpa said, his voice getting weaker.

Jimmy looked at him and saw his eyes roll back in his head as he slumped over against him. Gently he pushed him back until he lay against the other door. He pushed the clutch in again and started the truck. This time he let the

Lost Feather

clutch out real slow and the truck moved forward. But it seemed to be crawling toward the highway in front of him.

The load of ties on the truck made it sway gently back and forth. He turned the steering wheel to miss a hole. The truck rocked back and forth and almost turned over. His grandpa rolled back toward him, so he turned the steering wheel back a little and his grandpa slowly rolled back against the door.

He came to the road, turned the steering wheel again, and soon found himself on the highway. He turned the steering wheel back and headed down the middle of the white line toward Mercer. The truck moved along at a snail's pace. There must be something to make it go faster, he said to himself. He looked down at the floorboard of the truck. He pushed on the pedal next to the clutch and the truck stopped and the motor died again.

He frantically pushed the clutch in, then the starter button, and the motor started running again. He let the clutch out and the truck slowly moved down the highway. There had to be something to make it go faster. He now weaved back and forth on the highway as he looked at the floorboard of the truck, then up at the road. They were barely moving down the highway but at least they were moving. He stayed in the middle of the road most of the time. When it did get near the side of the road he turned the steering wheel and soon was back in the middle. His grandpa groaned and he looked over at him.

He had to go faster, and decided to try the other pedal on the floorboard and see what it would do. This time, he would do it slowly.

He pushed on the other pedal and the truck picked up a little speed. So he pushed the pedal down a little more and got a good hold on the steering wheel. He soon found he was getting more confidence in his driving ability as the

Lost Feather

truck moved along. He pushed the pedal down even further, the truck picked up more speed, and now they were making good time. Then he saw a car coming towards him. He took his foot off the gas pedal and the truck slowed down. As it slowed, it swayed back and forth. To his horror, the car was coming at him at a high rate of speed. The driver honked and shook his fist at him as he went by. Jimmy wanted them to stop, but he didn't know how to do it all at the same time. He must go on.

He pushed down on the pedal and the truck picked up speed again as it swayed back and forth down the highway. Ahead he saw the railroad crossing. As he neared the crossing the truck swayed off the right side of the road. Jimmy pulled on the steering wheel as hard as he could, but the truck was off the shoulder of the road. He looked up and saw the railroad crossing sign coming at the truck.

He took his foot off the pedal, and jerked the steering wheel as hard as he could. He managed to get the truck back onto the road, but not soon enough to miss the sign. The right rear fender hit it and the fender snapped. The truck shuddered a little but kept on moving down the road. Only now there was a loud banging noise. "Mr. Wilson and Grandpa just repaired that fender over at Mr. Wilson's garage after it cracked and banged for months," Jimmy thought, "Now he and Grandpa will have to fix it again."

Down the road Jimmy went, weaving from one side of the road to the other. "Where is that bridge?" he thought. "Come on bridge," he said out loud. Time seemed to slow down for him as he drove down the highway. Then, off in the distance he saw the bridge. Next came the problem of driving across it. The truck kept swaying back and forth as he neared the bridge. He pulled the steering wheel hard to the right and then the left. He thought the truck was going

Lost Feather

to turn over, but it didn't, so he took his foot off the pedal and the truck straightened up. It slowed down to a crawl and he safely crossed the bridge.

The road up to his grandparents' house came in sight. He steered the truck to the left side of the road as he came close. A car honked at him as it went by, but he paid no attention to it. He slowed down and turned the corner and caught his breath. He was afraid the truck was going to turn over. He took his foot off the pedal and the truck straightened again as it crept on around the corner. Then he pushed the gas pedal down again as he headed for the house at the end of the road.

Again he heard a horn honking, but he drove until he was in front of his grandparents' house. He put his foot on the brake as hard as he could and the truck came to a quick stop and the motor died. Jimmy started to open the truck door but found it pulled out of his hand.

"What are you doing driving your grandpa's truck?" Mr. Wilson asked, as he pulled Jimmy out of the truck. You've almost torn the fender off, that we just fixed yesterday."

Jimmy's grandpa slid off the seat and onto the floor. Mr. Wilson turned and looked at Tom lying there, then at Jimmy. He pushed Jimmy away and ran around the truck and opened the other door. He pulled Tom up off the floorboard and dragged him out of the truck. He turned around and placed Tom's arms over his shoulders and bent over.

"Alice!" he yelled as he bent over and picked Tom up off the ground and headed for the porch steps.

The screen door opened and Alice came running out. "What's wrong?"

Lost Feather

"A black widow spider bit Grandpa on the neck," Jimmy yelled, running toward her. "We were loading railroad ties -"

His grandmother turned around and ran back and opened the screen door for Bill.

He carefully carried Tom up the steps and across the porch.

Jimmy stood trance-like as Mr. Wilson carried his grandpa into the house.

"Put him on our bed, Bill," she said, as they disappeared into the house.

The screen door banged shut. Jimmy was left standing there. He realized he was alone and hurried up the steps and into the house.

Bill carried Tom through the living room and into his bedroom. He laid him gently on the bed and stood there looking at him. Jimmy stopped at the open door and looked at his grandpa. Alice brushed past him with a pan of water in one hand and some bottles clutched against her body with her other hand.

"Close the door, Bill," she said, as she placed her articles on the table next to the bed.

Mr. Wilson came over and looked at Jimmy. "I'm sorry I got onto you, Jimmy," he said, and grabbed him by the shoulders and looked him in the eyes. He patted him on the back. "We'll talk later." He went to his grandparents' room, closed the door and left Jimmy standing there. He could hardly believe he was shut out. He felt that old feeling of not being wanted rise up inside of him. He turned and walked over to the window and stood and looked at his grandpa's truck. The back fender looked awful.

He walked over and sat down on the sofa. He sat with his head lowered, looking at the pattern in the rug. It was a big rug that covered most of the floor. A little wood

Lost Feather

showed around the edge next to the wall. The wood had a nice shine to it from the love and care his grandma gave it. His eyes followed the loops and curves running all around the edge with tassels tied evenly every couple of inches. He followed the pattern slowly around the room with his eyes, trying to see if there were any places that were different. They were all the same.

His eyes got heavy as he looked at the rug. His head suddenly jerked and he almost fell off the sofa. He placed his hands under his chin. He was so tired and sleepy. Carrying the ties drained most of his strength. Having to drive the truck with his grandpa sick was another drain on him. Then when Mr. Wilson scolded him like he did - - all of that took its toll on his energy. On top of all that, he felt like he wasn't wanted.

The door to his grandparents' room opened and Mr. Wilson came out. "I'm going to go call the doctor, Jimmy," he said as he rushed by him. "You stay here and help your grandmother. I'll be right back," and he hurried out the front door.

Jimmy got up and watched Mr. Wilson. He got in his car, started it, and sped off down the lane towards the main road. He went back over and sat on the couch again, wishing his grandma would at least call him so he could do something, but she didn't. He sat with his back against the sofa thinking about the trip back home. He began to feel a little better.

It was kind of funny, now that he looked back on it. That old fender really banged against the truck after he hit that sign. A slight smile appeared, then, the more he thought about it, he got tickled and laughed out loud. The sound of his laugh caused him to sit up straight. It was quiet. He smiled again as he wondered if he had broken the sign. His smile disappeared. "If I did, will I have to pay for

Lost Feather

it?" Jimmy wondered. He'd have to check on it later. He began to worry about his grandpa.

It wasn't long until he began to drift off. His head nodded and fell on his chest a couple of times, and he sat up with a jerk and looked around. He leaned over and put his head on the sofa pillow. It felt good. He was soon asleep.

Jimmy didn't hear the car pull up outside, but the heavy footsteps on the porch woke him. He opened his eyes and the bright light caused him to squint. He put his hand on his forehead and closed his eyes.

Mr. Wilson came in with Dr. Bixler. The screen door banged as it closed, and he rolled over. The two men looked down at him and smiled as they walked past him toward the bedroom.

"I believe that boy saved his grandfather's life today, Doc," Mr. Wilson said, as he opened the door to the bedroom.

"I surely hope so," Doc replied as he hurried into the bedroom. Mr. Wilson looked down at Jimmy sleeping on the sofa.

"So do I," Bill said, and closed the door. Jimmy rolled over and sat up. He was stiff from lying on the couch. He went to his bedroom and got undressed. His bed was cold when he lay down, but it soon warmed up. Shortly, there was the sound of soft breathing as he drifted off to sleep again.

Lost Feather

CHAPTER V

It was after midnight, and Alice sat next to the bed where her husband Tom lay asleep. The doctor came again, but told her there was nothing to do but wait. He complimented her on how well her salve worked in the past for different ailments, and now he hoped it would work the spider venom out of Tom's body. He said he would come back the next day and see how he was doing, then he left. He hoped Tom would be O.K. Alice was worried that too much time elapsed between the time he was bitten and the time she treated him.

As she looked at her husband, she smiled now and then. The memories came of the many things that happened in their lives as they grew up on the Taos Indian Reservation. It was so peaceful sitting there that she dozed off several times. She woke with a start each time Tom made the slightest noise.

A loud grunt woke her at 3 A.M. She sat up straight and looked at Tom. The color of his face changed from pink to a light gray. She bent over him and took a closer look. Something was not right.

Again he grunted and his whole body jerked. "Oh Lord," she said. "What's wrong with my husband?" She turned his head and looked at the spider bite. It was a deep blue color and looked infected. The venom was attacking his whole body. "I need something to fight it, but what?" Alice thought. She searched her mind, trying to remember anything her grandmother taught her about remedies for spider bites.

Again Tom grunted and then threw up a yellowish substance. His body jerked a couple of times and he stopped breathing. Alice grabbed him and shook him but it

Lost Feather

didn't help. With her right hand flat she hit him in the middle of his chest.

He took a deep breath and started breathing slowly. She cleaned his mouth and around his chin. His breathing seemed to be getting slower and she heard a slight rattle each time he took a breath.

She put her ear on his chest and listened. His heartbeat was too slow. She raised her head, but kept her hand on his chest and closed her eyes. "Please don't leave me, Tom," she said sadly, as tears formed in her eyes. "Don't leave me."

"Lord, I don't know what I would do without Tom," she said, "You know we have been friends since we were little children and then husband and wife. Help me to remember what will stop the poison in his body. Please help me, Lord. Please don't take my love from me. Not now. Please."

She stood up and wiped her eyes. Tom grunted again and his body jerked. Yellow liquid came out of his nose and mouth. This time he didn't stop breathing, but he wheezed loudly. She cleaned him again and sat down.

She closed her eyes real tight and tried to think. There must be something she was taught that would reverse the poison in Tom's body. She shook her head from side to side and tried to get calm enough to think clearly. Tom grunted again and his body jerked. He gagged, but nothing came out of his nose, or mouth this time.

Alice stood up and thought, "Why didn't I think of this before?" She hurried out of the bedroom and into the kitchen. She pulled one of the chairs over to the cabinet, climbed up on it and opened the top right door. She pulled all of the boxes and bottles out, put them on the counter top, and got down.

Lost Feather

She rushed over to one of the drawers and got out some spoons and knives. Opening a lower door, she took out a thin dishtowel.

She jerked another drawer open and grabbed a couple of rubber bands. Finally, she opened another cupboard door and added a medium-sized bowl to everything on the countertop.

She quickly but thoroughly looked through the boxes and bottles, separating one from the others now and then. When she finished she had two boxes and one bottle. She opened another drawer and quickly took a small set of metal measuring spoons from their hiding place. She placed them on the countertop and closed the drawer with a bang.

She hurried off to the bedroom to check on Tom. He still wheezed each time he breathed. She listened to his heart, but it still beat too slowly. She straightened up and shook her head. Again she rushed to the kitchen.

She used a middle-sized spoon and took three spoonfuls from each box and bottle and put them in the bowl. She mixed it well and looked at how much there was. She decided to add three more spoonfuls, then, after mixing, another three spoonfuls.

When they were well mixed she laid the dishtowel flat on the countertop and poured the contents of the bowl on it. She picked up the ends and moved the contents so they were all together, then twisted the towel so it was in a small ball. She finished by placing a rubber band around the ball.

Over to the stove she went and picked up a large box of tea bags. She touched the teakettle on the back of the stove, and it was warm. She carried them both over to the counter top and placed them next to the bowl. She reached into the open cupboard door and picked up a large

Lost Feather

coffee cup. Placing one tea bag in the cup, she poured warm water over it, filling the cup to the brim.

She replaced the teakettle on the front of the stove, put in a few sticks of wood to heat the water, picked up the coffee cup and dishcloth with the herbs in it and hurried back to the bedroom. As she set everything on the nightstand next to the bed, Tom coughed hard. A small amount of yellow liquid came out of his mouth and he gagged.

"You hang in there, Tom!" Alice said, wiping his mouth with a clean cloth. She pried his mouth open and tried to clean it out. Before she could pull her finger out he bit her.

"Let go, Tom!" she yelled. She grabbed his chin with her other hand, pulled it down, and pulled her finger out. She unwrapped her finger and looked at it. "It's O.K., Tom. Don't you worry, it's O.K." Tom did not answer.

She went over to the dresser and got a handful of handkerchiefs out of the top drawer. She put them on the nightstand and picked up the dishtowel with the ball of herbs in it. "I've fixed a small medicine ball for you, Tom. We're going to beat this awful spider bite, my love. No nasty little old spider can separate us. No sir. Not us."

She pulled the medicine ball out of the cup of tea. She grabbed his chin and opened his mouth with one hand, held the medicine ball over his open mouth, and gently squeezed it. Drops of tea and herbs fell into his mouth and flowed down into his stomach. The rattling stopped for a second, then started again.

Alice placed the medicine ball back in the cup of tea, picked up a handkerchief, and wiped her eyes. "We've got a long way to go, my love, but we are going to get there. The Lord is on our side. Here we go," she said as she

Lost Feather

picked up the medicine ball and squeezed a few more drops into his mouth.

Minute after minute the drops fell into his mouth until the cup was empty. Then she rushed off to the kitchen to refill the cup with a new tea bag and warm water. Upon her return, she checked his breathing and heartbeat. Slowly his breathing rhythm grew stronger, and his heart started sounding more normal.

She returned to the drop from her medicine ball of herbs. After an hour passed, she saw a little color coming back into his face. She felt that with each drop he got better.

She kept up the routine for another hour, then stopped and checked his pulse. It was normal. His suntanned face returned to pinkish-brown. She sunk down in her chair and took a deep breath. Closing her eyes, she whispered, "Thank you, Lord."

Her eyes got heavier and heavier and her head rested on the back of her chair. The tension in her body slowly gave way and she fell asleep - - a nice, warm, peaceful sleep.

A funny noise caused Alice to stir. Then she heard it again and sat upright in her chair. She looked over at Tom and saw him lying there with his eyes wide open looking at her and not moving. "Oh, no!" she shouted, and jumped up.

Tom jerked back and looked at her. "What's the matter with you?" he squeaked.

"What?" Alice said.

"Are you deaf," he squeaked again. "I'm hungry."

"You will have to speak louder, Tom. I can't hear you."

"I'm hungry!" he yelled. "Can you hear that?" he yelled.

Lost Feather

Alice fell back in the chair and put her hands over her ears. "Yes, dear. I can hear you very clear. In fact, I'm sure that everybody in town heard you."

"Well, if that's what it takes to get something to eat around here I'll do it again."

"You do, and you won't get anything to eat."

"Yes, dear," he said softly. "Just be sure the plate is full. I'm starved."

Alice hurried out of the room and into the kitchen. It wasn't long until he heard pans and plates making their usual noise when she fixed breakfast. He smiled. "Maybe I ought to shout like that more often," he thought. "It sure did work this time."

He lay there and thought about it, then shook his head. He was lucky and knew he got by with it this time. "Well, once is better than none."

Alice soon returned with a bowl of chicken soup on a tray and set it on the night-stand beside their bed.

Tom looked at it and then at Alice and didn't say anything.

"Tom, you have been very sick and throwing up and you don't need any heavy food for a while," she said.

"I've been real sick, Alice? I feel fine. How come I was sick?"

"A black widow spider bit you on the neck and it poisoned your entire body," she said, brushing his hair back off his forehead. "I love you Thomas, very much."

"Oh, yes. I remember," Tom said smiling up at her. When she called him Thomas he knew she was serious. "Help me sit up so I can eat my soup, Mother," he said.

Alice nodded her head and smiled. He's going to be just fine," she said to herself. She helped him sit up and placed a pillow behind him.

Lost Feather

She sat down and watched him eat his soup. Leaning back in her chair, she said a little prayer of thanks. Her man was going to be fine.

When Jimmy woke up, he turned over and looked toward the slightly opened window. Sunbeams danced across his desk. A slight breeze moved the curtains oh, so gently, causing a beautiful display of light around his room. He overslept again. Then he remembered what happened. He jumped out of bed and put on his clothes as fast as he could. He ran out the door towards the kitchen.

His grandma sat at the table in the kitchen. Her elbows were on the table with hands folded together under her chin with her eyes closed. She looked as if she was asleep, but as Jimmy came into the kitchen she looked up at him. Jimmy's heart sank when he saw the look on her face. She looked worn out with dark circles around her eyes and her face was all puffy. He walked over and put his arm around her.

Alice smiled at Jimmy and said. "I want to thank you for what you did yesterday, Jimmy. We almost lost your grandpa, but your getting him home when you did saved his life. I don't know how you drove that old truck home, but I sure am glad you did. I love you so much, Jimmy."

Jimmy's heart felt good. Her words eased all of his bad feeling about himself. "I love you too, Grandma," he said, hugging her. He looked down at her and asked, "Is Grandpa all right?"

"Yes, Jimmy," she said, and grabbed him and hugged him hard. "He is going to be fine. That was a very poisonous spider that bit him. If there are no complications he'll be fine in a few days. A few days in bed are what he needs now. I've been telling him he needs a rest. It

Lost Feather

probably won't interfere with his job, as Saturday is five days away. He should be up and around by then."

"May I see Grandpa?" Jimmy asked.

"He's sleeping right now, Jimmy," she answered, smiling at him. "He asked about you when he woke up. He didn't come out of his fever until three o'clock this morning. Don't you worry, though; the first chance I have, I'll get you two together."

She got up and went over to the stove. "I have some oatmeal ready for you, Jimmy. You get the milk, butter, and jelly out of the refrigerator, and I'll fix the toast and get your bowl."

"Have you been up all night?" Jimmy asked.

She turned and grinned at him. "Yes. I'll get my sleep this afternoon when you and your grandpa get together. Then you can tell all those tall tales of how you two worked so hard yesterday. Then how you drove the truck home. Don't forget to tell your grandpa how you almost knocked off the rear fender."

Jimmy's smile disappeared from his face. He hung his head as he looked up at her. She noticed the change, but said, "Mr. Wilson drove back up the road to see what you hit. He knew it had to be fairly large to tear the rear fender loose like it did. He told me he saw where you drove off the road, then back on just in time. He said it could have been real bad if you hadn't gotten the truck back on the road like you did.

'The signpost at the railroad crossing was bent over pretty bad, but he fixed it. He said no one would know it had been hit unless they got out and looked real close. Then they might see a few paint scratches on the post, but they'd have to look real close."

The smile returned to Jimmy's face. "Grandma sure knows how to cheer me up," he thought. "I'm glad to hear

Lost Feather

that," he said. "If I had to pay for that railroad crossing sign, I'd have to sell something to raise the money. I'm glad Mr. Wilson could fix it like he did."

He sat at the table with his grandma and felt a weight lift from his shoulders. She asked the blessing on the food before they ate. They looked at each other now and then and smiled. Words were not needed for the way they felt.

They heard steps on the porch. Then someone knocked on the door. "Yes," Alice said.

The screen door opened and Mary Wilson stepped in. "It's just me," she said, smiling at them. "I came to see both of you, but especially Jimmy." She walked over to the table and sat down.

"We're glad you came by, Mary," Alice said. "Would you like for me to leave so you can talk to Jimmy?"

"Oh no, Mrs. Warrior," Mary said, embarrassed. "I just wanted to tell Jimmy how proud I am of what he did yesterday. Last night my father told me what he did, and I wanted to let him know how proud we are of him." She stopped and looked at Jimmy. "My father said you were so tired last night you fell asleep waiting outside your grandfather's room." She paused again as she sat there looking at Jimmy. "My father is telling everyone in town how you drove that old truck home even though you didn't know how to drive."

Jimmy turned red as he listened to Mary. Every time he started to say something, Mary praised him more. When she quit talking he said, "Have you looked at the right rear fender on the truck lately, Mary? It's almost torn off and I don't know how it can be fixed."

Alice and Mary looked at each other and laughed. Jimmy didn't think it was very funny, but finally grinned a

Lost Feather

little. "I looked at the fender, Jimmy, and you're right, it's in sad shape. But what really counts is that you did your best and it turned out good. I'm proud of you no matter what you say," she said.

Jimmy looked at his grandma and she just smiled at him.

They heard steps again on the front porch and then a knock. This time Alice got up and went to the door. "Oh, hello, Dr. Bixler. Come on in, please."

"Hello, Alice. How's our patient this morning?" he asked.

"He's sleeping right now," she replied.

The doctor looked over at the table where Mary and Jimmy were. "Hello there, you two," he said, walking over to them. He pulled up a chair and sat down. Alice sat down beside him. "Well, young man," he said, looking at Jimmy, "I'd like to let you know that your quick reaction to what happened yesterday saved your grandfather's life.

'I'm not saying this so you will get a big head. But you can be proud of what you did. Tom was in bad shape when I got here yesterday afternoon." Looking at Alice he continued, "Your grandmother made a salve and placed it on that bite. It drew most of the poison out. All I had to do was give him a shot of penicillin and he was on the road to recovery. Both of you sure made my job easy."

"Thank you, Dr. Bixler," Jimmy said, then, looked at his grandma. "What did you put on grandpa?"

Alice looked at Jimmy very seriously. "It was an Indian herb salve that my mother used to help people get well. She passed the formula on to me, plus many other things. I used the salve a few times many years ago to draw out poisons when an insect or snake bit someone. I'll pass that knowledge on to you one day when the time is right."

Lost Feather

The doctor looked at Jimmy and nodded his head. "You'll have to earn that honor. It's only given to a very few people, Jimmy," he said. "Only those who earn it are chosen by those who know the secrets of herbs. Learn how to use it to help your fellow man, Jimmy.

'I tried for years to get your grandmother to teach me what she knows about herbs, and other things, but she put me off every time. Now she has chosen you to pass her knowledge on to. I was beginning to wonder if she'd ever find one she felt worthy to tell them to. What Alice does is not witchcraft, Jimmy. She just helps people get well, like I do, every chance she gets."

Again he stopped for a moment, then, continued. "It's not only an honor, Jimmy, it's a responsibility to your fellow man." He turned to Alice and smiled real big. "Look at me carrying on, Alice."

"Thank you, Dr. Bixler," she said. "You paid me a very nice compliment. She looked at Jimmy. "If my grandson wants to learn the small amount of things that I've been taught, I will gladly teach him all that I know."

Alice reached out and took Jimmy's hand in hers. "It's up to you, Jimmy. Would you like to learn how to help others with some of the herbs that I know of? Like the doctor said, there's a responsibility you must accept if you do."

Jimmy looked at his grandma. "I think I would like to learn all I can so I will be able to help others, Grandma. If it's like helping Grandpa, then I want to learn everything."

His grandma looked at him for some time. She took hold of his other hand and smiled real big. It felt like electricity was flowing into both of Jimmy's hands as he stood there. Alice turned and looked at Dr. Bixler. "I'll wait

Lost Feather

a few days and see how Jimmy feels about it then. If he's still interested, I'll start then."

"That's fine, Alice," Dr. Bixler replied.

Alice released Jimmy's hands. The door to the bedroom opened and Tom came out. He walked over to the table, pulled up a chair and sat down.

"Tom," Alice said, "What are you doing up? You get back in bed this instant. You need a few more days' rest."

The doctor started to say something but Tom stopped him with an upraised hand. "I know. I know. I'll go back to bed in a couple of minutes, but I heard you talking in here and wanted to come out and see what was going on. I was hoping someone would come in and see how I was doing but no one did. I decided no one cared, so I got up and put on my robe and slippers. Now that I've said my piece I'll go back to bed, and be a good boy."

He stood up and smiled at them and started to leave when his gaze fell on his grandson, Jimmy. He walked over and put his hand on his shoulder. "Thank you, Jimmy," was all he said. He turned and walked back to the bedroom and started to close the door.

Jimmy got up and ran over to his grandpa and put his arm around him. They walked into the bedroom and Jimmy helped him take off his slippers and lie down on the bed. Not a word was spoken, but love flowed between them like a gentle river as they looked at each other. "You're welcome, Grandpa," Jimmy said, softly touching his grandpa's hand.

Tom took both of Jimmy's hands in his as a tear ran down his cheek. "I'm a little more tired than I thought I was, Jimmy. It sure is funny how your grandma is always right. But we know why, don't we? She knows what's best for us and she loves us so much that she automatically tells

Lost Feather

us what we should already know." His eyes slowly closed but he still held onto Jimmy's hands.

Jimmy enjoyed holding his grandpa's hand. Finally he slowly slipped his hands out of his grandpa's. He watched his grandpa drift off to sleep. "Grandma's not the only one who loves you," he thought to himself, "I love you too, Grandpa."

Jimmy closed the door and went back into the kitchen. Mary stood up as he came in. "I've got to go, Jimmy," she said, walking towards him. She smiled as she walked past him and over to the front door. "I sure am proud of you."

Jimmy blushed a little. "Thanks, Mary," he said. He changed the subject. "I plan on working Lady Samson and Lady Gwen tomorrow. Do you want to work Lady Joan? We'll give them a good workout. They need it, you know."

"That would be great," she said. "I forgot all about the hawks. I'll be over as early as I can. I've got to help around the house a little first, but I'll come over when I get through."

"That's great," Jimmy said, giving his best grin. Mary's excitement was catching and Jimmy felt it.

"Grandpa looks like he's going to be up and about real soon. I was wondering if he would be off work this coming weekend, but Grandma fixed him up real good. He'll need some meat, though. Everything is turning out fine."

Mary opened the door and started to leave. She paused and looked at Jimmy. "Good," she said. "I'll see you tomorrow. Bye," and she was gone.

Jimmy walked back into the kitchen. No one was there. He looked toward the front bedroom. He saw Dr. Bixler and his grandma come out. She closed the door quietly, then she and Dr. Bixler came over to him.

Lost Feather

"It looks like your grandpa is doing really well for his age," the doctor said to Jimmy. "Take care of both of them for me, Jimmy. Make sure Tom gets plenty of rest. They're very special to me. Will you do that?"

"Yes, sir," Jimmy said, surprised. "I sure will."

Dr. Bixler saw the surprise look on his face. "Your grandparents helped me out a few years ago when I was having some personal problems. Their love and caring saw me through it all, and I have a good practice now. I look forward to each day now instead of dreading it."

Jimmy listened quietly. He realized his grandparents were special to a lot of people around there. They helped many of their friends overcome some of their bad thoughts about Indians.

Dr. Bixler shook Jimmy's hand and turned to Alice. "I don't think I'll need to come back, Alice. Tom looks good. But if anything should change, you get Bill Wilson to call me at once. I'll come anytime he calls. But as I said, I don't think I'll have to."

Alice walked up to Dr. Bixler and hugged him. "Thank you, doctor," she said. "I hope we won't need your services either. There's nothing I like less than having one of mine sick. But when they are, I work hard at helping them get well, and then just as hard at keeping them well."

The doctor walked over to the front door with Alice. They said good-bye and the doctor left. Alice came back to where Jimmy was, and said, "We'll talk later about your learning some of my Indian ways, Jimmy. You may change your mind after you think about it for a while. There are some drawbacks to it, so give it plenty of thought."

"I will, Grandma," he said. Jimmy knew she was serious by the sound of her voice. "I'll go to my room for a

Lost Feather

while and think about everything that's happened the last couple days. I don't want to make a wrong decision."

Alice smiled and nodded. It surprised her how grown-up he sounded.

Jimmy went to his room and Alice went into the kitchen and started fixing something to eat. She knew that when her husband woke up again he would be hungry.

Jimmy closed the door to his room and turned around. With his back to the door, he looked around the room. His eyes stopped as they passed the window. It was like a large picture that someone painted on his wall.

Slowly, his eyes traveled from the window to the rest of his room. He never thought that someday he'd have such a nice room all to himself.

He walked around the room and looked at the pictures on the walls. Beautiful pigeons looked back at him from their frames. Jimmy's father was one of the best homing pigeon trainers around that area. He won many races with them, and some beautiful trophies.

He walked slowly, looking at everything. When he came to the mirror over the dresser, he looked at himself. "Do you really want to learn the Indian secrets that Grandma knows?" he thought.

It would be great to know something many people didn't. But would it be worth it? Some would understand, but others wouldn't. He thought about his grandpa, and decided what to do. He'd take the chance and learn what his grandma would teach him. He looked close into the mirror, then smiled at his reflection. "I'm glad that's settled," he said out loud.

His eyes moved to the wooden plaques that Mr. Miller made for him. One said, "Strong Feather Jimmy Warrior," the other "Strong Feather Lady Samson." They both hung on the wall next to his bed. Jimmy smiled as he

Lost Feather

remembered how Lady Samson, his first falcon hawk, won the falcon contest at the Air Force Academy in Colorado Springs, Colorado.

His hawk won over many other large, beautiful hawks. The judge first picked another hawk for first place. But the owner told them his hawk pulled some of her wingtip feathers out a couple of days earlier and he sewed them back in place. They were her feathers and he didn't see why that would matter. It was just a stupid thing for her to do.

The judge discovered what he did at the last moment and disqualified his hawk. Jimmy's hawk, Lady Samson, then won first place.

Jimmy's mind was awhirl with the thoughts of that wonderful day. He looked across the room from his bed to the other wall. He had two more wooden plaques that Mr. Miller made. One was Strong Feather Lady Gwen, and the other, Strong Feather Lady Joan. They were the two babies of Lady Samson.

Mary and Jimmy captured and trained them, and now showed them with their mother, all over Colorado.

Jimmy looked at his bed. It looked so inviting. He sat on the edge of the bed and took off his shoes. He leaned back and looked up at the light fixture hanging on a brass chain from the ceiling. The light fixture itself consisted of four lights at the ends of four brass tubes. The tubes curved down and then up, to make a tulip type shade around the bulbs.

Small crystals hung from other parts of the fixture, giving off different colors when he moved his head. Jimmy's eyes slowly closed as he watched the colors change. It felt good to just lie there and rest. Sleep came before he knew it.

Lost Feather

Someone tapping on his door woke him. The door opened and his grandma looked to see if he was awake. "Yes, Grandma," he said, having a hard time getting his eyes open.

"It's time to eat, Jimmy," she said. "Hurry. Your grandpa is going to eat with us, so get washed up." She closed the door and left.

Jimmy put his shoes back on and went into the bathroom. He cleaned up and made his way into the kitchen. His grandpa and grandma sat waiting for him. "Hi, Grandpa," he said and walked up and hugged him.

"Hello, Jimmy," Tom replied. "Looks like you and I snoozed a little. I surely needed mine. How about you?"

"I think I could have had a longer one than I did, but it felt good," Jimmy said, smiling. He went around and hugged his grandma. "I want to learn whatever you want to teach me, Grandma," he said before he went around the table and sat down.

His grandma didn't say a word. She just passed the food. But his grandpa grinned at them. "I'm sure glad you two are getting along so good. You're especially good at keeping secrets from me. But it wouldn't be much fun around here if there were not a secret or two between a grandson and his grandma. Sure hope I earn that privilege one of these days and can have a secret with my grandson---one that his grandma doesn't know anything about.

They all laughed. Tom sat and waited for them to tell him their secret. But they didn't. So he decided he might as well take some of the food Alice tried to give him. She got tired of waiting for him to take it and set it down in front of him.

"I'm hungry as a bear," he finally said. "Don't tell me. I don't care - much."

Lost Feather

Jimmy and his grandma snickered this time and went on eating. "Secrets are wonderful things to have," Jimmy thought, "especially with a grandma like mine."

Lost Feather

CHAPTER VI

Jimmy rose early the next day. He got dressed, washed up, and went into the kitchen. To his surprise his grandma was not there. He looked around and went over to his grandparents' bedroom door. He smiled when he heard them talking inside, and went back to the kitchen. He got the milk out of the refrigerator and fixed himself some dry breakfast cereal. When he finished eating about half of his food, his grandma came out of her bedroom. "Good morning, Jimmy," she said with a big smile. "Your grandpa had me in there for over an hour trying to find out what our big secret is. He finally gave up."

Alice made herself busy around the kitchen and Jimmy finished his cereal. "You know, Jimmy, it's good to have a secret with you. It's been such a long time since I've had a secret with someone. I guess it was when I was a young girl. Yep. It has been a long time."

"Mary and I are going to work with the hawks today, Grandma," Jimmy said as he washed his bowl and spoon in the sink. He placed them on the counter top next to the sink, then walked over and picked up the milk off the table. "We're going to do some hunting this morning. The hawks haven't worked much lately and it will be good for them and us."

Jimmy put the milk in the refrigerator and closed the door. His grandma watched him. "Thank you for putting up the milk and washing your dishes," she said.

Jimmy shook his head at her. "I'm learning," he said, with a smile. "It's good to have a secret with you, Grandma. Thank you for letting me share one with you."

Alice nodded at him as she got busy in the kitchen. Jimmy walked to the back of the house and opened the door. He took a big breath of the cool air. Colorado had the

Lost Feather

best air of any place he'd ever been. It seemed to wake every part of him as he stood and looked around. He jumped off the steps to the ground. He walked over to the hawk pens and looked at the three hawks inside. They seemed to be as glad to see him, as he was to see them.

Jimmy got busy working around the pens for about an hour. The hawks watched every move he made, letting him know they appreciated his presence in their cages. He neglected them last week and they were now letting him know they liked having him around. After he did everything that needed to be done, he closed Lady Samson's gate and went over and sat down on one of the railroad ties across from the hawk pen.

After a few minutes he got an idea. The stack of railroad ties he sat on grew smaller since he'd been there. It was his job to cut them up for kindling for the cook stove. Making sure the wood box behind the stove was full all the time was also his job. The ties that he and his grandpa loaded onto the truck the other day were not yet unloaded. He smiled as he thought about the truck sitting out front where he left it.

He got up and went into the house and asked his grandma if it would be all right to drive the truck around back and unload the ties. She told him it would be fine with her. Since he drove the truck home after the spider bit his grandpa, she figured he could drive it to the woodpile out back.

She got the keys out of the bowl in the cupboard and handed them to him. She watched him take them and head for the front door. She heard the truck start right away.

Jimmy did all the things he remembered to do to start the truck. It was driving around to the back yard that took some time. Turning it around was next, which

Lost Feather

included backing it up to the pile of ties. He didn't know where reverse was.

After much grinding of gears he found reverse. Then came many starts and stops, jumps and groans. He turned the motor off and got out many times to see where the ties were, and where the truck was. He gave up when he finally got it fairly close. Somehow driving was a little harder today than it was a couple days ago. He was glad when he turned the key off and the motor stopped.

He climbed up on top of the ties on the truck and rolled all he could onto the ground near the woodpile. He got down and pulled them onto the top of the woodpile. Slowly he got them in a neat pile where he wanted them.

He sat down and looked at the ties still on the truck. He needed to get the truck closer. He got back in the truck and started it. This time he found the truck moved easier and did what he wanted. With less weight on the truck, it handled better. He drove it forward a little and stopped, then with a great grinding sound from under the truck, he found reverse.

Slowly, he backed the truck up, stopped within a foot of the woodpile, and turned the motor off. He got out and looked at what he did. He was proud of how he backed the truck up. With a big grin, he climbed up onto the pile of ties and looked around.

He jumped down and started dragging the railroad ties off the truck. It was quicker to do it this way. It took a lot of tugging and pulling, but all of the ties were finally stacked neatly on the woodpile. Jimmy sat down and rested. He looked up. His grandpa stood at the back door. He didn't say a word, just gave him the thumbs up sign, letting him know he'd done real good. Jimmy nodded his head and gave it back. Tom turned and went back into the house.

Lost Feather

Jimmy climbed down from the woodpile and got in the truck. He started it and put it in first gear with no noise at all. He let the clutch out slowly and the truck moved forward nice and easy. "It sure is nice to know how to drive now," he thought.

He drove it slowly around the house with the fender banging. It did make a lot of noise, but he knew it would be fixed. He made a large turn in the front yard, drove the truck into the garage, turned the motor off, and got out. He felt proud of himself. "It's easy when you know how," he thought.

He handed the keys to his grandma and she rubbed the top of his head. "You'll be a man before you know it, Jimmy. I'll be as glad to see that day as you will, but enjoy this time in your life, also. No matter what age you are, it's a wonderful age. Enjoy every second. It won't come again."

"I'm enjoying it, Grandma," Jimmy said. "I really enjoyed driving the truck."

"Yes, I know Jimmy," she said. "I could tell."

Jimmy walked to the front door and looked down the road. He stepped out onto the porch and stood there. Alice came out and stood beside him and smiled. "Here comes Mary on the run with her Cocker Spaniel, Goldie."

Jimmy saw her and waved. It amazed him how fast she ran. He smiled because he knew that she was good at a lot of things. Especially hawks.

"Hi you two," she said running up to the porch. "Sorry I'm late, but my mother needed me to help her finish cleaning up the house. I'm sure that I live in one of the cleanest houses in Mercer. But you know what? I wouldn't have it any other way."

Jimmy looked at his grandma and she stood there smiling at him. "I know what you mean, Mary," Jimmy said. "The only difference is that Grandma knows better

Lost Feather

than to ask me to help her clean up the house. I don't know much about cleaning a house. I know how to get it dirty, though."

Alice nodded her head in agreement, then, looked at Mary. "You know what, Mary? That's a great idea. It sure would cut down on my work around here. I know that Jimmy learns real fast, and after a few months I'm sure he will be one of the best house cleaners in Mercer. In fact, we could start today."

Jimmy frowned at his grandma, then looked at Mary. "I ah-h, I don't know. We were going to go -" He looked back at his grandma and saw a big smile.

"Maybe we can start tomorrow. What do you think, Mary?" she asked.

Mary laughed at the look on his face. "If your grandma wants you to help her clean the house, Jimmy, I'll come over and help a little."

He shook his head. "A lot of help you are, Mary. I mean you would be a lot of help, but that's not what I meant."

Alice and Mary started laughing. He started to get mad, then realized they were kidding him. "OK, you two. I know when I'm being kidded." He then looked at his grandma. "You are kidding aren't you?"

They both laughed again. "Yes, Jimmy," she said patting him on the shoulder. She winked at Mary and went back inside.

Mary reached up and grabbed Jimmy's hand and pulled him down the steps. "Let's go get our hawks and put them in the air."

They ran around the house with Goldie right behind them.

They stopped in front of the hawk pens and Mary asked, "Which two?"

Lost Feather

"Let's put the two youngsters up first. I'll hunt with Lady Samson later today."

He opened Lady Joan's and Lady Gwen's pen, and they soon had their hoods on them. They put on their heavy gloves and got them to come to fist. They both smiled when they walked out of the pens with the two most beautiful hawks they ever saw sitting on their fists. Of course they were kind of partial, since they were their hawks.

Goldie ran on ahead of them and checked out every bush as they made their way out into the near by field. The hawks looked like two statues carved in stone as they carried them on their gloved hands. Goldie ran back and walked along with them.

The sky was a beautiful blue with only a couple of clouds. As they moved towards the hawks' hunting grounds, Jimmy looked off towards the mountains. He saw clouds forming above the majestic Rocky Mountains. Then as they passed over the foothills heading for the open plains they grew into big beautiful billowy clouds. The awesome white against the beautiful blue of the sky was a sight to behold.

From the town of Boulder to the Colorado border it was known as the plains. If the upper air was dry, the days were nice and warm. But if there was a lot of moisture in the upper air, this brought on the rains the farmers prayed for.

Jimmy pointed at the clouds and said, "If people would take the time to sit down and watch the clouds, they would see an awesome sight. On a warm day like today the clouds that formed over the mountains moved eastward due to the rotation of the earth. As the clouds moved over the foothills they expanded into beautiful billowy cotton balls. But the dry air that lay in front of them on the plains seemed to nibble on them until they disappeared. If one

Lost Feather

took the time they could see the cloud from its formation over the mountains, all the way to its disappearance over the plains."

"Jimmy, you know a lot about the clouds. Where did you learn all that?" Mary asked.

"I really don't know that much about them, Mary," he answered. "I just spend a lot of time lying on my favorite hill over there across the creek. I do a lot of thinking and watching everything around me. The clouds are one of my favorite things to watch."

Mary smiled at him and took the hood off of her hawk, Lady Joan. She held her left hand up above her head and Lady Joan took off, flapping her wings. She swooped down low near the ground. She kept flapping her wings and soon gained altitude. Higher and higher she went until she was high above them.

She then gave Goldie the command for her to hunt. She ran off looking for some type of game in the bushes. They followed her quite some time before a good-sized rabbit was flushed out from under a bush.

Lady Joan saw it and folded her wings. She went into a steep dive and opened them when she came close to the ground. She caught the rabbit. Mary ran over to her, took the rabbit and laid it aside, then had her come to fist on her glove. She placed the hood on her and picked up the rabbit. She held them both up for Jimmy to see.

"That's a good size rabbit, Mary," Jimmy said smiling. "Let's see if Lady Gwen can do the same."

He took the hood off of Lady Gwen. She nodded her head back and forth, telling him she, too, was ready to hunt. He raised his gloved hand up above his head. She took off and swooped down towards the ground with her wings spread out. She flapped her wings and rose higher and higher.

Lost Feather

It wasn't long until she was high above them, riding on the air currents. It looked like she was painted in the sky. He smiled remembering the first time he saw her mother, Lady Samson, high above him like she was. Like Lady Joan, she too was ready to hunt.

He looked at Goldie and gave her the command, "Hunt, Goldie," and off she ran. Back and forth through the field she ran but found nothing. She ran towards the creek and checked out the bushes and tall grass but still nothing.

Goldie then followed the creek as it wound back and forth. Up ahead, Jimmy saw the bridge on the highway. If she didn't find anything by the time she reached the bridge, they would then be near the front of his grandparents' house.

As Goldie came close to the bridge, a flock of blackbirds flew out of one of the tall trees. Jimmy watched the birds fly away and looked up to see what Lady Gwen was doing. She was in a steep dive. "Oh no!" he thought. "She's going to catch a blackbird. That's not much of a meal for a hawk."

She opened her wings not far from the ground and swooped upwards and caught something and flew a short distance and landed. They looked at each other and shrugged their shoulders.

"What did she catch, Mary?"

"It was a fairly large bird. I don't know what kind it was," she answered.

He ran as fast as he could and soon stood next to Lady Gwen. The bird wasn't as large as he thought earlier, but it was a good size. It looked something like a pheasant but was smaller. He'd never seen a bird like that.

Mary came walking up carrying her hawk and rabbit. "Wow," she said. "She caught a quail."

Lost Feather

"That's a quail?" Jimmy said, looking closely. "I've never seen one of them before."

"They say they are very tasty, Jimmy." she said. "I've never eaten one, though. My parents like them."

"That man that tried to take Lady Samson from me said that there were a lot of quails out on the farm where he took me. I never saw any out there, though."

"There might be, Jimmy," she said, thinking about what he said. "He could have been lying like he lied to you just to get your hawk," she said looking at the quail. "I'd say he was lying."

"Yeah," Jimmy said. "He did a lot of that."

Both of their hawks caught something to eat, so it was time to head for the house. He took the quail from Lady Gwen and put her hood on. He then took the rabbit from Mary and gave her the quail. She smiled, accepting the lighter catch.

They were both happy when they returned to the hawk pens, put them inside their own pens, and headed for the house. They had a surprise for his grandmother, and they were excited as they entered the house. They both giggled as they entered the kitchen, not knowing what she would say.

Alice was stirring a pot on the stove when they came in, and she just glanced up at them, then went back to what she was doing. They laid their catch on the table and stood waiting for her to turn around. When she did they smiled real big at her.

Alice looked down at the table. Her eyes got big; then a smile followed. "You've got a quail. I haven't seen one of them around here for some time. I did hear some people down at Mrs. Windell's store the other day mention that quails came back to this area. But I didn't think much about it. I sure am glad they have. We need them back here.

Lost Feather

"In my childhood there were quails all over Colorado and New Mexico. But when the depression came to our nation, there wasn't much to eat and quails were easy to catch. So the time came when there were no more of them around here. But look at this one you brought home with you. I sure hope they're back to stay."

Jimmy and Mary looked at each other, then at Alice. "I'm sorry that Lady Gwen caught this one, Grandma. I'll be more careful from now on."

"No, Jimmy," she said. "The Creator made them for man to eat. If they've come back into this area, I'm sure there will be enough of them for man to catch and eat. When things are not kept under control, they overpopulate the land. It's just as bad as eliminating all of them. We just have to be wise enough to maintain a good balance."

"That makes sense," Mary said. "I guess that's why there always seem to be rabbits around here for our hawks to catch. If our hawks didn't catch them they would soon overpopulate this area. One rabbit sure does have a lot of babies. So it makes sense about all types of game. If we don't keep them under control, it will be a mess around here."

Alice smiled, knowing they understood what she said. She looked at Jimmy and smiled. "Guess what?"

He stood there looking at her for a moment, then smiled. "We've got another secret, Grandma?"

Alice just smiled and said, "I'll go out and clean and dress the rabbit and quail. There's not much meat on that quail, so guess who's going to get it!"

"Not me," he said.

"Not me," Mary said.

"Not me," Alice said. "That only leaves the one who doesn't know we have it. Right?"

They all said, "Right!"

Lost Feather

Alice picked up the rabbit and quail and headed for the door. Mary & Jimmy followed her out onto the porch. She left them standing there.

"I've got to go," Mary said. "I'll see you tomorrow." She ran down the steps and out of the yard, headed up the road to the highway. She stopped and waved back at him, then disappeared behind the house on the corner.

Jimmy went back into the house to his room. He lay down on his bed and thought about what happened. It wasn't long until he was asleep.

His grandma knocked, opened the door and looked in. Jimmy raised himself up on one arm and looked at her. "I'll be right in as soon as I wash up, Grandma."

She left the door open, and he quickly washed up. He hurried down the hall and sat down at the table. He watched as his grandma placed different things on the table, but no meat. Tom sat there waiting for her to put the meat on but it never came. When Alice sat down he looked at her kind of strange. "Where's the meat?" he asked."

""What meat?" she asked.

"We've been having meat. Where's the meat? Oh, we don't have any? OK."

"Oh, that meat," Alice said smiling. "Jimmy, will you go get the meat out of the oven. Use the two pot holders on the counter so you won't burn your fingers."

"Yes, ma'am," he said, getting up. He hurried over and picked up the pot holders, opened the oven door and took the plate out. He set it down in front of his grandpa.

Tom looked at it and then at Alice. "What is that?" Then he saw them smiling. "Not another surprise," he said. "What is it? It's too big for a pigeon and too little for a pheasant." Looking closer, he sat back and grinned real big.

Lost Feather

"It's a quail. Man, oh man. I haven't had quail for a while. In fact, I can't remember the last time I had quail."

Alice looked at Jimmy and winked. She got up and took the pot holders over and opened the oven again. She took out the plate of rabbit. She put it in front of Jimmy and sat down.

"Now I don't know which one to eat," Tom said. "It's no fair putting my two favorite dishes on the table and making me have to make a choice. It's not fair."

"This is ours and that is yours," Alice said. She sat back down and put some of the rabbit on Jimmy's plate and the rest on hers.

Tom looked at his grandson and smiled. "That's what I like about your grandma, Jimmy. She knows how to make my mind up real quick."

Without another word they started eating and didn't speak again until they ate everything Alice cooked. It was a grand meal that wouldn't be forgotten for a long time.

After supper Alice washed the dishes and they sat around the table and talked about the day. Evening shadows brought the darkness with them. It was a busy day and it wasn't long until they each headed for bed.

Jimmy thought about how pleased his grandpa looked when he knew what was on the plate in front of him. He sure did love his grandparents.

Lost Feather

CHAPTER VII

The next morning Jimmy ate breakfast with his grandparents and remembered he did not take Lady Samson out to hunt yesterday. He would do that today for sure.

Tom looked at him and said, "You know what I'm going to be doing today? I'm going to help Bill weld that fender on the truck. You know, the one you tore loose when you hit that railroad crossing sign."

"How could I forget," Jimmy answered. "I didn't know you knew how to weld, Grandpa."

"I don't, but Bill is going to show me how. Or maybe I should say he's going to show me how to start; then he will let me finish welding the fender."

"Could I watch? I sure would like to know how to weld."

He looked at Alice, then Jimmy. "I don't see why not. You're the one that tore it off; it's only right that you get the pleasure of fixing it."

"Now, Tom," Alice said. "It's your truck. You need to be the one who learns how to fix it. Anyway, Jimmy didn't do it on purpose."

"I know, Alice. I was just having fun. But it wouldn't hurt if we both learned how to weld."

She looked at Tom sternly and Jimmy said, "I sure would like to learn how to weld."

"OK" she said. "You're getting to be so much alike, I don't know what I'm going to do with you."

"Please keep us," Tom said, laughing.

"You go on and get out of here and go play with your truck," she said, shooing them away from the table.

They hurried out the door and over to Bill Wilson's garage, talking and laughing and having a good time. When they got there Bill was putting gas in someone's car and he

Lost Feather

motioned for them to go on into the shop. They made their way into the shop and saw the truck near the back of the building. It was parked by a large worktable with a large roll-around tool cabinet next to it.

The left side of the truck was jacked up and the tire was leaning up against the workbench. They took a good look at the torn fender. It was bent back so the fender was close to the truck body. It didn't look like an easy job to them.

Bill walked up, pushing a standup dolly on wheels with two large metal tanks standing up on it. There were gauges on top of each bottle with rubber hoses coming out of the top of the gauges. The other ends of the hoses were wrapped around the tank with a funny looking brass apparatus connected to the hoses.

He set the bottles down next to the tailgate of the truck. He let the tailgate down, took the hoses from around the tank, and laid the brass apparatus on it. He hurried over to the workbench, got the roll-around metal workbench, and pushed it over to where they stood.

"OK, you two," he said. "I'm going to show you how to weld two pieces of metal together. Then I'm going to let you practice until you can do it. Then we'll weld the fender. Tom, you've watched me weld before, and you shouldn't have too much trouble; so you can show Jimmy how. OK?"

He nodded his head in agreement. Bill previously cut up some small pieces of metal. He showed them how to light the welding torch and how to set the gauges. They put on welding glasses, and Bill welded two pieces of metal together with a brass rod. It looked so simple.

And so it went for about thirty minutes. Tom did a good job but Jimmy took some time. He did fair when Bill

Lost Feather

came over and checked on them. He said, "You did fine, Tom. It's time to get the fender ready to be welded."

First, there was a lot of bending and banging with a large hammer. Then they used the smaller hammers until the fender was where Bill wanted it. He lit the torch and welded little spots along the tear in the metal. That held it together so he could weld it to fit. He welded a couple of places between the welds with the brass rod, then let Tom weld one. He did a good job. Jimmy was next, and Bill had to go back over it and fix it. The next one he welded better, and Bill let Tom fix it. Jimmy's third try was fine. Bill then let them trade off welding until it was done.

Then they did a lot of grinding and sanding. More welding was done, which was ground and sanded. Finally they stood back and looked at the finished product. "Not bad," Bill said.

Now they had to have a primer coat of paint. Tom went over to the paint cabinet and brought back a can of paint and a brush. It wasn't long until the whole fender was gray.

Bill came out of the office and over to the truck. He ran his hand over the welded area and smiled. "Not bad for a couple of amateurs. In fact, I think we all need a cold drink to celebrate. Yep, a Nesbitt Orange for me and one for Jimmy, and what would you like, Tom?

"Make it three," he said. He grabbed Jimmy and Tom around the waist and herded them back to the office. It was time to sit back and enjoy the fruits of their labor. With Nesbitt pops in their hands, they sat down and took a big drink. They each smiled. Then Tom sat back and laughed.

"OK, Tom," Bill said, "Tell me what you're wanting to tell me.

Lost Feather

"Well, Bill, you could never guess what I had for supper last night."

Bill held his hands up in the air and said, "Not again. If you think I'm going to sit here and play that game with you, I'm not. You can sit there in that chair until you're blue in the face and I'm not going to bite."

Tom looked at Jimmy and smiled. "He knows how to get me to tell him things doesn't he?"

"Yes, sir, he sure does."

"Well, I had quail, Bill. My grandson and your daughter caught a quail yesterday with her hawk. I thought they were gone from around here for good."

"No, Tom," Bill said. I've heard of them being east of here. A couple of people told me they saw quite a few coveys. Jim Brown said he has quite a few on his place."

Jimmy sat up and looked at Mr. Wilson. "That's where Mr. Lucas said there were quail when he tried to take Lady Samson from me."

Bill and Tom looked at him and didn't say a word, remembering what happened to him. "I guess he didn't lie about everything," Jimmy said.

"I don't know about that, Jimmy," Bill said. "All I know is he did lie about a lot of things. I didn't think I'd say anything more about that man. But what I did was because I'm the town marshal. I guess you need to know. I called your dad, Jimmy, and told him what happened. He was really mad and let me know that he hardly knew the man. He left without permission more than once, causing trouble for a lot of people."

"That man told you a lot of lies, Jimmy. "Your dad let me know he really appreciated my calling him and letting him know you were all right."

"I'm sure glad to know that, Mr. Wilson," Jimmy said smiling.

Lost Feather

"Me too, Bill," Tom said.

They thought about everything that happened. Then Bill said, "So you had quail last night for supper. Did you save me a piece?"

Tom laughed and looked at Bill. "Yep, and you can wait as long as I did for you to guess what I had to eat, before you'll get it."

They both laughed. But Jimmy thought about something. "If there are a lot of quail at Mr. Brown's farm, do you think he would mind if Mary and I went over there and caught some?" he asked.

"Now that's a great idea," Bill said. "Maybe I won't have to wait as long as you think, Tom, to get that tasty piece of quail." He went over and picked up the phone and dialed a number.

"Hello, John. This is Bill Wilson. I'd like to ask you a question. We're fine. I appreciate that. I'm glad everything turned out all right. Yes. You told me the other day that you had quite a few quail on your place. Would it be OK if my daughter Mary and her friend, Jimmy, come over there and catch a few of them?"

He smiled. "Yes, I said catch. They both have hunting hawks and they would like to see if they could catch some quail. I'm sure they can - right across from your place. O.K., John, they'll be coming over there tomorrow morning. Do they have to stop by and see you? Oh, you'll be busy. O.K. thanks. I'll talk with you later."

He hung up the phone and sat back down. He looked at Tom and then Jimmy. They both had big smiles on their faces. Tomorrow was going to be quite a day. A high adventure day for sure.

The next morning Tom, Mary, Jimmy, and Goldie got in Tom's truck and headed for Mr. Brown's farm.

Lost Feather

When they drove by, Jimmy pointed at the run-down place where Mr. Lucas took him.

Farther up the road they came to a nice looking farmhouse. He stopped the truck near the top of a small hill. They all got out. Lady Joan and Lady Gwen were both on log perches with their hoods on. Lady Gwen was the one that caught the first quail the other day when they hunted. It was amazing how one hawk was unable to turn as sharp as the quail and it would get away. But with both hawks hunting together when the quail tuned sharp to get away from one hawk, the other hawk caught it. They hoped they would work together the same way today.

With their hawks on fist and Goldie running back and forth ahead of them, they made their way out into a wheat field and headed for a row of small trees. They saw there was a lot of low-lying brush along the irrigation ditch.

They took the hoods off and the two sister hawks came alert to their surroundings. "You first, Mary," Jimmy said.

She raised her hand over her head and Lady Joan spread her wings and took off. She flapped her wings and swooped downward at first. Then slowly she rose higher and higher. High above she watched their every move, ready to hunt.

Mary gave Goldie the order. She ran into the bushes, coming out on the other side. Back and forth she ran in and out of the bushes. Nothing moved anywhere, but she didn't quit. She ran towards some high weeds by the edge of the wheat field.

All of a sudden there was a loud whirring sound. About a dozen quail flew a short distance and landed. Everybody stopped and watched, even Goldie. This was new to all of them, but Tom.

Lost Feather

They looked up to see what Lady Joan was doing. She was in a steep dive. With her wings folded back along her sides, she headed towards the spot where the quail landed. As she came close to them, they took off flying to the right, catching her off guard. She flapped her wings and flew off gaining altitude again.

"Send up your hawk, Jimmy," Tom said. "It's going to take two of them to catch those birds. They are a lot smarter than the pheasants."

Jimmy didn't hesitate. He raised his hand and Lady Gwen took off. She flapped her wings as she gained altitude. It wasn't long until both of them were high above.

"Hunt, Goldie!" Tom commanded, and off she went again. This was getting exciting and he liked it. He relived earlier days when he was a hunter. His eyes sparkled and his face had the stern look of a hunter.

The only thing was, he didn't have his bow and arrows. "Oh well, hawks will do," he thought. He smiled and looked up. Then he frowned as he looked around. "I sure hope they can catch at least one of them," he said. "I'm hungry for quail again."

They all laughed as they ran after Goldie. When they reached the place where Goldie flushed the quail out of the wheat, there was another loud whirring sound. Again the quail took off and flew a short distance and landed.

They looked up and saw the hawks dive. As they neared the area where the quail landed, they spread their wings and soared over the wheat. The quail took off and flew off to their left, only this time Lady Gwen was there and she caught one of them.

"You got your wish, Grandpa," Jimmy yelled as he ran over to where Lady Gwen flopped around on the ground.

Lost Feather

Mary was surprised to see that Lady Joan watched close by. She hurried over and took her to fist. "This is something new, and Lady Joan wants to do it, too," Mary thought. She didn't have to call her down with a lure. Their hunting together made them a great team.

Which hawk caught the quail depended on which way the quail flew off the second time. They watched the quail fly from the light cover of the wheat field to the more dense cover of the alfalfa fields. It was more work than they thought it would be, but they were so excited they kept hunting.

Tom finally stopped and looked at his watch. "I think I'm about ready to quit," he said, "We've been out here almost 2 hours."

"I agree, Grandpa," Jimmy said, looking at Mary.

She nodded her head in agreement and patted her game bag. It was full.

When they climbed into the pickup they were smiling. They had a dozen quail in the back with the two hooded hawks on their perches.

Tom started his pickup and just sat there a minute. "This has been a great day. One I will remember for a long time. How about you two?"

They both yelled, "Yes!"

He put the truck in gear and off they went, laughing. When they passed the place where Jimmy was held captive, he just glanced at it. "A good memory is a lot better than a bad one," he thought.

Tom pulled up at Mr. Wilson's garage. They were all in high spirits. Bill came out and looked in the back of the truck and gave a long whistle. "Now that's what I call a fine bunch of quail. I think I'll have quail tonight just like my best friend did last night.

Lost Feather

Tom got out and gave him six of them and patted his gray fender. "One good deed deserves another."

"That's right, Daddy," Mary said. "Mr. Warrior told us to send both of our hawks up to catch them, and it worked."

Bill smiled real big and Tom smiled back at him. Two young people, two hawks, and two families were going to enjoy a good meal that evening. What else could one ask for in the small town of Mercer, Colorado?

Lost Feather

CHAPTER VIII

The next morning Jimmy slept in. At nine o'clock his grandma knocked on the door and came in. Sleepy-eyed, he crawled out of bed and walked past her. She went back to the kitchen. He would be ready in a few minutes for the breakfast waiting for him.

She was right. When he came in he was all smiles and talked about last night's quail meal and how good it was. On and on he went about it. She set a bowl of oatmeal and toast in front of him. That ended his talking in a hurry.

When he finished he took the bowl and spoon over to the sink and rinsed them off. He looked at the clock above the sink and was surprised to see what time it was. "It's nine o'clock, Grandma."

"I let you sleep in today. With all you and your Grandpa did yesterday I decided to let you both sleep in. He's still in bed."

"Thanks, Grandma," he said, hugging her. She hugged him back. He looked out the window. "Mary was going to come over early this morning. I wonder what's keeping her. We're going to clean out the cages and see if we can find some better perches for the hawks to sit on. We talked about how it doesn't look very nice back there when someone comes by and wants to see the hawks."

"I agree," Alice said.

"It was Mary's idea. I didn't even think about it. It looked fine to me but I guess she knows best."

"I agree," Alice said again, as she headed for her bedroom.

Jimmy shrugged his shoulders and went out to the hawk pens. He cleaned up the place the best he could, but it didn't change the way it looked much. He worked some

Lost Feather

more and looked at what he had done and smiled. "Now that looks a lot better," he said to himself.

He went back into the house and stopped in his room first. He looked around and decided to clean it also. He moved a few things and put a few things in drawers. He stood back and looked at it. It now looked better. It was amazing how easy it was. He looked at the clock and saw that the morning was already gone.

He went into the kitchen where his grandma was busy cooking dinner. "I wonder where Mary is, Grandma," he said. He walked over to the front door and opened the screen door. He stepped out onto the porch and leaned up against one of the porch posts.

Alice came out onto the porch. "Oh, she'll be here when she can," she said. "You need to clean up. We'll be eating in a few minutes."

"Yes, ma'am," he said, as he headed towards the bathroom. After washing up he decided to go back out on the front porch to see if she was coming, but she was nowhere in sight. He walked over to the rocking chairs and sat down in his grandma's chair.

As he rocked, his eyes wandered to different things on the porch, then off towards the trees down by the highway. Out of the corner of his eye he saw something move. Looking in that direction he again saw something move to his left. "What is it?" he wondered. Then he sat upright when he saw who it was. It was Brad Bradley and Joe Crow standing in the shadows of a tree next to the alley. "What are those two doing around here now?" he thought.

Then he saw Mary come around the corner up at the highway, almost running toward his place. They saw her and quickly turned and hurried off down the alley. Then Joe stopped, turned and looked back at Jimmy sitting on the

Lost Feather

porch, and pointed at him. He heard him yell something; then they laughed and ran off.

Mary saw Jimmy on the porch and started waving and yelling at him. He couldn't hear what she said so he went down the steps and took off running to meet her. She came running up to him all out of breath. She stood there huffing and puffing and trying to get her breath, trying to tell him something. But Jimmy couldn't make out what she said.

Alice came out of the house to tell Jimmy that dinner was ready. She stopped when she saw Mary and Jimmy running toward each other. She hurried down the steps and ran to where they were. She took hold of Mary's arm. "Take your time, Mary," she said. "Take some deep breaths and quiet down. Then you'll be able to tell us what you have to say."

Mary took some deep breaths and it helped. She looked at them and started to cry. Again she started to tell them something, but now they couldn't understand her because she was crying. Jimmy didn't know what to do, but his grandma kept calm. She grabbed her by the arm and led her back to the house. They walked up the steps and onto the porch. Alice led Mary to a chair, then went over and sat down in her rocking chair and waited. Mary's crying soon ceased. She wiped her nose with her handkerchief, looked at them and gave a little sob.

"They're going to take our hawks from us, Jimmy," she said very low. "The game warden came to the garage this morning and told daddy! He talked and argued with him all morning. The game warden found out from those two guys that were down by your alley a while ago. They told him that we've been using hawks for hunting. He says it's against the law to use hawks to hunt with in this area of Colorado. Have you ever heard of anything so silly?"

Lost Feather

Jimmy sat down in his grandpa's chair. "What?"

"That's right, Jimmy," Mary said, only this time she didn't talk low. She was mad. "My daddy told him over and over about how we got our hawks, and that if it hadn't been for them your grandparents would have had a real hard time. But all the man says is, 'It's against the law.' Daddy doesn't know anything else to say or do."

"I wondered what Brad and Joe were laughing about." Jimmy said. "I heard them talking about something when they walked down the side street over there. They disappeared real quickly when they saw you come down the road. I surely don't know what I ever did to get those two mad at me. Why are they mad at me, Grandma?"

Some people don't need a reason to be mad at someone, Jimmy," Alice said. "Just being an Indian is enough for some people."

"Daddy is still talking to him over at the garage," Mary said. "Mr. Miller is there with them. They're trying to get everyone around town to come by and talk to the game warden. They're all hoping they can get him to change his mind."

Tom was in the house listening to everything. He opened the screen door, came out onto the porch and reached down and patted Mary on the shoulder. "It's not going to change the law, Mary, is it?" he said softly.

Mary didn't say anything as she slowly shook her head.

"No. The law is the law." Tom continued. "We abide by the law. So if it's against the law to use hawks to hunt with in this area of Colorado, then it's against the law. No matter how much talking is done, it's not going to change it."

Jimmy's mouth fell open. How could his grandpa say such a thing? It would mean that he would have to give

Lost Feather

up Lady Samson and her chicks, Lady Gwen and Lady Joan. He'd never had anything of his own before he caught Lady Samson. She'd brought him through some tough times since he came to Mercer. Now that things were finally going good for him his grandpa had to spoil it all by not wanting to fight for him to keep his hawks.

"But, Grandpa," Jimmy shouted getting up from his grandpa's chair, "Lady Samson is all I have. Not only that, I'm the only thing she has. She was treated so mean by her first owner, and now she has the love she needs. I love her, Grandpa. You can't let them take her away from me now. She's all that I have."

"No, she's not, Jimmy," his grandpa said. "You have much more here than just a bird. You have your grandma and me. We love you. But we cannot break the law, Jimmy. You understand that don't you?"

"No, I don't," he answered angrily. "I don't understand at all. I would think you would try everything so I can keep my hawks. Mary's father is trying right now to help Mary and me keep our hawks. But you don't seem to care."

"I do care, Jimmy," he said looking him in the eyes. "If there was any way you could keep them, I would fight for your keeping them. But Mary said the game warden said it was against the law. I've known for some time that it was against the law. But everyone around here went along with what you were doing, so I said nothing. But it is against the law to use hawks of any kind to hunt with."

Jimmy stopped and looked at his grandpa. "You knew it all the time. Why didn't you tell me? You said that you wished that we could have a secret like grandma and I have. But you kept it to yourself and now I have to get rid of Lady Samson. I could have hidden her. There are a lot of things I could have done. Why didn't you tell me? You

Lost Feather

should have told me! Especially, after what I did for you. You should have told me!"

His grandpa did not say a word. Jimmy saved his life and he knew it. All he could say now to his grandson was, "It's the law."

Alice took hold of Jimmy's shoulder and shook him hard. "I should spank you for what you just said to your grandpa, Jimmy. You wanted me to teach you things that only I know. You should never brag about helping someone. You never hold it over their heads that they owe you a favor. You will have to change your attitude if you ever want me to teach you what I know. Do you understand me?"

Jimmy couldn't believe he was being scolded by both of his grandparents. He shrugged his shoulders and the attitude he had on the streets of Newark, New Jersey, came back. "I don't need either one of you. I can get along on my own. I've survived on the streets before and I can do it again. I've helped you both ever since I've been here, and this is the way I'm treated for it. Well, you both can go back to the way you were living before I came here. I'll go back to Newark. At least I'll know who'll rat on me there," he told them.

Jimmy turned and ran into the house and straight to his bedroom. He got his suitcase out from under the bed and opened the clothes closet. There were all of his clothes, hanging pressed and clean. He reached for them and stopped. He stood there with his hand out, not moving.

There was a tap on his bedroom open door. He turned to see Mary standing there. Tears ran down her face, but not a sound came from her. She walked over to the bed. She couldn't look him in the eye.

"I've come to say good-bye, Jimmy," she said slowly. "I'm sorry that I brought bad news to you. Bad

Lost Feather

news seems to have explosive surroundings. Everyone's trying to change the game warden's mind. But even if they don't, they will have tried. Not for themselves, Jimmy, but for you. They all know how it will hurt you if you lose your hawks."

Jimmy's hand was outstretched toward the closet. He lowered it slowly and turned to face Mary, but he could not speak.

Mary's tears ceased and she dried them with a handkerchief. "You know, Jimmy, the people are trying to show you they like you. They don't want you going back to the big city where you came from. They want you to stay here. The hawks are important to both of us, but not enough for me to run away from home. My home is very precious to me. It's more precious than a bird, or a dog, or anything else. These hawks will die one of these days, Jimmy, and we won't have them then. Will you run away from home when they die?"

"This is not my home," Jimmy said.

"Yes, it is, Jimmy!" she said angrily. "You know it is. Home is where you're loved, and you are loved here. There is no one more loving than your grandparents. They love you so much. But they will not let you break the law. You should be proud of that, not angry. Some people don't care if their family breaks the law. They have no love for them if they do or if they don't. Those two boys who told the game warden are like that. I've been told that their parents let them do what they want, even break the law. That's not love, Jimmy, and you know it."

Jimmy walked back to the bed and looked at the suitcase. He reached down and closed it, picked it up and put it back under the bed. He slapped his hands to his side and with a look of desperation he said, "Mary, what am I going to do now? I said a lot of things that I shouldn't have

Lost Feather

a few minutes ago. I can't take them back. I might as well go ahead and leave."

He started to reach under his bed again but Mary stopped him. She took Jimmy's hand and shook her head. She led him out of his bedroom and into the kitchen. Jimmy's grandparents quietly sat at the table. With tear stained faces, they both looked up as Mary and Jimmy came into the room. A smile came across their faces as they looked and saw no suitcase in Jimmy's hand.

"Jimmy has decided to stay," Mary said with a quiver in her voice.

Jimmy's grandparents got up and hugged him. "I don't want to go anywhere," he said, looking at them. "If I have to give up the hawks, then I'll give them up. I'm sorry I said the things I did."

Jimmy's grandparents didn't say a word, but their faces showed they were pleased. Mary took Jimmy's hand again and they went back out onto the porch.

Mary sat down in Alice's chair and Jimmy sat down in his grandpa's. For a long time, they said nothing. "I'm glad you're not going to leave," Mary said as she turned and looked at him.

"So am I," Jimmy replied. "I don't want to go back to Newark. My mother doesn't want me. It would be nothing but trouble. I'm also glad that I'm here in Mercer, where people care enough to stick up for me."

The screen door opened and Tom and Alice came out onto the porch. Mary and Jimmy got up. They both sat down in their chairs and Alice rocked slowly back and forth. Mary and Jimmy smiled at each other as they went over and sat down on the porch steps. "Jimmy," his grandma said.

"Yes, Ma'am," Jimmy answered and turned and looked at her.

Lost Feather

Smiling at him, she said, "That's the first time you've said ma'am to me, Jimmy. Your daddy used to say that to me a lot." She rocked a couple times and said. "A lot of things were said a few minutes ago, Jimmy, that needed saying. The air is clear now. With that said, we can see clearer now than before. I ask you not to dwell on it too much. We need to remember and do better. Do you understand what I'm saying, Jimmy?"

"Yes, Ma'am," he said.

Tom got up and looked down their lane. He watched as a car turned off the highway and came down the road. It stopped at the lane leading up to their house. Whoever it was, he was looking for something, or somebody. Slowly it moved along; then it entered their lane and drove up to the house.

It stopped in front of the house. A young man got out of his car and closed the door. He walked around his car and up to where Mary and Jimmy sat. He smiled at them and raised his head and looked at Tom and Alice. He tipped his hat to Alice.

"Good afternoon," he said. "I'm Dale Walton, the game warden for this county. I'm told this is the Warrior house."

Tom got up and stepped between Mary and Jimmy's legs to get to the bottom of the steps. "I'm Tom Warrior, Dale, and this is my wife, Alice," he said, and shook his hand. "Come up and sit down. Jimmy, go get a chair for this man."

Jimmy got up and went inside and brought out a folding chair for the game warden. "Would you like something to drink?" Alice asked.

"Yes, I would," he replied. "I've been talking for almost four hours down at Mr. Wilson's garage. I surely could use some lemonade if you have some."

Lost Feather

Alice got up and went inside. As he sat there they could hear her making it. The ice rattled as she filled the glasses. "So you're Jimmy," the game warden said, looking at him.

"Yes, sir," he replied, and stood up and shook his hand, then sat back down.

Dale turned and looked at Mary. "I saw you down at the garage, Mary. You're Mr. Wilson's daughter."

"Yes, sir," she replied smiling up at him.

Dale looked at both of them, and then back at Tom. "I'd say you know why I'm here, so I won't go into all I've been through at the garage. It's against the law to hunt with hawks. I'm not here to fine you because it was minors who broke the law, but I'm here to see that it's stopped. Where are the hawks?"

"The hawks are out back in their pens." Tom said, pointing.

Dale's mouth fell open. "You mean after all the time they kept me down at the station so they could warn you, you didn't hide them?"

"No, sir," Tom answered, only this time he smiled. "If it's against the law to hunt with hawks, then we won't hunt with them. It was Jimmy's idea. He said he didn't want to break the law and you could take them if you want."

He was about to say something else when the screen door opened, and he stopped.

Alice came out with a tray of glasses and a pitcher of lemonade. She set it down and poured a glass for everyone. Dale just sat there looking at each of them. He'd shake his head now and then as he sipped on his lemonade. He then looked at Alice. "This surely is good lemonade, Alice."

Lost Feather

"Thank you, Dale," Alice said, looking him in the eye. "What do you intend to do with my grandson's hawks?"

"Well," he said, squirming around in his chair. "Well, to tell you the truth I didn't think you'd give them up so easy. The way everyone stood up for what Jimmy did to supply meat for you when Tom couldn't work, I just thought you'd hide them, or turn them loose, or something. I didn't know you'd just give them to me."

They all sipped on their lemonade for some time. Alice got up and filled Dale's glass each time it got empty. They all waited for Dale to say something, but he was in deep thought about what to do. Finally he shook the ice in his glass and looked at Jimmy. "They tell me you won a contest at the Air Force Academy at Colorado Springs."

"Yes, sir," Jimmy said, beaming a little.

"I tell you what," Dale said. "Let me check around and see if I can find a home for your hawks. They need new hawks now and then down at the Academy. Since their judge gave your hawks first place, well, we'll see. Let me check it out and I'll get back to you."

Jimmy looked at Mary. They were glad everything turned out the way it was.

Dale drank the rest of his lemonade in one gulp and set the glass down on the tray. He looked at Jimmy and Mary. "I want you to promise me that you won't hunt with the hawks again. If you'll promise, I'll leave them here for a few days. That will give me time to find a good home for all three of them."

Jimmy looked at Mary and then looked up at Dale. "We were going to go hunting this morning, but your coming put a stop to that." He looked at his grandparents and they shook their heads in agreement. "OK, we won't hunt with them again."

Lost Feather

"Good," Dale said, as he got up and made his way down the steps toward his car.

"I want to thank you, Mr. Walton," Jimmy said, as he got up and followed behind the game warden.

Dale turned in surprise. "You want to thank me, Jimmy?"

"Yes, sir," Jimmy replied. "Thanks for leaving the hawks here for a few days. If I hadn't had a chance to say good-bye to Lady Samson I don't know what I'd have done. But you've been nice enough to leave her here so I can do that."

Dale put his hand on Jimmy's shoulder. "You're welcome, Jimmy. I tell you what, I'll phone Mary's father when I hear from the Academy. Would you like that?"

"Yes, sir," he said, "I would, and Mary would, too. I think she loves her hawk as much as I love mine."

Dale stuck his hand out and shook Jimmy's hand. "It's a deal then." He turned, walked around his car and opened the door. He looked over the car at everyone. Then he looked down at the ground by the car and scratched some dirt with his foot. He looked up.

"Jimmy, you and Mary will have to feed those hawks every day. I realize that you use some of what the hawks catch to feed them. So if you'll let your hawks hunt for their own food I could go along with that. No need for them not to eat like they should. Would that be O.K. with you two?"

Jimmy looked at Mary and she nodded her approval. "Yippee!" Jimmy shouted.

"That would be great," Mary said. She ran around the car and gave Dale a peck on the cheek. She stepped back. "I thank you, too," she said.

Dale got into his car and started it up. He sat there a few seconds, put the car in gear and drove on around the

Lost Feather

circle, then honked his horn at everyone and waved as he headed out onto the road. He turned right on the highway and headed off down the road towards Denver. He was soon out of sight, hidden by the trees that lined the road. He wouldn't forget this day for some time.

Mary looked at Jimmy and smiled. "Let's go put those hawks up in the air. They won't be with us much longer, and we need to give them as much freedom as we can. It could be a long time before they'll ever hunt again."

"Wait, Jimmy, have you forgotten we haven't eaten yet?" Alice asked, "It's probably cold by now, but let's go in and eat before you and Mary go work with the hawks."

"O.K., Grandma, with all the excitement I did forget about dinner," Jimmy answered, "I am really hungry. Mary, can you eat with us?"

"I think it will be alright," she said, "I'm sure my parents have already eaten and they know where I am."

After dinner, Jimmy and Mary ran around the house to the hawks' pens. After Alice cleaned the kitchen, she and Tom went out on the porch and sat quietly for some time. Alice rocked back and forth, and Tom just leaned back, enjoying his comfortable chair. They heard Jimmy and Mary talking behind the house. Now and then one of the hawks screeched. Tom smiled and looked at Alice.

"Everything turns out for the best when love is expressed. Look at how Dale turned out when he was shown a little love. And look at Jimmy, Alice. I love him so much sometimes it hurts. He reminds me of Tommy when he was Jimmy's age. I thank the man above for giving us a chance to raise another boy. Some people never get a second chance like we've been given."

Alice kept on rocking. Not a word was spoken as they sat and thought of many things. She rocked slower and

Lost Feather

slower until the rocker was sitting still. She got up and looked up towards the sky. "I thank you, too," she said.

She reached down and placed her hand on her husband's shoulder. "It hurt me the same way, Tom. I'll go fix supper," she said, as she opened the screen door. "They'll both be starved again when they get back."

She paused and looked back down the road where the car went. "We almost lost him today, Tom. Mary was the key. We both sat, but did nothing and would have let him go back to the big city. He would have been lost among all of that mass of people. Not wanted, and alone. There's no telling what he would have become. My heart just broke. We must never do that again. The next time we might lose him for good; then we'd all be losers."

Tom hung his head and said nothing. The grief in his heart showed on his face. What if he left? "Yes," he thought, "today would have been a sad day instead of a great and joyous day." Sitting in his chair he moved his feet back and forth.

"I'll fix Jimmy's favorite dessert," Alice said, joyfully. "It's yours too, Tom---cherry pie." She turned and went into the house, humming as she went.

Tom's face turned from a frown to a smile. Cherry pie, now that should drive away any sadness that anyone around here could ever have. Tom smiled as he leaned back in his chair. He was suddenly very tired.

A lot happened that day, and he wasn't completely over that spider bite. He lay his head back on the cushion on the top of the chair and closed his eyes. His head nodded a couple of times and he was asleep.

Lost Feather

CHAPTER IX

The days went by slowly for Jimmy and Mary. Each day they took their hawks out to let them hunt. They caught enough food the first day to last two days. Dale Walton, the game warden did not call Mr. Wilson. They enjoyed every moment they spent with their hawks. Everything looked so good the day Dale was at Jimmy's house. But now doubt arose in their minds. "What will happen to the hawks?" they wondered.

One day when Jimmy and Mary finished their hunt with the hawks, they both felt great. Each hawk caught a large jack rabbit. As they walked back to the pens with the hawks and their catch, Mary looked at Jimmy. "Are you ready for school to start?" she asked.

It caught Jimmy off guard. He forgot all about school. He thought about it a few times earlier that month, but when the problem arose about the hawks, he blanked it out of his mind. "I forgot all about school, Mary. When does it start here?"

"All schools in Colorado start the day after Labor Day," she said. She noticed the frown on his face.

When he opened the door to his hawk pen he was in deep thought. He placed Lady Samson on one side of the pens. Mary walked around the pens and put Lady Joan in her pen next to Lady Gwen's. Jimmy looked at Mary through the small chicken wire that separated the two pens. "I don't have anything to start school with, Mary," he said. He walked back out of the pen and placed a lock through the hasp on the door and locked it.

Mary locked her pen and they sat down on the sawhorse next to the pile of railroad ties. Mary finally said, "Jimmy, you don't need anything to start to school in Mercer but a couple pencils and a notebook with paper.

Lost Feather

That's all anyone that I know has when they start school," she said.

Jimmy shook his head as she talked. "No, Mary, that's not all they have. They also have nice clothes. I don't have anything nice to wear to school. I don't have any money to buy any either."

"That's not the way it is here in Mercer, Jimmy," Mary replied. "A lot of people here don't have much money. They do the best they can for their kids. Everyone knows that and accepts it. You don't have to dress up to go to Mercer High School. You'll see next week."

What Mary said helped him feel a little better. But still he didn't want people to look down on him or his grandparents. If he could find a way to get some new clothes he would do it. He'd look around and see if he could earn some money.

They heard a car pull up in front of the house. They jumped off the pile of wood and ran around the house to see who it was. It was Mary's father, Bill Wilson. He was standing on the porch when they came running up. "There you two are," he said. "Mr. Walton, the game warden, called me a while ago, and asked me to come tell you two something. Do you want to know what he had to say?"

They both said, "Yes," at the same time.

"Well," he said slowly, "Maybe I'll wait until I have some of Alice's lemonade. Dale told me she made the best lemonade he ever tasted. Not that I didn't know that already."

"All right, Bill," Alice said smiling. "I'll go in and get you some. But you can't tell anyone anything until I get back."

They all laughed except Jimmy and Mary, who flung up their hands in desperation. "Take it easy you two," Mr. Wilson said laughing. "I'd do anything to get some

Lost Feather

lemonade right now. Just sit down for a minute and you'll be glad you waited. It's good news."

Jimmy and Mary sat on the edge of the steps and waited. Alice soon appeared with a tray with glasses for everyone. A big pitcher of lemonade splashed back and forth when she set it down on the porch. She then quickly filled each glass with lemonade and sat down in her chair, "Now, Bill, what's the news?" she asked.

"Well," Mr. Wilson said slowly after he had taken a big drink. "I think I may have forgotten."

Alice got up and took the glass out of his hand. "Oh, now I remember," he said laughing. Alice put the glass back in his hand as he kept on laughing. Alice looked at him as if she would take the glass away again, and he pulled the glass back and stopped laughing.

Everyone was now laughing. Bill smiled at them and said. "Mr. Walton told me that he went down to the Air Force Academy a couple of times since he was here. He worked out a deal with them for you to give them your hawks." He looked at Jimmy and Mary. "All three of them," he said.

Jimmy and Mary jumped off the steps and started dancing around in the driveway. Bill waved them back toward the porch. They came back and sat down. "Mr. Walton said they remembered your hawk. He also talked to Mr. Archer, who was a judge at the show. They want you to bring the hawks next Monday. Next Monday is Labor Day, you know, and they plan to have a ceremony of some kind when you present your hawks to them as a gift. He said he was pleased to let you know your hawks will have the best homes a hawk could ever have. They will get excellent care there at the Academy."

"That's great," Jimmy said. "I'd like for Mr. Miller to go with us. He's the one who took us down there the first

Lost Feather

time. We owe him a lot for all he's done for us, and I'd like to do that for him."

"That sounds like a real good idea, Jimmy," Mr. Wilson said. "I'll talk to him about it. I'm sure he'll want to go. We'll have two cars going, which means we can take everybody. We'll make it an all day affair, might even take a picnic lunch with us, and eat it after you give your hawks to the Academy."

Tom and Alice smiled at Bill. It had been a long time since they were in Colorado Springs. It sure was beautiful country down there, and just the idea of going back brought back fond memories of their childhood. They lived in that part of Colorado when they were younger, and to see it again would be a blessing for both of them.

The next day, Jimmy took Lady Samson out into the field behind the Warrior house by himself. He wanted to do something different that would surprise everyone. He grabbed the leather thongs tied to Lady Samson's feet with his left hand, then took off her hood. She looked at him as he took his comb out of his back pocket. He talked softly to her as he rubbed the feathers on her neck with the back of his comb. He was so proud of her. He put his comb back in his pocket and raised her up to eye level. It was time for her to learn one more thing before he let her go.

He ran across the field with her on his gloved fist. She opened her wings a little to keep her balance as he ran. Jimmy stopped and talked to her in a soft, low voice as he stroked her with his fingers. Then he started running again. Each time he did this she stretched her wings out further and further, until at last her wings were fully extended. He was so pleased with her performance he gave her a big hug when they finished which surprised her and she fluttered backwards a little.

Lost Feather

He decided he wouldn't do that again. He ran and repeated the lesson, only running a short distance each time. He didn't want to tire her too much. The next day he discovered she remembered what he taught her. When he finished that day he felt they would have a nice surprise for everyone at the Air Force Academy if everything worked out like he hoped it would.

Time once again seemed to slow down for all of them. They took a lot of walks, then sat around and talked about all of the things they were going to do. The little things they did with the hawks now seemed less important, and they were more interested in going to Colorado Springs than anything else. Jimmy and Mary were seen now and then, just walking along together daydreaming, and not saying a word.

Alice and Tom spent a lot of time sitting on their front porch. They, too, said very little as their minds wandered over the memories of their younger days in Colorado Springs. Bill Wilson and Chuck Miller were a little better at not showing their eagerness to go. Their work helped them cover it up so others didn't know how anxious they were for Monday to get there.

Bill fell over backwards in his chair in the office one day. He leaned back thinking about the trip, and his chair toppled over. He had a red face when he got up and looked around to see if anyone saw what happened. He laughed out loud when he realized that he was alone.

Chuck Miller drove his tractor into the creek one day. He had to go back to the barn and get another tractor to pull it out. He, too, was daydreaming while he was plowing, and ran through the fence at the end of a row. The fence was right along the edge of Mercer Creek, so down the tractor went with him standing on the brake trying to

Lost Feather

stop it. It was funny after it was over, but he felt different at the time it happened.

Jimmy slept in that Saturday morning. When he got up he stayed around the house for a while then decided to walk over to Mr. Wilson's garage. Mary would probably stop there before she came to help work with the hawks. He'd get to talk to Mr. Wilson a little more about the trip.

As he walked out of their lane and onto the road, an old car turned the corner off the highway and headed toward him. He stepped off the road and waited for it to pass. But instead of passing him, it pulled up beside him and a young kid stuck his head out the window and looked at him. "You Jimmy Warrior?" he asked.

"Yes," Jimmy replied.

"I'm Don Nix. I saw a couple of guys I know heading for Sand Rock Cave with your hawks awhile ago," he said.

"What?" Jimmy yelled turning and running back toward his house.

Don shook his head as he watched Jimmy disappear around the house. "You're welcome," he said. He put the car in gear, turned around, and drove off.

When Jimmy got to the pens he found the locks had been torn off the cages. The doors were open and all of the hawks were gone. "What am I going to do now?" he wondered. "Where did he say they took them? Sand Rock Cave. Where in the world is that?"

He ran back around the house and found that Don already left. He ran until he got to Mr. Wilson's garage. He rushed into the office and looked around for someone. No one was there, so he went through the office and into the garage. Mr. Wilson was in the grease pit draining the oil out of his car. He was getting it ready for the trip Monday.

"Where's Sand Rock Cave?" Jimmy yelled.

Lost Feather

"What?" Bill asked, turning around and letting some of the oil drain onto the floor. He quickly turned around and kept his mind on his business. "Quiet down, Jimmy," he said, watching the oil slowly come to a stop. He put the plug back in the oil pan and tightened it up with a wrench.

He took a rag out of his back pocket and bent over and cleaned up the oil spill. Jimmy was ready to burst when he looked at him again. "O.K., Jimmy, tell me what happened."

Jimmy told him what Don Nix told him, and Bill's face got red. "Those two are going to get in trouble over this little prank." He walked into the office and picked up the phone, then put it down. He looked out his office window and saw Brad Bradley and Joe Crow walk by. He ran out the office door and up to them. They backed up a little and Joe got behind Brad. Jimmy stood in the office door and watched them. Brad looked at Mr. Wilson and then glanced at the garage and saw Jimmy standing in the doorway.

"What is it you want, old man?" Brad said with his hands on his hips. "You don't scare me at all."

We'll, I'm going to do more than scare you this time, Brad," Bill said. "I'm going to talk to your dad about putting you and Joe in jail for a couple of days. Someone saw you steal Jimmy's hawks this morning."

"How could anyone see us steal something we didn't steal, old man?" Brad replied. "I wouldn't advise you talking to my old man either. He's planning on being appointed marshal next month, and you'll be out of that job. He's got a lot of friends in town and he's got it all sewed up. So if you know what's good for you, you'll shut up, or I'll get mad and have you put in jail when he's marshal. How do you like that, old man?"

Lost Feather

Brad's not backing down surprised Bill, but he'd dealt with braggarts like him before. "We'll see about that young man," Bill said.

"Yeah, we will," Brad replied. "Oh yes, old man, we saw someone put some hawks in Sand Rock Cave about an hour ago." He then looked at Jimmy. "If you and your Indian friend want them, you know where they are." He turned and walked off with Joe following close behind. After they went a few steps they started laughing. They did it again and they felt proud of themselves.

Bill shook his head as he walked back to Jimmy. "Let's go get your hawks, Jimmy," he said as he put the sign "Gone To Lunch" in the window. They hurried out of the office and got into his truck. Brad and Joe stopped and watched them drive by. They laughed at them as they passed. Brad turned and walked down the street toward the beer joints, and Joe followed. Jimmy watched as they went into the first one they came to and shut the door behind them. "What mean things those two do for fun," he thought to himself. He turned around and noticed Mr. Wilson watching them in the rear view mirror.

They arrived at the cave about a half-hour later. They went in slowly, checking everything. They didn't know what Brad and Joe might have done to the birds. The cave got smaller and smaller as they walked into it, and they finally bent over so their heads wouldn't hit the roof of the cave. It was harder on Mr. Wilson than it was on Jimmy.

Then up ahead in the shadows Jimmy thought he saw some movement. He stopped to make sure. Then he saw them. They stood on the ground huddled together with hoods over their heads.

"What a cruel thing to do to these beautiful birds," he thought. "They would have starved to death inside the

Lost Feather

cave because they could not get their hoods off." He shook his head. He would have to thank Don Nix for telling him where they took the hawks.

"There they are, Mr. Wilson." Jimmy pointed to where they stood in the back of the cave. They walked slowly up to where they were huddled together. "How are we going to get them out of here? We need gloves, Mr. Wilson."

"I think those are gloves over there," Mr. Wilson said, pointing at something on the ground. "Yep. They brought them in here and threw the gloves over there before they left."

They put the gloves on and Mr. Wilson took the two young hawks while Jimmy got Lady Samson. He was glad to see her and have her on his fist again.

Lady Samson responded by shivering. Jimmy was glad to get her off the cold damp ground. He talked to her as he carried her out of the cave. By the time they reached the entrance, she quit shivering and was calm.

The heat from the sun helped warm them up as they carried them to the truck. Jimmy sat in the back of the truck with the three hawks, while Mr. Wilson drove back to Mercer. When they got to Jimmy's house, Mary came out of the front door waving.

"Hello, you two," she yelled, with a smile. "What have you been doing with the hawks?"

Bill waved at her as he drove around the house to the pens, and Mary followed.

"Well?" she asked as she walked up to the truck. Jimmy slowly got out of the back of the truck with Lady Samson on his gloved hand. She followed as he went inside the pen and put her on her perch.

"Brad and Joe stole our hawks this morning, Mary," Jimmy said, closing the pen's door. He pointed at the gate.

Lost Feather

"They tore the locks off the pens, took all three of them and put them in Sand Rock Cave. We were lucky to find them. A guy named Don Nix came by this morning and told me he saw them putting them in there. Your father and I went and got them. They would have been in bad shape if we hadn't found them when we did."

"Those two should be put in jail," Mary said. "Daddy, you need to put those two in jail."

"He told them he was going to do just that," Jimmy said. "But Brad told him his dad is going to be appointed marshal, and your dad will be out of that job. He said that he has it all sewed up. He said he would have his dad put your dad in jail if he messes with him. Then he told us they saw someone put the hawks in the cave."

Mary looked at her father and he looked back at her. "When he told me he saw someone put the hawks in the cave, Mary," Bill said, "that cleared them of anything I could do to them. It would be their word against Jimmy's, and I doubt that Don Nix would testify against them. Brad's a smart kid. He just says and does stupid things. Too bad he doesn't know how to put his intelligence to good work."

When the hawks were back in the pens, the three of them stood back and looked at them.

"You won't have to worry about those two again," Jimmy said to the hawks. "Saturday you'll be in Colorado Springs. Nobody will mess with you at the Air Force Academy."

Lost Feather

CHAPTER X

Saturday came and everyone got together at the Warriors' house after church. They made plans for what foods to take, who would bring what, and how much. It would be a great day if it didn't rain. Picnics usually brought rain, but they sure hoped it wouldn't this time. They hoped it would be a beautiful day.

Bill's wife, Helen, and Chuck's wife, Jackie, were there. They were as excited as the rest. "The excitement around here is catching," Helen said to Jackie, as they decided what they would bring for the picnic.

"It sure is," Jackie said, with a smile. "I watched those two kids work with the hawks around our barn for some time. They helped us a lot. The rats were getting quite a few of our eggs, plus a lot of the baby chickens we raised. I'm grateful for what those two did around here. They could have turned out like some of the other kids that seem to do nothing but get in trouble."

"Thanks," Helen said, patting Jackie on the shoulder. "I needed that. I'm proud of them, too. You're right. They could have been destructive instead of constructive." She looked around and then said, "I sure do like picnics---if it doesn't rain and the wind doesn't blow too hard and there are no ants."

"I agree," Jackie said, and they laughed.

The men wondered what they were laughing about. Bill and Chuck just shook their heads and continued talking. With everything decided, the Wilsons and the Millers left. The Warriors ate supper and sat around the house not saying much until bedtime.

The alarm beside Jimmy's bed went off at five o'clock that morning. Most of the time he would have just reached over, turned it off, and gone back to sleep, but not

Lost Feather

today. He jumped out of bed, turned off the alarm with one hand, and reached for his clothes with the other. He dressed as fast as he could and ran into the bathroom. Grandpa shaved earlier and the mirror was still steamed up. He heard Jimmy's alarm go off and left a few seconds before he got there.

Jimmy cleaned up, brushed his teeth and hair, and was ready for breakfast. He went into the kitchen. His grandma stood by the table, and his grandpa sat and looked out the window.

"It's going to be a beautiful day, Jimmy," his grandpa said. "Look at that orange glow in the east. There are only a couple of clouds off in the distance. I'd say we're going to have a nice day. Maybe a little warm, but probably not too hot."

"I hope you're right," Jimmy said, as he sat down at the table. His grandma put a stack of pancakes and two eggs on his plate. He reached for the butter, but just as his hand touched the butter dish he remembered and pulled it back. His grandpa smiled, then gave thanks for the food, and everything they had, and everybody they knew.

He finished and reached over and passed the butter to Jimmy. "Thanks, Grandpa," Jimmy said, "for everything."

Tom sat and watched Jimmy pile the butter on top of the pancakes. "You're welcome, Jimmy," he said, after a while. "I'd like it if you'd leave me a little butter for my pancakes," he said laughing.

Jimmy stopped putting butter on his pancakes and looked down at them. He was so excited he didn't realize what he was doing. He started to scrape some of it off, but it was melting and running down the sides and onto his plate. Tom now laughed harder at the sight of Jimmy trying

Lost Feather

to pick up the butter with his knife and put it back on the butter dish.

Alice came over and watched her grandson; then she reached down and picked up the butter dish and passed it to Tom. "Don't worry about it, Jimmy," she said, smiling. "You eat. We have a lot to do before we're ready to leave."

With breakfast over, they got busy packing a large basket Grandpa brought in from the garage. It slowly filled up until there was no more room. Alice said she still had two more things that needed to go. Tom went back out to the garage and looked around. He came back with an Easter basket. Alice smiled as she picked it up and looked at it. She put it on the counter and filled it up. Everything fit just right. She got a dishtowel and tucked it around the items in the basket. "That was just what I needed," she said. "One of the bowls in the basket has boiled eggs in it. Now that's what an Easter basket was made for."

A car drove up outside. Jimmy got up and rushed over to the door. "It's Mr. Miller," he said. "He hooked his trailer onto his car." Jimmy stood there thinking. "The Wilsons should be here pretty soon. I'll go out and load the hawks into the trailer. Jimmy took a deep breath to help calm down, then turned and ran out the back door to get the hawks.

First he unlocked all of the pens; then he put hoods on each of the hawks. He carried Lady Samson out and put her on her perch in the back of Mr. Miller's trailer. Lady Gwen was next, and she gave him a little trouble, as she wasn't used to being bothered that early in the morning. Then Lady Joan flapped around when he put her in beside the other two, which disturbed them. He talked in a calm voice and soon had them calm. He closed the trailer door and took another deep breath of the cool Colorado morning air. "Nothing like it," he thought.

Lost Feather

He enjoyed the thought of all that was happening. He saw a couple of stars. The sky in the east started to change from black to gray. He turned and walked up the porch steps, and smiled when he heard his grandparents talking.

"Everything's ready to go, Tom," Alice said. "Are you feeling all right? We surely don't want you to overdo it today."

"I'm feeling good all over," Tom said. He went over and started to pick up the big basket she packed. Alice slapped his hand. He drew it back with a hurt look on his face. "You let someone else carry that heavy basket," she said. She reached over and got the small basket. "You can carry this one. I don't want you hurting yourself."

Jimmy came walking into the kitchen and smiled at his grandparents. He walked over and tried to pick up the large basket, but it was very heavy. He shook his head, wondering what his grandma put in it.

Mr. Miller came up onto the porch and knocked. "Come on in here, Chuck," Alice said. "I need you to carry this heavy basket out to your car for me."

Chuck came in and picked up the basket. "This thing is heavy, Alice," he said. "Jimmy, you give me a hand. I'm not as strong as your grandmother thinks I am. You grab the handle on that end and I'll grab the one on this end."

They carried the basket out to his car. Chuck opened the trunk before he came in, and all they had to do was put the basket into the trunk. They breathed a sigh of relief as they headed back towards the house. The Wilsons drove up and parked behind the truck.

Tom came out with the Easter basket in his hand. He swung it back and forth as he walked. His face had no smile on it as he walked over and set the basket down in the

135

Lost Feather

trunk, turned and said, "I'm taking my Easter basket with me, and don't any of you laugh."

Bill and Helen got out of their car. Jackie, Chuck, and Jimmy looked at Tom. It was an invitation to laugh. But they didn't know if Tom was serious or not. Slowly a smile came across his face. Chuck and Bill went over and tried to pick him up and put him in the trunk with his Easter basket.

After the joking and laughing was over, they all went into the house where Alice was about ready. "Is everyone ready to go?" she asked.

"I am," Jimmy said, as he went over and opened the door. The sun came up as he looked out. "It is a nice day, Grandpa, just like you said it would be."

"Dale Walton called me right before we left," Bill said. "He will be waiting at the gate for us. He said it looks like it will be a nice day down there, too." Everyone smiled at that good news.

That seemed to be the signal they needed to leave. They all went out, got into the cars, and drove down the lane and onto the road. As they turned onto the highway Chuck and Bill started blowing their car horns. It was an exciting time for all of them, and they wanted everyone in town to know it.

Mile after mile began to roll by. Denver came into view and then disappeared behind them. Castle Rock was the next town. It, too, soon appeared in their windshield, then, disappeared in their rear windows. They made good time. The next town they came to would be their destination, Colorado Springs.

The Air Force Academy was on the north side of town. They would come to the Academy before they arrived in Colorado Springs. Jimmy and Mary rode with Mr. Miller, and Tom and Alice were in Mr. Wilson's car.

Lost Feather

Jimmy and Mary remembered Mr. Miller told them about the church on the Academy grounds. "It has high peaks on its roof and a spire," he said, "which can be seen from the highway long before you see the Academy buildings."

Jimmy mentioned it to everyone the day before. He told them they strained their eyes looking for it that time when they went to the hawk contest at the Air Force Academy.

So it was only natural that everyone looked for a church with high pointed peaks on the roof when they got close to Colorado Springs. When the church spire came into view, Jimmy and Mary pointed and said at the same time, "There's the church."

They drove until they came to the main entrance ramp off the highway to the Academy. Chuck slowed down and turned off the highway at the Academy exit. Bill Wilson followed him to the main entrance. As they drove up, Jimmy smiled. Dale Walton stood next to his car. He was dressed up in his uniform.

"There's Mr. Walton," Jimmy said, and pointed in his direction.

Chuck pulled up beside him, with Bill Wilson right behind him. Dale saw who it was and came up to the window. "Hello there, everybody. I'm glad to see you made it here safely. I have it worked out with the guards to let you go in without any trouble. He gave each of them their pass.

He then went back to Bill's car and talked to them and gave them their passes.

Walking past Chuck's car, Dale said, "Just follow me." He got in his car and drove up to the guards, who motioned for everyone to go on through. They soon arrived at the building in front of the football stadium. It was where they brought Jimmy's hawk, Strong Feather Lady Samson,

Lost Feather

and was where she won first place. It brought back memories to Mary, Mr. Miller and Jimmy. They got out of the cars and met beside Dale's car.

A lot of men in Air Force uniforms milled about outside the entrance to the stadium. Some went in, but the others seemed to be in charge of those who were going in. Those in charge saw that everything was done correctly. Jimmy stood there and smiled as he watched with pride. Then he asked, "Mr. Walton, what's going on at the stadium?"

Dale turned around and looked. "Oh that. You'll see in a little bit, Jimmy." Changing the subject, he asked, "Are the hawks in the horse trailer?"

"Yes, sir," Jimmy said. "They're hooded and ready to be taken out any time you want. Will we be taking them into the same place we did the first time we were here, Mr. Walton?"

"Yes, Jimmy," Dale said. "Mr. Archer is in there waiting for us. Can you bring them in without any trouble, or do you need some help?"

"No trouble at all," Jimmy replied. "When they have their hoods on, they are easy to handle." Jimmy walked around to the back of the trailer and the rest followed. Mr. Miller opened the sliding door on the right side of the trailer and peeked in.

"They're sitting on their perches just like they were when we left Mercer," Mr. Miller said. "Looks like they had a good trip."

Jimmy opened the other door slowly and looked in. They showed no ill effects from traveling. He stepped up and into the trailer and picked up one of the gloves. He put it on his left hand and placed his hand behind Lady Samson's legs. He moved his hand forward until it touched Lady Samson legs. She stepped back and onto his hand.

Lost Feather

Jimmy made his way out of the trailer with Strong Feather Lady Samson perched on his hand. She was a beautiful sight. Some of the cadets walked over and stood and looked at Jimmy and his hawk. He looked at them and smiled.

Mary went in and brought out Strong Feather Lady Joan of Arc on her gloved hand. Mr. Miller went in last and brought out Strong Feather Lady Guinevere on his glove. The three of them stood there while the hawks sat on their fists like they were at attention. With their hoods on they looked like three beautiful hawk statues.

"Which door do we go through, Mr. Walton?" Jimmy asked.

"That one over there," he said, pointing to the small side door.

Jimmy looked around at the cadets that watched them. "Now for the surprise," he thought. He took off Lady Samson's hood and took off running toward the door. Lady Samson spread her wings out to the fullest. He'd never run that far with her before, and as he approached the side door he felt both of his feet leave the ground now and then. Lady Samson's large wingspan caused him to become airborne.

The cadets cheered each time his feet left the ground. When Jimmy neared the closed door to the stadium he stopped. Lady Samson folded her wings, and he walked the rest of the way to the door. He was not only out of breath; he was surprised at what happened.

He started to open the door but stopped, turned and lifted his hand above his head, letting everyone get a good look at Lady Samson. He lowered her and replaced her hood, opened the door and waited for the rest.

Mary ran up to Jimmy and jumped up and down, disturbing her hawk on her gloved hand. She was so

Lost Feather

excited. "That was great, Jimmy," she said. "When did you teach Lady Samson to do that?"

"The other day after you went home," Jimmy said grinning.

The rest of the group came up, commenting on what Jimmy just did. Jimmy was proud that Lady Samson looked so good to the cadets. Even though he was going to have to leave her there, he wanted them to know that she was something special to him.

"Hello, Jimmy," a voice said behind him. He turned around and saw Mr. Archer, the falcon judge. He stood there with a big smile. "You just won the hearts of all of those Air Force cadets out there when you ran across with your hawk. What I would like for you to do a little later, is to run with Lady Samson up and down the football field, like you just did."

"Yes, sir," Jimmy said smiling. Then he thought about it. "I don't know, Mr. Archer. My feet came off the ground a couple times before I got to the door. I might fly most of the way down the football field if I go that far."

"That would be all the better," Mr. Archer said laughing.

Jimmy looked at him and smiled. "OK, if that's what you want."

Mr. Archer walked over to where three perches were placed. Beside each perch a cadet stood at attention. "You can put your hawks on these perches," he said.

After each hawk was placed on its perch, Mr. Archer said, "Jimmy, I want you and Mary to stay here with your hawks. They have a place for your family and friends up in the stands. If they'll follow those cadets over there, they'll take them to their seats outside in the football stadium."

Lost Feather

As they left with the cadets, they looked back at Jimmy and Mary and waved. "OK you two," Mr. Archer said. "We'll each take a hawk into the stadium. Which one would you like for me to take?"

"You can take Strong Feather Lady Gwen," Jimmy replied pointing at her.

Mr. Archer put on the glove Mr. Miller gave him. He soon had Lady Gwen on his fist. "Let's go," he said.

Jimmy and Mary got their hawks and followed.

As they came near the opening that led out into the football field, they saw a lot of cadets lined up along each side of the entrance to the stadium. Jimmy looked at Mary and then at Mr. Archer. "What are they doing, Mr. Archer?"

"Oh, it is just a little thank you get-together," Mr. Archer replied. "All of these cadets want to thank you for giving them your prized falcon hawks. Dale Walton talked to me about the problem you had. I talked to the base commander, and he told me that a couple of their falcon hawks died not long ago. They've been looking for some real good ones to take their place.

"When I told him that you two had three of the best falcon hawks I'd ever seen, he was interested. When he found out why you had to get rid of them, he decided that they'd show their appreciation by this little get-together. I'm sure you're going to be overwhelmed standing in front of all of those people out there. Just remember that everyone out there is there for one reason---to thank you personally, and this is the only way they can, all at once. Give them your best smile and let's go."

Jimmy and Mary walked beside Mr. Archer through the opening and out into the football stadium. All talking stopped as the cadets watched the three of them carry three of the largest falcon hawks they'd ever seen. They walked

Lost Feather

over to where the base commander stood. The quiet in that stadium could almost be heard. When they stood in front of him, Mr. Archer introduced Jimmy and Mary.

"General, this is Jimmy Warrior and Mary Wilson. Jimmy and Mary, this is General John West."

"I'm very glad to meet you," the general said. "You have three of the largest hawks I've ever seen." He paused, then continued. "We'd like to have a small ceremony in your honor. It will be an acceptance ceremony and a thank you ceremony all in one."

The three cadets, who stood inside by the perches, followed them out into the stadium and brought the perches with them. They again stood at attention beside the perches.

"I have something to show you and your cadets, General," Mr. Archer said. "Would it be all right to show it now?"

"Yes, Mr. Archer," the general replied.

The three of them walked over near the perches. Mr. Archer turned to Jimmy, and said, "We'll put our hawks on their perches, Jimmy, but I'd like for you to run up and down the field a couple of times. You don't have to go all the way, but enough for them to see Strong Feather Lady Samson in flight. When you feel like it's enough, just bring her back here to her perch."

Jimmy nodded and walked about twenty feet into the football field. He stood there and looked at the cadets in the stands. To his surprise, there were a lot of civilians there also. For a minute he just looked at them. Mr. Archer got his attention with a wave of his hand. Jimmy waved back and everyone in the stand stood up and waved at him, then sat back down. With a big smile he took off Lady Samson's hood and turned to face the breeze blowing across the field.

Lost Feather

He grasped the leather thongs hanging from Lady Samson's feet, took a deep breath and started running. Lady Samson opened her wings to the fullest. As he ran, he again could feel his feet leave the ground now and then. It didn't slow him down so he kept on running.

Every cadet in the stands stood up to watch as he ran down to one end of the field. When he turned and started back they started yelling. When he reached the other end of the field, all the cadets yelled and slapped their fellow cadets on the back. It was something they'd never seen before. Jimmy held his hands up high and it looked like the hawk was flying off with him. He was too big for her to carry him off, but when the conditions were just right she had a lot of lift in her wings. It was a sight to behold.

Jimmy stopped at the end of the field to rest. He was tired. He turned and heard the crowd yelling, and he found new energy. Again he ran back down the field to where the general stood and stopped. Lady Samson folded her wings and sat on his fist and looked at him.

General West came up to Jimmy and shook his free hand. "She's the most beautiful falcon hawk I have ever seen, Jimmy," he said smiling and shaking his head in disbelief of what he just saw. "The cadets and I thank you. I can truthfully say this is a day we'll never forget, Jimmy."

General West went over to the microphone and turned it on. He spoke about how happy he was to accept these three fine falcon hawks. "They'll make the academy proud," he said. "I know that each cadet here would like to thank Jimmy and Mary personally, but since that would take too long I will do it for you." He then turned to Jimmy and Mary. "We all thank you for all the hours of work you've spent training these beautiful hawks. And now, for letting us reap the benefits of that work. On with the ceremony!" he yelled.

Lost Feather

Everyone in the stands applauded and then sat back down. Jimmy walked over to where the cadet stood next to Lady Samson's empty perch. Lady Samson was now watching every move Jimmy made. The surroundings were strange to her and she relied on Jimmy to let her know what to do. Jimmy looked at her with so much pride that he felt like his heart would burst. He would have to let her go, and it hurt so much, deep inside.

Jimmy moved into position with the cadet so he could take her off his glove. As the cadet's hand came up behind her and touched her legs she grabbed hold of Jimmy's glove even tighter. It was the first time she ever did that. She looked at Jimmy and didn't move. Jimmy reached up and stroked her gently with his free hand. "I know how you feel, lovely Lady. I don't want you to go either," he said softly to her. "They'll treat you good here. It won't be like it was with Mr. Ross, your first owner. They like you here and they'll learn to love you just like I do. Wait and see."

Lady Samson didn't move. A bond of love grew between them and she felt the sadness of Jimmy's voice as he talked to her.

"I want you to go with this cadet, Lady Samson," he said finally.

She turned her head and looked at the cadet. She acted as if she understood exactly what Jimmy said. She then looked back at him.

He nodded his head and she stepped backward onto the cadet's gloved fist. Jimmy lowered his hand and stood there looking at Lady Samson on the cadet's glove as tears streamed down his face. The cadet grabbed the leather thongs on Lady Samson's feet and held her high above his head. Everyone in the stadium stood up. He then turned and ran along the sidelines of the football field with her held

Lost Feather

high. She opened her wings like she had for Jimmy, and the cadets yelled and clapped.

When the cadet came back to where Lady Samson's perch was, Jimmy was yelling and clapping, too. The cadet placed Lady Samson on her perch and tied the leather thongs to it. She sat there looking around at everything. When she saw Jimmy her head stopped. Jimmy walked up to her and took out a pencil and stroked her a few times with it. He then handed it to the cadet. Lady Samson watched very carefully. The cadet then stroked her a couple of times with the pencil and Jimmy stepped back. She seemed to know what that meant. The cadet was now her new master. Jimmy handed her hood to the cadet, with her watching his every move.

The cadet moved to place the hood over Lady Samson's head but she moved and the hood slipped off to one side of her head. She moved her head back and forth until she could see Jimmy clearly. When she could see him she stopped. On the next try the cadet got her hood on. She straightened up and looked like the most beautiful stone statue that had ever been carved sitting there.

"Would you, Jimmy, and you, Mary, step over here," the general said.

Jimmy and Mary walked over to where General West stood. "I have a small check here for each of you. It's not that we are buying them from you. It's just that we want to thank you for raising them. We'd like to give you a little gift for doing that for the Air Force." He handed each of them a check for $100.00.

Everyone in the stands stood up and clapped. Jimmy and Mary didn't know what to say or do. General West lowered the microphone so that Jimmy and Mary could say something to the people in the stands.

Lost Feather

Jimmy stepped up to the microphone and said, "Thank you for the check. Now I can buy me some new clothes for school," and stepped back.

Everyone laughed and clapped. Mary then stepped up to the microphone but didn't say a word. Everyone got quiet waiting for her to say something. Then, oh so softly, she said, "Jimmy and I have trained these hawks together. They are very dear to us. Please take good care of them. We're going to miss them so much. Please, don't be mean to them like Strong Feather Lady Samson's first owner was. Jimmy loved her so much that she'll do anything for him. You just saw what she did. She'll do the same for you, too, if you'll just love her. That's all I ask of you. Please. Just love our gifts to you. Thank you."

This time there were no cheers or applause. Tears ran down the cheeks of many of the cadets. They knew what she said. It wasn't that long ago since each one of them left something they loved very much back home, when they joined the military.

General West stepped up and put his arm around Mary's shoulder. "I give you my promise, Mary, that these beautiful gifts that you and Jimmy gave us will never be treated mean. They'll be treated with much love and care by their new trainers. I will see to it. You have my word."

Then from the cadets in the stands, "And ours, too, Sir!"

General West came to attention and saluted Jimmy and Mary. The cadets saluted, also. He then walked with them over to the passageway they came in. When they were back in the place where they met Mr. Archer, everyone shook hands. The three cadets came up to them with the three hawks on their gloves. "I'd like to thank you again," General West said. "I'm sorry to have to leave such good company, but duty calls. What are your plans?"

Lost Feather

"We're going to have a big picnic, General West," Jimmy said.

"That's a great idea, Jimmy," General West replied. "Sorry I can't join you. But remember, any time you're in the neighborhood, drop in and see your falcons. We'd love to see you any time. Thanks again."

He walked away with several officers who were gathered around them. Jimmy's grandparents, the Wilsons, and the Millers came to where they were standing. They were so happy and full of praises.

"Let's go have that picnic," Jimmy said.

"Yes, let's go," they all chimed in. They hurried out to where the cars were parked.

Dale Walton was standing by his car when they got there. He was kind of choked up when he congratulated Jimmy and Mary.

They thanked him for everything and hurried over and got into their cars. As the Millers and the Wilsons drove out through the Academy gates, there was a feeling of pride. They now had contributed just a little to those who served their country. It felt good.

They stopped at the first picnic area they came to. They quickly unloaded all of the food and put it on a table. Everyone ate and ate, and all agreed that Alice was the best cook in the world. The baskets were a lot lighter when they went back into the trunks than when they came out.

With the picnic over, they got into the two cars and drove off, headed back to Mercer. Time flew by as they talked about what happened that day. Before they knew it, they were home. Mr. Miller's car was unloaded at the Warriors' and Mary got into her parents' car. Everyone said goodnight with a little sadness. It had been a great day, just like Tom said it would be. They would remember it for a long time.

Lost Feather

As Jimmy lay in his bed that night before drifting off to sleep, the events of the day came to his mind like pictures painted by an invisible hand. It had been a great day for everyone. Then a shadow crept into the last picture he saw. It was a shadow of a large bird taking off in flight and flying alone. He wondered as he saw the shadow slowly disappear out of sight. He then knew that he lost his feathered friend for good, and that it was he who was flying away, not the bird. He would be lost without Lady Samson. A tear ran down his cheek as he drifted off to sleep. He would soar no more.

Lost Feather

CHAPTER XI

The Warriors slept in the next morning. It was 9 A.M. when Alice knocked on Jimmy's door. She opened it and peeked in to see if he was awake. He rolled over and looked at her. "Good morning, Jimmy. Breakfast will soon be ready."

He sat up, rubbed his eyes and smiled at her. "I'll get dressed, Grandma."

She closed the door and walked back to the kitchen. Jimmy got dressed. After he brushed his teeth and combed his hair, he hurried into the kitchen. His grandpa sat at the table reading the comic strips. He got the paper from one of the places he worked the week before. Jimmy also enjoyed reading a few of them.

Pancakes and eggs waited for Jimmy, and a large glass of milk to wash it all down. He sat down and smiled at his grandpa, who winked at him and laid the paper down. He scooted his chair up to the table and looked at his grandma.

Alice came over to the table with the syrup and sat down. "I hope this food will fill you two up."

They all grinned as they grabbed hands and Tom said the blessing.

There was no talking as they ate. Tom picked up the paper and started reading again. They finished eating and Alice sat and looked at Tom, not saying a word. The silence caused him to look at her. He smiled, put the papers down and got up, and hurried off to his bedroom. Today was one of the three weekdays he cleaned one of the beer joints in town.

Jimmy sat there until Alice looked at him. He got up and disappeared into his room.

Lost Feather

She stood there smiling, then, thought, "I should have waited until they put everything up and washed the dishes."

She hurried around in the kitchen and soon put everything away and the dishes were washed and drying on the counter drain board.

Jimmy made his bed and cleaned up his room. With everything put in order, he went out the back door and over to the hawk pens. The hawks were gone, and the pens needed to be cleaned. He stood and looked at the two empty pens for some time. He slowly shook his head. Lady Samson was gone for good this time. There was an empty place in his life now and he didn't know how he could fill it.

He walked around the house to the garage and opened one of the doors. He picked up a shovel and rake, and went back to the pens. Opening the gate to the first pen, he leaned the shovel up against it to hold it open. He went inside and raked the ground. He soon had a good size pile of all kinds of things.

Jimmy stacked boxes and boards in one corner. He placed feeding trays and cans on top of the boards. He stopped and looked around the pen. It looked good.

He picked up the water bucket, went behind the pen, and emptied it. He returned and replaced the shovel with the rake. He soon had the bucket full, and carried it over behind the railroad ties and dumped it into the fifty-five-gallon barrel they put their trash in. It was about full and he knew he would have to burn it later.

As he headed back to the pen, the back door opened and Mary came out. She hurried down the steps and over to where he was.

Lost Feather

She smiled at him. "I sure enjoyed the great time in Colorado Springs yesterday. But I feel kind of empty."

"Me, too, Mary," he said.

"My parents noticed it this morning when we had breakfast. We talked about it and decided we need to do something together. They called my grandmother down in Denver, and her brother is going to go pick her up and take her to his farm near Greeley. So we'll be driving over there.

'Some of my aunts and uncles and cousins will also meet us there and we'll have a big picnic this afternoon. We have so much fun when we get together. One of my uncles always brings his guitar and another brings a violin. They play and we sing. Some of the songs are old songs my great-grandma sang when she was my age."

"That sounds great, Mary," Jimmy said, thinking about having another picnic.

"We are going to bring my grandmother back here for a week," Mary said, "We always go see her. In fact, I stay with her a lot in the summer when school is out."

Jimmy smiled. "I remember that you just came back from seeing your grandmother when I first met you at your father's service station."

"That's right, Jimmy. So you can see why we want her to come and stay with us for a while."

"Where is their farm located?" he asked.

"Well, you go through Longmont and up to Fort Collins, then turn right and go about fifteen miles to Greeley. I don't know exactly how far it is. They live on a farm north of town. It's dry land farming up there. If it rains, they have a good crop. If it doesn't, they have a hard time making it until the planting season the next year."

"I've never heard of a dry land farm," Jimmy said, looking at her.

Lost Feather

"There are a lot of them around here, especially out by the coal mines. There are no streams up on those hills to irrigate their crops. Most of the wheat grown around here is on dry land farms. The only difference between here and there is that we are closer to the mountains. We get a lot more rain here than they do. In fact, a lot of their land can't be planted at all. It's just hard dry land with cactus and weeds," Mary said.

"I sure am glad we live by the mountains, Mary," Jimmy said, and turned and looked at them. "I'd like to go up there some day, up where all of the snow is. It would be great to play in the snow right now, even build a snowman. Today, in August."

"Yes, it would be fun," she said, following his gaze off towards the mountains.

"I came out to clean up the pens. With our hawks gone, there's nothing to put in them. I'm sure my grandparents will find something to put in there."

"I'm sure they will. I felt like you might be out here cleaning the pens. So I told my parents I'd come over and help if you were."

"OK, I appreciate the help and your company," he said, and went into Lady Samson's cage and got the shovel. He came out and handed it to Mary. He got the rake and closed the gate.

Mary opened the gate to the other pen and waited for Jimmy. He handed her the rake and took the shovel and placed it up against the gate.

She took it and started raking the ground while he picked up everything that was loose and started stacking it on one side. It wasn't long until they finished.

Jimmy got the shovel and soon had the bucket almost full. Another trip to the garbage barrel finished the job of cleaning the hawk pens.

Lost Feather

Mary stopped and stood there in the middle of the empty pen. Her hawk, Lady Joan, and Jimmy's, Lady Guinevere, were gone. Tears formed in her eyes and ran down her cheeks. She wiped her eyes as she looked at the empty pen. She put her hands up and covered her face so Jimmy wouldn't see her crying.

She couldn't take it any more and ran out of the pen and over to the porch. She sat looking at the ground and cried.

Jimmy put the bucket down and walked over to her. He wanted to say something, but couldn't, and his eyes filled with tears. He didn't want Mary to think he was a sissy. He tried hard to hold back the feelings of loss, but waves of emotion washed over him as he choked back his tears. He lost both of his parents, his hawk, and his home in Newark, New Jersey. Lady Gwen once, and Lady Samson three times. After a while one learns to bury one's deep hurts. He found it hard to let this one go. He realized that it wasn't working as he wiped his eyes with his shirtsleeve.

Mary stopped crying and dried her eyes. "I'm sorry, Jimmy. I don't know what we're going to do. We had so much fun together with the hawks, and now they are gone. What are we going to do now?"

"We will find something, I'm sure," he said. "Just wait and see."

She looked up at him and smiled. "OK. We will still be friends."

"Sure we will. Good friends."

She stood and walked back to the pen, closed the gate, and latched it. Jimmy followed her and closed the other gate and latched it. Their job was finished, and now they would look forward to happier times, like those in the past.

Lost Feather

The back door opened and Alice and Mary's mother, Helen, came out and looked at them. Helen came down the steps and walked over to where they were.

"Mary," her mother said softly.

It snapped them out of their daydream. They turned and saw her mother take a handkerchief out of her purse. She gently wiped the tears stains on Mary's cheeks. "There, that's better. I know it's hard to lose your hawks, but after a while there will be other things to take their place."

"Yes, Ma'am," Mary answered, "That's what Jimmy said, and I agreed."

Helen smiled at Jimmy, then looked back at Mary. "It's time to go."

"Yes, Mother," she answered.

"I've got to go, Jimmy," she said, smiling.

"OK. I'll see you when you get back," he answered. "Have a great time."

"I will," Mary said. She walked over to the bottom of the steps with her mother. "We've got it all cleaned up, Mrs. Warrior."

"Thanks, Mary," Alice said. "I'm glad you came over and helped Jimmy. He needed you to help him as bad as you needed him."

Mary smiled. "You're right. We needed each other today."

"You'll have to excuse us, Alice," Helen said. "We've got to hurry."

"Come back and tell me all about your family reunion, Helen" Alice said.

"I will," she replied as she turned and they both hurried off around the corner of the house.

Alice looked at Jimmy, while he looked at her. "After you put your tools away, come in the house. I've just baked some oatmeal cookies," Alice said.

Lost Feather

"Yes, Ma'am," he said. He picked up the rake and headed around the other side of the house towards the garage. Oatmeal cookies and a big glass of milk were exactly what he needed.

As Alice walked back into the house, she felt better knowing she got his mind off of losing his hawks. It was amazing how oatmeal cookies with raisins in them did that for young boys. It worked with her son, Tommy, and it worked with his son, Jimmy. Must be something in the family bloodline, or maybe it's something that's planted in young boys. Whatever it was, she would keep doing it.

"Of course, I kind of like them, too," she thought.

Jimmy hurried back to the pens, picked up the water bucket, and put it on top of the boards behind the pens. He checked to see if there was anything else that he needed to do. It looked good. Then he saw the shovel on the ground outside Lady Samson's pen and smiled.

He latched the gate, picked up the shovel, and went back around the house to the garage. He made sure the shovel and rake were in their place. He closed the garage door and hurried up the porch steps into the house. He ran to the bathroom to wash his hands. "Those oatmeal cookies called," he thought. Then after he ate, he lay down and took a long nap.

Jimmy woke up from his nap and felt good. He got up and went into the kitchen and found it empty. "Grandma and Grandpa must have gone somewhere," he thought. Then he heard someone talking out on the porch. He hurried over to the open front door and looked out through the screen. They were in their rocking chairs.

He went back into the kitchen, picked up a chair, and carried it out onto the porch. When he sat down his grandpa said, "Some people have it made around here,

Lost Feather

Alice. How come I don't get to take a nap when I want one?"

"I believe I woke you up yesterday in that chair you're sitting in." Alice said.

"I was just resting my eyes," he said.

"You were not resting your nose from snoring."

"Of course not. Who ever heard of resting one's nose?"

The three of them laughed. It was nice to have some fun now and then.

It was a nice, bright, sunny August day. They enjoyed their time on the front porch. Time passed slowly and a nice gentle breeze passed by now and then.

Alice sat back in her rocker and took a deep breath. The quiet all around her gave her peace.

Tom slowly rocked back and forth. He closed his eyes and his rocking got slower and slower, then stopped.

Jimmy thought about not having anything to do. He unbuttoned his shirtsleeves and rolled them up. It was a time to rest and count one's blessings, instead of worrying.

Alice rocked and looked around. She enjoyed this time with her two men. A lot happened in the last week and they needed to draw back and take some much needed rest. She enjoyed this time in her rocking chair.

She looked at her grandson and said, "Jimmy, would you go into the house and get your grandpa and me a couple of hand fans? I'm too hot and I know he is."

Tom heard his name and opened his eyes. He looked around to see what was going on. Alice looked at him and shook her head. He closed his eyes again.

Jimmy got up and went into the house. Tom and Alice heard him talking to himself as he tried to find the fans. There was silence, then the screen door opened and he

Lost Feather

came out with three fans. He gave each of them a fan and went over and sat down. He never used a hand fan before.

He fanned himself, and it cooled him. His chair didn't rock, but that was O.K. He enjoyed the time just being with his grandparents.

Alice's rocking got slower and slower, then stopped. She put her hands on the rocker's armrests. "I've heard that a woman's work is never done," she thought. "Now, let's see, how does that go? *'A man works from sun to sun, but a woman's work is never done.'* Yes, I surely agree with that," she thought, and pushed herself up.

She looked at her two men again and nodded her head. "I wouldn't have it any other way."

She was soon in her kitchen making all kinds of noise. She always made a lot of noise when she fixed something to eat.

Tom and Jimmy fanned themselves. It was another hot August day. There was a familiar tinkling noise coming from inside the house. They looked at each other and smiled, then put their fans down and looked over at the screen door.

The door opened and Alice came out with a large tray. On it were three glasses and a large pitcher filled with lemonade. The two of them sat up straight as she handed them each a glass.

She set the tray down and picked up her glass and the pitcher. The glasses were soon filled, and she sat down and joined them in drinking a refreshing glass of lemonade. The fans were set aside until the lemonade was gone.

Tom looked over at Jimmy and asked, "Did you clean out the hawks' cages this morning?"

"Yes, Sir. I did. I even had some help. Mary came over and helped me clean out the pen her hawk was in. I sure was glad to have the help. I needed someone to talk to

Lost Feather

about not having the hawks around anymore. We both have an empty place in us. I hope I can find something to fill that place.

"I understand," Tom said slowly. "I understand."

It was after supper at the Warrior house and the three of them were in the front room reading the newspaper. Jimmy finally got his turn to read the funnies. He enjoyed reading nearly all of them. When he read the Katzenjammers' comic strip he almost laughed out loud at the things the two young boys did to the Captain.

Alice went over the different store ads while Tom read the sports section. All of their peace and quiet was suddenly interrupted when they heard tires skid around the corner, coming off the highway. They looked at each other.

Who is that, Tom?" she asked.

"I don't know, but it looks like someone is in a big hurry," he said, and got up from his chair.

Then they heard the roar of the engine. The car sped down the road towards their house. It continued on into their yard, and the horn started honking as the car slid to a stop in front of the house. Someone jumped out and yelled, "Alice! Alice! Alice!"

Tom and Jimmy headed for the door, but Alice headed for her bedroom. Somebody needed her and that meant only one thing. Someone was in bad trouble. It happened many times before. Whatever it was, she knew it wasn't good.

Tom opened the door and Helen Wilson ran up the steps and shouted, "Where's Alice, Tom?"

"She's gone to get her bag, Helen," he said. "Calm down. Tell us what's wrong."

"Something happened to my mother. She may have had a heat stroke, Tom," she said. "It was so hot at her

Lost Feather

brother's ranch, near the end of the day she got dizzy and fainted. We worked with her and she regained consciousness and soon sat up. She said she was all right but was very tired. She looked pale and didn't seem like her old self.

"We started home and just outside of town she fainted again and we can't revive her. Bill called Dr. Bixler, but it will take a long time to come over here from Longmont. I would like for Alice to come right now. She'll know what to do."

"She's in the bedroom getting things together," Tom said. "I'm sure she heard you, Helen. Calm down. I'll drive you back. I don't want you to have an accident driving back to your place."

He turned to Jimmy. "You go help carry your grandma's stuff for her."

"Yes, Sir," he said and went into their bedroom.

Alice pointed at a bag and he picked it up and she picked up a smaller one. "Let's go, Jimmy," she said.

They hurried out into the front room and Jimmy followed Alice to the car, got in and closed the door. Helen was already in and waited for them. Tom put the car in gear and drove towards their house.

When they got there, Bill stood outside on the curb and opened the door for Alice. He led her into the house. Tom and Helen hurried in after them, and Jimmy followed.

Mary sat in a chair at the kitchen table. Tears ran down her cheeks. Jimmy walked up to her, but he didn't know what to do or say. She wiped her eyes and motioned for him to sit down. They sat looking at each other for a while. There was nothing they could do. Jimmy leaned back in his chair and looked out the window.

Mr. Wilson rushed out of the bedroom door and went over and opened the refrigerator door. He took a tray

Lost Feather

of ice cubes out of the freezer and hurried back into the bedroom, leaving the refrigerator door open. Mary got up and went over and closed it.

There was a lot of talking, and then Mr. Wilson and Tom came out of the bedroom and closed the door. They walked over and sat down at the table. Mr. Wilson sat looking down at the floor. He took quick glances at the closed bedroom door.

The four of them sat there for what seemed an hour. They heard Alice talk now and then, and Helen answered. This went on for a long time.

Then there was someone laughing. It was a beautiful melodious laugh that filled the room. Bill smiled and said, "That's Helen's mother." Everyone at the table stood up and headed for the bedroom door. It flew open before they got to it, and Helen ran out and grabbed her husband around the neck.

"She's going to be O.K., Bill," she said, hugging him again. Big smiles appeared on everyone's face. They all went into the bedroom, and there sat Helen's mother, Ruby, smiling at everyone. "What's all the fuss about?" she asked. "I'm all right. I feel fine. In fact, I feel better now than I have all day. I had a good nap."

"Her temperature is now normal and she's doing fine," Alice said. "All it took was a few ice cubes to bring it down."

Ruby started to get up, then lay back down. "Well, I thought I was feeling O.K."

"All you need is some rest and a good night's sleep and you'll be doing everything you were doing before this happened."

Ruby looked at Alice strangely.

Ruby looked around the room and saw Mary's red eyes. "What's this, Mary? You come over here and sit by

Lost Feather

me. Now you stop your crying. I'm sorry I went to sleep but I was really tired. I'm wide-awake now. Both of us need to sit around and talk. That is the reason I agreed to come home with you. There are so many things that we need to talk about. We always talked when you came to see me but you're getting older and becoming a young lady so we'll be having more talks about different things.

"You need to hear about your great-grandparents and their lives - where they came from, where they lived, who they were and the things they did. Then there are many things we haven't discussed about my and your grandpa's lives. It's time for your mother and me to teach you our family's history and some of the things that happened that have never been discussed - things that only we know. We want you to know how to deal with worldly problems that will come your way as you become a woman."

Mary looked at her mother and she nodded her head. "That would be nice, Grandma. I've always wanted to know more about all that you mentioned. Mother taught me a lot of things, and so has Mrs. Warrior. She is very knowledgeable about a lot of things that only she knows."

Ruby looked at Alice and smiled. "I sure would appreciate it if you'd help me teach my granddaughter some of the things you know."

"I would be glad to," Alice said. "First things first, though. I'm Alice Warrior and that is my husband, Tom, and our grandson, Jimmy, next to him."

"Of course, Alice," Ruby said. "And I am Ruby Jones."

"It's a pleasure to finally meet you, Ruby. I've heard a lot about you."

"I'm sorry about that, Alice. It seems like I have expected my daughter and granddaughter to always come

Lost Feather

and see me. I am going to change that. They'll have to put up with me now, instead of my putting up with them."

Everyone laughed. Everything was turning out fine. "It's good to meet you and your husband, Alice."

"Thank you, Ma'am," Tom said, smiling.

"And you, Jimmy. I've heard nothing but good things about you from Mary."

Jimmy looked at Mary and smiled. Her face turned a bright red. "Thank you," he answered.

Alice closed her bag and looked at Helen. "I'll drop by tomorrow to check on Ruby. I'll bring something to help her get her strength back faster. You probably should call Dr. Bixler and let him know that her fever is down and she is doing fine."

"That's right, Alice," she said. "Bill, would you please go call Dr. Bixler?"

"Be glad to," Bill answered and left the room. They soon heard him talking to someone on the phone.

"I'll see you tomorrow, Ruby," Alice said, and motioned for Tom and Jimmy to follow her.

"I will be honored to have you come see me, Alice. Thank you for everything you did for me and my family."

Helen and Mary got up and followed them into the kitchen. Bill hung up the phone and said, "I talked to Dr. Bixler's wife. She said he was out on another call and she would try to get in touch with him."

"Good," Alice replied. "I'll come back tomorrow and check on Ruby. Helen, see that she gets lots of liquids. She looks good and I believe the dizzy spell she had is just lack of liquids in her body."

"I'll do that, Alice," she said. "Thanks again for coming over like you did."

Lost Feather

They all said their good-byes and Bill walked out to the car with them. They got into the car and drove slowly back to the Warrior house. It was a very exciting day.

After breakfast was over and Alice washed the dishes and put them away, she went into her bedroom. She picked up her small bag and thought for a minute. She looked around the room and tried to think if she needed anything else. She smiled, turned and walked back into the front room and out onto the front porch.

Tom sat rocking in his chair. He stopped and stood up. "You stay here, Tom," she said. "I'm just going to check on Ruby and I'll be right back."

Tom thought about what she said, and then sat back down. "Oh," he said. "It's going to be a woman thing. No men allowed."

"That's right. We girls need some time together, too. Just like you men," Alice replied.

"You're right, my love. Have a great time. Tell them some of your great stories about yourself, so they'll ask you to come back."

"If I tell them some of those, Tom, they might not ever ask me to come back. But if I tell them some about you, they'll have me back every day for a month."

Tom smiled at her. He knew she was teasing him. He liked it. "Thanks my love. I love you very much."

"Me too, you," she said, and walked down the steps, swinging her bag back and forth. It was good to be loved, especially by a man like Tom.

It didn't take her long to walk the three blocks, and she soon knocked on the side door of the Wilson's house.

Helen opened the door and smiled. "We've been expecting you, Alice," she said. "My mother and Mary are in the front room talking. I just finished putting everything

Lost Feather

up after breakfast and I'm ready to join them. Come on in and we'll see what kind of stories my mother is telling Mary."

Alice followed Helen into the front room. She was pleased to see Ruby dressed and looking good. "Good morning, Ruby," she said. "I see you're doing fine."

"Yes, Alice. I was told that you were the one that got my temperature down. I want to thank you for that. I didn't know I passed out. I thought I just fell asleep. I didn't understand what all of you were talking about last night. Helen and Mary filled me in on everything that happened."

"You're welcome," Alice said. "I'm glad I was here to help."

"Mary told me about giving her hawk to the Air Force Academy last week. I, of course, told her my daddy used to shoot chicken hawks when I was a kid. We didn't know we could train them to hunt. If we had known that, we might have treated them differently."

"That is true," Alice said. "There are good and there are bad hawks. There are small hawks and there are large hawks. The ones Mary and Jimmy trained are called Grand Hawks. You must start training hawks when they are young. Just like any type of animal, even children. Be honest and always be there for them. Give them plenty love along with the discipline."

"I know that to be true, Alice," Ruby replied. "I know from the way my mom and dad raised us children when we were young. We were in big trouble if we didn't follow the instructions they gave us."

Mary looked at her grandmother and frowned. "What kind of instructions did they give you, Grandma?"

"Well, Mary," she said. "We moved a lot and were on our own a lot. We could have gotten lost real easy, been

Lost Feather

bitten by snakes, or eaten the wrong things. We could have even lost our lives."

"All of those things, Grandma?"

"I don't believe your grandma told you where she was born, Mary," Helen said.

"No, she hasn't," she replied, looking at her. "Where were you born, Grandma?"

She smiled at Helen, then, looked at Mary. "I was born in a dugout on the Kansas prairie."

"In a what?" Mary asked.

Alice smiled as she sat listening. This was something she wanted to hear.

"Well, Mary," Ruby said, smiling. "A dugout is a hole in the ground that you live in. My daddy dug a big hole in the ground on a large piece of land he traded for. He was always trading for something. There wasn't a house on the land, and out on the Kansas prairie there is what is known as a tornado. You've probably heard of them. They are big winds that go round and around, usually on a zigzag path, tearing everything up as they go.

"Most people who live on the prairie dig a big hole in the ground that they call a storm cellar. They dig the hole, put a roof over it with a cellar door on it, and cover all but the door with dirt so it is flat with the ground. That way the tornado can't blow it away.

"Well, a dugout is nothing more than a big storm cellar. My daddy made it big enough for us to live in. We had a stove, tables, chairs, beds and everything else we needed to live in it. My sister Dixie was also born there.

"After my daddy finished the dugout, he started building our two-story house. It took him quite a while, but eventually he got it built. Then, a short time after that, he traded it for a house in Topeka, Kansas. That was the way he did things.

Lost Feather

"There was an oil boom in Oklahoma, so we moved to the small town of Blackwell. Dad got a job in construction, and mama got a job cooking for a boarding house. There were a lot of men staying there and all of us kids had jobs."

"Wow!" Mary said. "That's a great story, Grandma."

Ruby looked at Alice and smiled. "Where were you born, Alice?"

"I was born in a tee-pee on the Taos reservation in New Mexico," she said.

"Wow!" Mary said again. "In a tee-pee. That's exciting, Mrs. Warrior."

"Nothing like your grandmother's story," she said, looking at Ruby. "I grew up with a lot of other Indian children in our village. Instead of tornados, we had a nice life. The only thing that caused us a lot of trouble was the big snowstorms. Taos is near the mountains and we got a lot of snow some years.

"The most important thing was staying healthy. I was blessed. A very caring woman taught me how to help myself, and my people, with herbs and salves. With this knowledge, and other things she taught me, I have been able to help a lot of people."

"I know that," Mary said, grabbing her hand. "I remember how your herbs saved Mr. Warrior's life. Also, they helped Jimmy get well from his beatings."

She looked over at her grandmother and smiled. "You also helped my grandmother get over the heat stroke last night. I sure was worried about her, and in just a short time you had her temperature down and she sat up in bed. I want to thank you for that, Mrs. Warrior."

Helen took Mary's hand and said, "I thank you, too, Alice."

Lost Feather

Ruby reached over and placed her hand on top of theirs. "Just think, Alice," she said. "It all started in a teepee on an Indian reservation and a Kansas dugout."

They all thought about what Ruby said.

Alice placed her hand on top of Ruby's. "It all started a long time before that. It started when a rib was taken from man and woman was made----created to take care of those about us who need our loving touch."

"That's true," Ruby said, as they leaned back. Our life has been an adventure."

"It sure has," Alice said. "We've both had an interesting life."

"Will you tell us something about your heritage, Alice?"

"I'm a Taos Indian, Ruby. The Taos Indians are different from all the other tribes. We have a council of men who are our leaders. The highest is the tribal Holy Man, our spiritual leader whose position is passed down to males only in that family. Next we have the tribal President, Chief and War Chief. These positions are rotated to other members of the council. Only male members of these families can be tribal council members. They make all of the decisions for the tribe.

'I learned how to weave blankets and work animal skins for clothes when I was very young. Then later I was chosen to learn how to use different plants and their fruit to help people get well.

'My father was one of the council leaders. He was a good leader and the best hunter of the tribe. Tom's father was a great leader but a poor hunter. So my father would get an extra deer now and then and give it to his family. Tom and I grew up playing together and became good friends.

Lost Feather

'The only problem that arose when we became teenagers was that all of the parents of the tribe decided who their children would marry when they were born. Families would get together and come to an agreement, and that was whom you married. It worked O.K. for some people, but not all.

'It didn't work for Tom and me, which meant we either followed our parents' wishes, or we could stay single.

'Tom and I found ourselves madly in love and, being teenagers, we rebelled. That, of course, was not tolerated. We were separated and I had to move in with my cousins on the other side of the reservation. One evening Tom showed up and asked me to go with him. So we ran off and left the reservation.

'We made our way up to Colorado where one of Tom's friends lived. He and his wife did the same thing. He got a job working in a coal mine in Aguilar, Colorado. We got married and found a small shack to live in. We were two happy newlyweds.

'The coal mines shut down in the summer time because there is less demand for coal. Tom heard of a job on a farm up near Boulder and we moved. He got a job on a farm where they had a nice house for hired hands. We loved it there. The same mountain range that runs through our reservation and Aguilar, runs through Boulder.

'I loved getting up in the morning and stepping outside and looking at the beautiful Rocky Mountain range. I still like to go out on the back porch and just sit there and relax. We are blessed to live here.

'One of the problems was that the farms were not worked in the winter. So Tom went back to work in the coal mines. That's when we moved to Mercer. Our son, Tommy, was born here and married a Taos girl he met

Lost Feather

when we went home to visit one year. She, too, was the daughter of one of the religious council members.

'We found out that nothing changed on the reservation after all of the years we were away. It was like we stepped back in time.

'Jimmy was born in Denver, and Tommy and Jimmy's mother, Mable, moved off to New Jersey. I didn't get to see my grandson after that. But he came back to us and has brought a lot of joy to my and Tom's life.

'We've had a good life here, even after Tom found out that he had black lung from breathing coal dust in the mines. He decided to quit, and I'm sure that is why it didn't affect him as bad as it did some of the men he worked with, that worked a lot more years than he did. I, too, have had a very interesting life, Ruby."

"You sure have, Alice," she said.

"That is very interesting, Alice. What was your last name?" Helen asked.

"It is the Spanish name, Montoya," Alice answered.

"A Spanish name," Ruby said. "That sounds so exciting. A lot more exciting than my being born in a dug out."

"Grandma," Mary said, frowning. "How did you live in a hole in the ground? What did you do? You didn't get to look out since there were no windows. And it must have been awfully dark. And how did you keep warm?"

Ruby laughed. "You make it sound like it was terrible, Mary, but it wasn't. We opened the large door that was over the entrance and we had plenty of light. When we closed the door we had coal oil, also called kerosene, lamps, and a lantern for light. We had a wood cook stove, and we had plenty to do.

'My mother was a schoolteacher before she married my dad. He was an inventor, carpenter, and trader. His

Lost Feather

trading is what caused us to move so much. It seemed we were always moving.

'My father built the house and we moved out of the dug out. It was a nice house. But it wasn't long until he traded it for a house in Topeka. He invented a hay stacker and showed it at the county fair. But a big company came out with the combine and dashed his dreams.

'Dad heard of the big oil boom in Oklahoma and we moved to Blackwell, Oklahoma. There was no place to stay, so Dad found a farmer that let us stay in his barn. He went to work in the oil field and Mama started growing vegetables for the farmer. She put up a roadside vegetable stand and started selling her produce.

'When it got cold they moved to town. Dad quit the oil field and went to work as a carpenter. Mama got a job at a boarding house as a cook with room and board. We were sure glad to move out of that barn. It wasn't long until she put all of us kids to work. That was where I learned to cook and clean a house.

'We came out to Denver to visit one of dad's brothers, who was sick, and we stayed. Dad heard about a three-story house in Boulder that was for sale, and we moved again. It wasn't finished, no windows or doors. So we all helped dad finish it. It was nice when we got through.

'My moving days ended soon after that. My two oldest sisters and I met the men we married.

'Back to your question about what we did in the dug out, we seemed to always be doing something. We made all of our own clothes. Dad bought fifty pound bags of flour, and sometimes feed for the animals, in sacks that were made of nice print material. We used those sacks to make our clothes.

Lost Feather

"One thing that our mother taught us to do, that I would like to teach you, is to quilt. I have my quilting frame in our attic in Denver, and I'm going to bring it with me next time I come."

Mary looked at her mother, and smiled.

"I learned to quilt when I was about your age, Mary," Helen said. "All of my sisters and I used to get together and quilt. It is a lot of fun."

"You can make a quilt, Mother?" she asked.

"Yes, I can. Wait and see," Helen said. I know how to build a house, can food, and sew; and I'm a good trader. Your grandpa traded some land to a man who had six popcorn machines like the large ones you see at the movie theaters. Well, the Maytag washing machine man came by our house one day and I traded my popcorn machine for the washing machine that we still have. It is the only one in town that has a separate spin cycle attachment that spins the water out of the clothes."

"I never knew that, Helen," Ruby said. "I'm proud of you."

Helen smiled at her mother. "See there, Mary. My mother's proud of me just like I am proud of you."

"I'm proud of you, too, Helen," Alice said. "In fact, I believe I'll bring all of my wet clothes over to your house and let you wring them out for me. I get tired of doing it by hand."

They all laughed, knowing what she meant. It takes a lot of effort to wring the water out of a large load of wet clothes.

"Anytime you want to use my spin wringer you're welcome to bring your wet clothes over here."

"Well, thanks for the offer, Helen," Alice said. "But it would probably take me more time to haul them over here, wring them out, and haul them back home. I

Lost Feather

appreciate the offer, but I guess I'll continue to wring them out by hand. Just look at the good exercise I get."

They laughed again. It felt good just to sit around and enjoy time together. A bond developed among the four of them.

Mary looked at each of them and smiled. She was going to learn how to make a quilt. She could hardly wait.

Lost Feather

CHAPTER XII

The first day of school found Jimmy in the best old clothes he owned. He didn't want to go to school dressed in his old clothes, but Mr. Wilson promised he would take him and Mary to Longmont the next weekend so they could buy a few new clothes. He would take them, that is, if they went on to school the first week without fussing about it. They agreed after talking it over at the picnic.

The first week of school was a getting-acquainted period for Jimmy. The school had three large rooms with two classes taught in each room. They put him in the eighth grade and told him they'd send back to Newark, New Jersey, for his records. If he had enough credits he would stay in the eighth, but if he didn't he'd have to go back into the seventh.

He told them he didn't want to go through the seventh grade again. He was fourteen in August and should be in the eighth grade. He was smart and was doing the work of their eighth grade that was what the seventh grade did back in Newark. Why they wouldn't believe him he didn't know.

Jimmy had trouble in school in Newark, but he knew he passed. How many credits he earned, he didn't know. He just hoped Colorado would accept all of his credits so he could stay in the eighth grade.

After talking with his teacher, Miss Davis, he felt better. Mary was a year behind him, which put them in different rooms. The next year they'd be in the same room.

When Saturday finally arrived, Jimmy and Mary met at her father's garage. Mr. Wilson had a few things to do before they left, so they went out and got in the front seat of his car. Jimmy's grandpa was going to watch the

Lost Feather

garage and pump gas for him while he took Mary and Jimmy to Longmont to buy clothes.

Jimmy gave half of his money to his grandparents. They accepted it, and thanked him. It would help pay the bill they owed Dr. Bixler. He would send a bill, not expecting to be paid for some time. "He sure is going to get a surprise," Jimmy said.

They waited in the car for Mr. Wilson to finish up. Jimmy's grandma and Mary's mother came and got into the back seat. Jimmy and Mary sank down in the front seat. They hoped to buy what they wanted, but it didn't look like that would happen now.

Mary's mother, Helen, said, "We just want to go see what you're going to buy. We like to shop too, you know," and they laughed.

They got most of the things they wanted for school, but not all. They did get a banana split with lots of ice cream and nuts on it. That made up for what they didn't get.

It turned out to be a good trip, and Jimmy and Mary got several new clothes. When they got back they both went home and tried them all on, just to see how the clothes looked with the sales tags off. Their new winter coats looked great and felt good.

New snow could now be seen on the tops of the high mountains. Jimmy's grandpa told him before he left the house that morning that the cool mornings were a good sign that winter was not far off, especially since there was already so much snow up in the high mountains. If he was right it wouldn't be long until there was snow in Mercer.

All of the kids he knew seemed to look forward to it, but Jimmy had mixed emotions. When it snowed in Newark it was a mess. You could hardly dress for it, as the air contained a lot of moisture. The streets were nothing but

Lost Feather

slush. All of the exhaust from the cars turned the snow a dark, dirty color. The idea of snow didn't leave a very nice picture in his mind. He would have to wait and see what it looked like in Mercer.

The school received Jimmy's records from Newark, and all of his credits were accepted. He felt good about not having to go back a grade, even though he would have been in the same class with Mary. He would have liked that, but decided it was better for him to be a grade ahead of her since he was a year older.

Days turned into weeks and soon a month passed. Jimmy went out behind the house now and then and looked at the hawk pens. He sat on the pile of railroad ties and daydreamed of the times he had with Lady Samson. He recalled how he helped his grandpa get the load of railroad ties. He thought about the time his grandpa was bitten by a black widow spider and he had to drive the truck back home, not ever having driven before.

He laughed when he remembered how he drove all over the road. Then he thought of the railroad tracks where he hit the railroad crossing sign and ripped the back fender almost off the truck. His grandpa and Mr. Wilson just fixed it the day before that happened.

Memories flooded his mind, but his thoughts always came back to his hawk. He was lonely for the days when he hunted with Lady Samson. Those were the best days of his life.

Jimmy finally stopped going out to the hawk pens. It was getting colder, and he started staying in his room more and more. He did his homework at night, which helped occupy his mind most of the time. But there were the other times, especially the weekends, when he lay on his bed and daydreamed all day. It got to where he seldom

Lost Feather

came out of his room. When his grandparents tried to find out what was wrong, he wouldn't talk.

Mary came by to see him and he talked to her. But as soon as she left he went back to his room. Alice and Tom often talked about how they hoped Jimmy would come out of the deep depression he was in. They felt like they should do something, but what?

One day they decided they would try again to get him to talk. It was now too cold to sit out on the porch in the evenings, so they moved into the kitchen and sat around the table. Tom and Alice started out by telling stories about their life and some of the people that lived in Mercer. Jimmy liked to listen to them and seemed to start coming out of his shell. But when asked to talk, he still wouldn't. It wasn't long until he started daydreaming while they talked.

They tried for a couple of weeks, and then Jimmy retreated back to his room. One day Tom talked to Chuck Miller down at the garage. He told him that Jimmy stayed in his room all the time. He told him they tried to get him to come out of his shell by telling him stories, but he always went back to staying in his room. They didn't know what to do to get him interested in life outside his room again. If he didn't change soon, they felt it might lead to something worse, and they didn't want that to happen. It worried them not knowing what to do.

Chuck thought about it for a while. "Tom," he said, with a smile on his face, "I think I know how we can get him out of that shell he is building around himself. I know one time in my life I was down in the dumps over my dad giving my dog away. It was the only dog he ever let me have. But it barked all night, and my dad got tired of it and gave it away the next day. I was all broken up over losing that dog. But, lucky for me, my best friend's dad saw the

Lost Feather

problem and helped me out. You know what he did for me, Tom?"

"No," Tom said. "But if you don't hurry up and tell me I'll go ask your wife. I'm sure she'll tell me and not keep me in suspense."

Chuck laughed. "He took me deer hunting, Tom. He got me out of the house and into the woods. With new surroundings, all my old thoughts disappeared and I forgot about my dog being gone. I didn't have time to worry about what my dad did. I thought about what happened around me, and if I would get a deer or not. It was great."

Tom thought about it for a while, then he said, "That sounds like a good idea, Chuck."

"It is, Tom," Chuck replied. "Hunting season opens next week. It will be open when the kids get their Thanksgiving holiday. That's less than two weeks away. I'll talk to him about it and see if he would like to go with me this year. I bought a cabin on twenty acres up above Ward, Colorado, last year. It's not too big, but the fellow I bought it from said he never failed to get a good-size deer each year. He told me that he took a lot of his good friends up there over the years and they always got a deer."

"OK, Chuck," Tom said. "You talk to Jimmy and see if you can get him interested. It just might be what he needs to get his mind off the things that happened that got him down. You know what a lot of those things are. I know if they happened to me, I'd probably feel the same way. We've got to do something to turn him around. I want to see him like he used to be. Yes, sir. I sure hope it works. It has to."

"I'm sure it will work, Tom," Chuck replied, with enthusiasm. "I'll go over and talk to him right now. I know he'll get excited about it because I've gotten myself excited.

Lost Feather

No one could keep from being excited if I'm excited. Right?"

"Well, I know one thing for sure, Chuck," Tom said. "You've got me excited."

Chuck went out the door of the garage laughing. "I'll see you later and tell you how it all turns out."

They laughed as Chuck got into his truck and drove off. He drove down the main street until he came to the last street in town, then, turned right. He drove down the street and up to the lane that led to the Warriors' house. He slowed down as he drove to the front of the house and parked so the driver's window faced the house.

He thought how he needed to handle this situation. He must get Jimmy excited about going hunting. He smiled and started honking his horn.

Alice opened the door and shouted at him to quit honking the horn and come on in.

"No thanks, Alice," Chuck replied. "I want to talk to Jimmy. Ask him to come out here so I can talk to him."

Alice nodded and disappeared. Chuck waited for a while, but Jimmy didn't come out, so he started honking his horn again. Pretty soon Jimmy came to the door with his grandma behind him. She pointed at the car and he heard her tell Jimmy to tell Chuck to quit honking his horn.

Jimmy came down the steps and walked up to the car. He looked like he was half-asleep. "What do you want with me, Mr. Miller?" Jimmy asked.

Chuck looked at Jimmy for a while not saying a word. Jimmy didn't look like he did a month ago.

Jimmy opened his eyes a little wider and looked at Chuck. "My grandma wants you to quit honking your horn."

"I'm just trying to wake you up, Jimmy," Chuck said. "I've come to shake you up a little and get you as

Lost Feather

excited as I am. I'm going deer hunting, Jimmy, and I'd like for you to go with me. Have you ever been deer hunting?"

"No, sir," Jimmy said, showing no interest at all.

"Well, I bought me a little cabin up in the mountains last year. The man who sold it to me told me there were herds of deer up there last year. I'm sure there are plenty still there. Now the deer-hunting season opens next week and runs to the first part of December. You get your Thanksgiving holiday in less than two weeks. That gives us just enough time to get everything ready."

Jimmy didn't know too much about what Mr. Miller was talking about, but his excitement was catching. He seemed to come alive a little as he listened. "I've never hunted deer, Mr. Miller," he said. "In fact, I've never hunted anything by myself - only with the hawks. They were the hunters."

"Well, it is time for you to be the hunter, Jimmy," Chuck replied. "We'll go up in the mountains for about a week. You'll have a lot of time to think things over up there. Your thinking will get straightened out in that clean mountain air. The air up at my cabin smells so fresh, and the trees and mountains are so pretty, you'll never want to leave. We'll have a good time, Jimmy, and if you get a deer you'll bring enough meat home to last all winter."

That was what Mr. Miller should have said when he arrived. Jimmy's face lit up. He'd not been able to supply any meat for the family, and it bothered him. He knew his grandpa needed to have meat to stay healthy. Jimmy looked at Mr. Miller. "I've never fired a rifle."

"We have over a week to get you used to firing a rifle. Not only firing the rifle, but hitting what you want to hit," Mr. Miller said. "I'll get everything together, and when you get out of school tomorrow, you come over to my farm and we'll go out and sight in a couple of rifles."

Lost Feather

Jimmy's eyes were now bright and he was wide-awake. He was getting excited about going deer hunting. "Yes, sir," he answered. "I'll be over right after school. Do I need to bring anything?"

"No, Jimmy," Mr. Miller answered. "Just yourself. See you then." He started his car and Jimmy stepped back. He drove around the circle drive and out onto the street.

Jimmy ran up the steps and into the house. His grandma was in the kitchen getting dinner ready. He sat down at the table and said, "I sure am hungry."

It took Alice by surprise. When she realized what he said, she went over and got some milk out of the refrigerator and poured him a glass. "Supper will be ready in a few minutes, Jimmy. Your grandpa will be here soon. You drink this and go get cleaned up. I've got your favorite tonight, spaghetti with meat balls."

Jimmy gulped the milk down like he hadn't had a drink in a long time. He got up and put the glass on the counter near the sink. "I surely do like spaghetti and meatballs, Grandma. Yes, ma'am, I sure do."

Just then the front door opened and Tom came in. He walked into the kitchen and looked at the two of them. "What are you two up to now?" he said, smiling.

Alice didn't say a word; she just smiled back.

"We're having spaghetti and meatballs, Grandpa," Jimmy said. "It's my favorite." He started toward the bathroom to get cleaned up, then stopped. "Mr. Miller wants me to go deer hunting with him up at his cabin. He wants me to come over to his farm tomorrow after school and learn how to shoot one of his rifles."

Alice started to say something but Tom beat her to it. "I'd like for you to take my rifle, Jimmy," he said. "You come by here first and get it before you go out to Mr.

Lost Feather

Miller's. If you learn how to shoot real good, learn all the safety rules, and get a deer, I'll give you my rifle."

"Would you, Grandpa?" Jimmy asked. "That would be great! I'll learn how to shoot, and I'll get you and Grandma a deer so we can have meat all winter." He turned and ran down the hall to the bathroom.

Alice looked at Tom.

"If that's what it takes to get that boy out of the sad state of mind he's been in for a month, I'll gladly give him my rifle," Tom said. "His happiness is worth a lot more to me than that gun. Anyway, when I'm gone someone needs to look after the Warrior rifles. I'll give them all to him if he proves to be worthy, Alice."

Alice nodded her approval, and went about setting the table. Tom sat down and waited for Jimmy. Jimmy hurried in, sat down, and looked around. Alice came over and set the food on the table. His eyes grew wide as he looked at all of that spaghetti in front of him. Tom asked the blessing on the food, friends, and family, then, sat back.

Alice and Tom watched Jimmy eat for a few minutes. It sure was good to see him eating like he should. After dinner Tom went into his bedroom and came out with a rifle. He handed it to Jimmy and waited for a response.

Jimmy looked at it, turned it over in his hands a couple times, then looked up at his grandpa. "What kind of a rifle is it, Grandpa?" he asked.

"It's a Winchester 30.06 lever action rifle, Jimmy," he replied. "One of the better weapons made. It's the right size for you, too. Not too big and heavy, but big enough to bring down a deer."

Tom reached over and took the rifle from Jimmy. "I'll let Mr. Miller show you how to use it, and then teach you all the safety rules. I could show you, but Mr. Miller

Lost Feather

agreed to do it for me. I saw him when I was coming home and he told me about you two going hunting."

"Yes, sir," Jimmy said. "I'm sure looking forward to going with him during the Thanksgiving holiday. I'll have about a week out of school." Jimmy paused. "Excuse me, Grandpa. I've got to go to my room."

Tom's face sagged a little. He thought maybe it had only been a short-lived excitement, and now it was over. "What's the matter?" he asked.

"I've got a lot of homework to do, Grandpa," he said, heading for his room. "I want to be passing when Thanksgiving gets here. I don't want to have to stay home and do extra work the teacher will be giving those who get behind."

The smile returned to Tom's face as Jimmy made his way to his room. He got up and walked over to Alice, who was washing the dishes. "I think Chuck and I have found the solution to help Jimmy get over the loss of his hawks."

"I sure hope so, Tom," she replied.

After school the next day Jimmy ran all the way home. He quickly put his books in his room and went back to the kitchen. Tom was at the table wiping off the barrel of the rifle. "I just cleaned her up for you, Jimmy. That's one of the things you must always do. Keep your gun clean. That way you won't have any trouble with it." He put his hand over his mouth, then, slowly took it away with a grin on his face.

"I told you I wouldn't be telling you what to do; Mr. Miller will do that. You run along and take the rifle with you, Jimmy," he said, handing him the rifle "Above all, Jimmy, be careful with any weapon. It's designed to kill things. Don't let it be a person, or maybe yourself."

Lost Feather

"Yes, sir," Jimmy replied, taking the rifle. "I'll be extra careful, Grandpa."

Jimmy started to leave, but his grandpa stopped him and gave him a box of shells. "Take these, Jimmy. It's hard to shoot the rifle without them."

Jimmy took the box of shells and put them in his pocket. Tom laughed as he ran out the front door. Jimmy ran for a block before he started walking. It felt good to walk with the rifle in his hand. He thought of all kinds of things he could shoot with it. He'd bring back all kinds of meat.

When he got to the Miller farm he found Mr. Miller waiting for him. Mr. Miller's rifle was larger than Tom's. "That's a fine rifle you have, Jimmy," he said. "I've seen your grandpa bring down a lot of game with it."

They got into his truck and drove out to one of his fields. A creek ran through the field, and they pulled up near the bank.

Mr. Miller brought along some targets that he put in the back of the truck bed. They got out, opened the tailgate and laid their rifles on it. Jimmy stepped back and watched Mr. Miller. Jimmy did everything Mr. Miller did.

"Let's set up the targets," Mr. Miller said. "I've also got a box full of old bottles we can shoot at later. But right now we need to get your gun sighted in. After that, you'll learn how to aim and fire it at a target. Then we'll shoot some bottles for fun."

After they set up the targets across the creek, Mr. Miller gave Jimmy a safety lecture on how to use and take care of his rifle. He was so serious Jimmy thought he was getting mad at him as he talked about safety.

"I mean what I say about safety, Jimmy," he said, at the end of his lecture. "One of my best friends was hurt bad

Lost Feather

by a person who didn't think much about safety. You can never be too safe!"

Chuck then smiled at Jimmy. "Let's see how good your grandpa's rifle is."

They walked to the back of the truck and got their rifles. Mr. Miller first showed Jimmy where to load shells into his rifle. He then showed him how to look down the barrel to the sight at the end. He loaded a shell into the chamber of Jimmy's rifle and sighted it at one of the targets. He fired, and the loud explosion surprised Jimmy. It made his ears ring. "You'll get used to it, Jimmy. Let's go see where I hit the target. It looks good from here."

Jimmy strained his eyes to see the target. "See that small, black place near the center of the target?" Chuck said. That's called the bull's-eye." They walked over to the target and looked. Sure enough, the bullet went through the bull's-eye.

"That's a fine rifle, Jimmy," Mr. Miller said again. "I'd like to have it myself."

Jimmy smiled real big knowing his grandpa's rifle was a good one. Some of his sadness left as pride filled its place.

They walked back to the truck. "Now let's see how you do, Jimmy," Chuck said. He loaded another shell into the rifle chamber and handed him the gun.

Jimmy put the rifle up to his shoulder. Mr. Miller moved his arms until he was satisfied. "Take a deep breath, then let some of it out. Keep the sight of the rifle in the middle of the bull's-eye. Then slowly squeeze the trigger, don't jerk it. If you can do all of that you'll hit the bull's eye like I did."

Jimmy took a deep breath, let some of it out, put the rifle sight in the center of the bull's-eye and pulled the

Lost Feather

trigger. The loud bang of the rifle, and its recoil against his shoulder, felt like someone hit him.

"Squeeze, Jimmy," Chuck said, "squeeze. You'll never shoot good until you master squeezing the trigger."

Jimmy put the rifle down on the tailgate of the truck and ran over to the target. There was still only one hole in the target, the hole Mr. Miller put there.

The next time he squeezed the trigger like Mr. Miller told him to do. When he checked the target he found two holes. His was a couple inches outside the bull's-eye. "You're shooting too high, Jimmy," Chuck said, looking closely at the target, "You jerked the trigger just a little. Work on squeezing the trigger and you'll hit the bull's eye every time."

As the afternoon passed, the holes on the target moved closer and closer to the center. Jimmy's confidence grew with each round he fired. After they practiced about an hour, Chuck went back to the truck and placed his rifle on the tailgate. "Let's break a few bottles, Jimmy, and call it a day."

Jimmy placed his rifle beside Chuck's. He was glad they stopped. His ears still rang.

When the bottles were all broken they picked up the pieces and put them into the sack they brought them in. They loaded the targets in the back of the truck with the sack.

They drove back toward the farmhouse and talked about how well Jimmy did. They got out of the truck and Jimmy put his rifle on his shoulder like a marching soldier. Mr. Miller's face turned red.

"Jimmy, when you raised your rifle to put it on your shoulder you pointed the barrel at me," he said sternly. "That's something you never do! You never point a weapon at anyone. People are shot and sometimes killed each year

Lost Feather

by someone who accidentally pointed a gun at them. The shooter thinks the weapon's not loaded. Weapons that people think are not loaded are the ones that kill. Many times it's one of their best friends."

Jimmy slowly took the rifle off his shoulder making sure he didn't point it at his good friend. "I'm sorry, Mr. Miller."

"Don't ever do it again, Jimmy," Chuck replied. He walked toward the house, then stopped, turned and looked at him. "Tomorrow's Saturday. Come on over in the afternoon, like today, and we will practice some more. Do you want to leave your rifle here?"

"Yes, sir," Jimmy said. "I'll be over about four tomorrow afternoon, Mr. Miller. I sure do thank you for teaching me how to use my grandpa's rifle."

"You're welcome, Jimmy," he said smiling, "I'll see you tomorrow."

Jimmy handed him his rifle. He ran all the way home. He hit the bull's-eye a few times. It was good for his first time, but he knew he could do a lot better.

\

Lost Feather

CHAPTER XIII

The Thanksgiving holiday came at last. School was out and Mr. Miller waited for Jimmy at Mr. Wilson's garage. He left the school building and headed toward the garage. Mary yelled at him, and he turned and waited for her.

"What's your hurry, Jimmy?" Mary asked. But before he could answer she laughed. "I know. You and Mr. Miller are going deer hunting. How can you shoot one of those pretty little deer?"

"I've never shot one, Mary," Jimmy said. "But it will help my grandparents have meat all winter, so I think I can shoot one. I don't know for sure, but I think I can."

Mary didn't say anything for a while as they walked together; then she shook her head in agreement. "That does make a difference, doesn't it? If it was the difference between my being hungry or shooting a deer, I think I could shoot one, too. But I'm like you; I'd have to wait until the time came to see if I actually could."

Jimmy agreed with a shake of his head. They walked towards the garage. Jimmy stopped and Mary took a few steps before she noticed he stopped. She turned to see what was wrong. "Have you gotten over the loss of your hawk?" he asked.

Mary hung her head a little. "Not really," she said slowly. "I know you haven't either. Everyone talks about how bad you've been taking it, but you're the first one to ask me how I feel. I loved her a lot. I loved the times I had with her and you and your hawks. It's a precious memory to me now, and it always will be."

Jimmy started walking again. Mary walked a little closer to him. They both lost something they loved, and they lost the fun times they had together with the hawks.

Lost Feather

Together they were deep in their own thoughts. Not paying any attention to what they were doing, they walked past the garage. Mr. Miller stepped out the office door and yelled after them. "Where are you going?"

Mary and Jimmy turned around to see who was yelling at them. Mr. Miller could see the sadness in their eyes. "Come on in here, you two, and have a bottle of pop," he said. "Come on, get happy. There are better times ahead I can assure you."

They smiled at him and followed him into the office. To their surprise, there sat Tom, Alice, Jackie, Helen, and Bill. A large cake sat on Bill's desk, and an ice cream freezer sat on the floor with a gunny sack over the top of it to keep it cold. Smiles came across the faces of Mary and Jimmy. "A surprise party!" they exclaimed at the same time.

The cake and ice cream soon disappeared as once again they enjoyed just being together. Then it was time for Mr. Miller and Jimmy to say good-bye. They walked out to the truck with everyone following. They drove off as everyone yelled and waved, which made Jimmy feel good inside. Jimmy hoped the sadness he felt would now go away and not come back. He waved his last wave out the side window of the truck, then turned around and watched the road.

They were soon out of town and headed down the road toward Denver. It wasn't long until they passed over the railroad tracks and then came to the place where he and his grandpa loaded his truck with railroad ties. It was also where a black widow spider bit his grandpa. As the memories of that day returned, his face started showing sadness again.

Lost Feather

Chuck saw what was coming and said, "We'll turn up here and go a different way, Jimmy. Have you ever been down that road?" He looked at Jimmy to see his reaction.

Jimmy looked at Mr. Miller and said, "What?"

"I just wondered if you were ever on the road we're going to be on in a few minutes," he replied. He looked at Jimmy to see if he was paying attention. "That road right up there. See it? We're going to turn there."

Jimmy looked ahead as the road came nearer. "No, sir," he said, "I've never been off this road to Denver." Chuck slowed down then turned. As the truck straightened out on the new road, Jimmy saw the mountains stretching across the sky in front of them. He looked at them a long time. Chuck began to wonder if he'd slipped back into his sad, daydreaming world again.

Then, Jimmy turned and looked at him and asked, "Where is your cabin, Mr. Miller?"

"Oh, you can't see it from here, Jimmy," he replied, with a grin. "But it's off to the right up there on those mountains. You see those two peaks that look alike? Well, they're called the Twin Sisters. Next to them on the left is Longs Peak, the big, high one there with all of the snow on it.

'A little to the left of it is Mount Audubon, named that because if you look real close, you can see that the shape of the snow makes it looks like a bird. If you look a little further to the left and down, you'll see a kind of a cup in the mountain. Well, that's just about where Brainard Lake is located. My cabin is in that area.

'The town of Ward is below it a few miles. We'll go through Ward, then wind around until we come to a little road that leads up to where my cabin is located. It's a few miles back in the trees after we leave the road."

Lost Feather

Jimmy's thoughts were now on the area Mr. Miller told him about. He wondered what it would be like to be miles off the road among all those big pine trees. His imagination began to run wild, and the excitement showed in his face as he thought about it.

The mountains came closer, and the road grew steeper. They weaved back and forth through a beautiful valley with hills on both sides. Mr. Miller slowed down and turned onto a smaller road. After a few minutes Jimmy saw a small stream through the trees that ran along beside the road. They crossed a small bridge and the stream could be seen bubbling over the rocks. Then they passed a place where tables were built next to the creek for people to have picnics.

"Have you ever had a picnic up here, Mr. Miller?" Jimmy asked, as he sat on the edge of the seat and looked at everything they passed.

"Sure have, Jimmy," he replied. ""My wife and I came up here many times when it got too hot down in Mercer. In fact, that's why we bought the cabin we have now. We were just driving around one day and stopped in Ward to mail a letter. There was a man in the post office talking to the mail clerk about how he wished he could find a buyer for his cabin. He was transferred back east and wouldn't be able to take care of it any more."

Jimmy turned his head back and forth trying to see everything. He saw big pine trees that grew straight out of solid rocks, and wondered how that happened. They grew straight up and their roots grew sideways into the side of the rocks.

Mr. Miller got excited as he watched Jimmy. "Would you like to know a little history about this area, Jimmy?" he asked.

Lost Feather

"Yes, sir. I sure would," Jimmy said, his eyes taking in everything in sight.

"Well, Jimmy," Mr. Miller started, then stopped. Jimmy looked at him to see why he stopped. He saw that he finally had Jimmy's attention and continued. "When the white man first came into this area, there were Indians all around here. The Indians were not warring Indians, but they'd fight if they needed to, just like anyone else. The chief who lived in this area was left handed, so the white man named this canyon we're driving through, Left Hand Canyon."

"Wow," Jimmy said. "Indians lived up here! Wow!"

It seemed he wouldn't have to worry about getting Jimmy over his sadness any more. He continued his story. "The town of Ward that we'll be going through in a little while was a gold mining town in those early days. Gold was discovered above Boulder, which is about ten miles from here. We'll soon pass near the little town of Gold Hill. It's off this road about a mile. They're still mining some gold there.

"If we had stayed on the road back there where I turned, we would have gone through another gold mining town. The people call it Jimtown, but its correct name is Jamestown. Don't ask me why they prefer to call it Jimtown, they just do.

'A lot of gold was mined there in the old days. Hundreds of thousands of dollars worth was dug out of those mountains. You'll see a lot of places as we drive along, where miners dug holes in the side of the mountains. Below the entrance to the mines you'll see where they dumped the rocks they dug out. That rock is called tailings. You can't miss it, as it's kind of a gold color. Some say the gold is almost all gone now.

Lost Feather

'Like I said, there's one mine still being worked up near the gold mine town of Gold Hill. Some say there's not enough to bother with now. But I kind of doubt they've found all of the gold around these parts.

'OK. See that little road up ahead with the bridge across the stream? That goes up to the town of Gold Hill I told you about. That road is called Lick Skillet Road. Some say it's the steepest road in Colorado, and others say it's the steepest one in the United States. It drops a thousand feet in less than a mile."

He had Jimmy's attention now. "That creek that's running along side this road is called 'Left Hand Creek'; I wonder why."

He pulled up and stopped so Jimmy could get a good look and also he wanted to sit there and enjoy the sound that only a creek can make as it moves down a mountain.

Jimmy smiled and said, "It's named after Chief Left Hand." Jimmy's eyes took it all in. Then he heard the gurgling sound the water made as it passed under the bridge. It was a nice soothing sound. Everything around them was so quiet except for the water talking to them as it moved down the mountain, making its long journey towards the sea.

"The town of Ward is about four miles up this road, Jimmy. Ward was a big gold mining town. In fact, they built a railroad up to Ward just to pick up the gold they dug out of the mountains around there.

'The railroad is another story in itself. The train hauled more than just gold out of these mountains. They had grand sightseeing trips on weekends for those who wanted to take a train ride through the mountains. It wasn't long until it got the name Switzerland Trail Railway because some who rode it said it looked like the scenery

Lost Feather

they saw on train rides they took over in the country of Switzerland in Europe. It was what they call a narrow gauge railroad, Jimmy. The iron railroad tracks are a lot smaller and they are placed closer to each other than the ones the large trains run on.

'They brought Chinese laborers in to build the railroad. It is hard work building a railroad on the open plains, but going through these mountains was really hard work. They used dynamite to blast the rock to make a large enough place for a train to pass through. Then came leveling the track bed and laying the railroad ties and iron tracks. You've seen ties like they used when you and your grandpa got those ties for firewood. When the railroad was complete, the Chinese took up panning for gold.

'The rains wash the gold down into the streams, and if you know how, you can find it. You pan for it in a stream like his one. That means you dig up some of the creek sand and rocks and with a certain type of pan you slush it around and find small amounts of gold. The more you pan the more gold you have. It adds up.

'The Chinese were all over these mountains where there was a creek, searching for gold. There are a couple of men in Ward that still do some panning for gold."

Jimmy looked at the creek. "I wonder what it looks like," he thought.

"Oh yes, Jimmy," Mr. Miller continued. "The town of Ward has a couple of good stories. I guess the best one is that the town was first built on top of the hill above where the town is now located. The old railroad station is still up there. One night there was a large roar and almost all of the houses slid down the side of the hill into the valley. Many of them were destroyed, but some survived in good shape. The people took it as a sign to not build on top of the hill, so the town is now in the valley."

Lost Feather

Mr. Miller sat back and said nothing more until they drove into the city limits of Ward. "This is Ward, Jimmy. There's not much to it, but it is a nice little town. Nice friendly people."

Chuck slowed down as he drove through town, letting Jimmy get a good look. They came to the edge of town, and Chuck pointed at a house and said, "That is where a friend of mine, Pete Steel, lives."

Jimmy looked at it but didn't say anything. "This is interesting," he thought, "a real gold mine town." The road then started upwards out of town, switching back and forth like a snake, as it went higher until they came to a stop sign.

"This is the Peak to Peak Highway," Chuck said, and looked both ways. He turned right and increased the speed of the truck. He was getting excited and wanted to get to his cabin. A little over a mile down the road, he turned off the highway onto a dirt road. It was only wide enough for one car. If you met anyone coming toward you, you'd have to pull off to the side and let them go by.

"I'm sure glad the snow melted," he said, as he looked in between the trees for snow, as they drove along. "It's a lot better like this. It's not as cold and it's not muddy."

The trees grew almost up to the side of the road. Now and then one of the tree branches brushed against the truck making a scratching noise. They drove for some time until Chuck said, "It won't be much further now, Jimmy. That trail off to the left up there is the road to the cabin."

Chuck turned to the left and slowed down. The trail was less traveled and, like the small road, just wide enough for one car to travel on. Two ruts in the road showed where cars traveled going to and coming from his cabin.

Lost Feather

Now and then they came to a clearing where there were no trees. The grass was a couple of feet high, and it was the lightest green he'd ever seen. The dark green of the trees and the light green of the grass was a beautiful sight.

"The cabin is up ahead, Jimmy," Chuck said, pointing. A couple minutes later he said, "There it is. It's not much to look at, but it's beautiful to me."

He drove the truck up near the cabin and stopped. They got out and walked up to the front door. Chuck got out his keys and opened the padlock on the door, removed it, opened the door, and stepped back. "You first, Jimmy. Welcome to 'Miller's Mountain Cabin.' "

Jimmy walked in and looked around. They stood in a large room with a large fireplace at the far end of the room. Two bedrooms were off to the right with a bathroom in between. A large kitchen was to the right of the front door. "This is great, Mr. Miller," Jimmy said.

"Yeah it is, isn't it?" he said, laughing. "I sure do love it up here."

They walked through the cabin and checked it out. No one had broken in. Everything was just like he left it. "The front bedroom is mine, Jimmy," he said, "and the one next to the kitchen is yours. Let's bring our stuff in and put it up. Then we can think about what we're going to have for supper. Are you a good cook?"

"I cooked hamburgers when I lived in Newark, but that's all," Jimmy said.

"Well, I guess you'll just have to put up with my cooking," he said, laughing again. "I'm not a good cook either. Sure hope my wife put in a lot of canned food for us. We might starve if she didn't."

They both laughed as they went out to the truck and unloaded it. It wasn't long until everything was put away, and Chuck let Jimmy cook some hamburgers. He wanted to

Lost Feather

see how good a cook he was. It surprised both of them when they turned out real good.

They washed and dried the dishes and put them in the cabinets. Chuck put some wood in the fireplace and lit it. There was no electricity in the cabin, so a Coleman lantern was lit and placed in the kitchen. It was turned down so it wouldn't interfere with the glow from the fireplace in the front room. Quiet settled down around them as they sat in two easy chairs and watched the fire.

In the light of the fire's glow, Chuck told Jimmy tale after tale of the great deer and elk hunts he and his friends had been on. He told him that after they mounted the horns of some of the deer, they had to be turned sideways to get them through the door at their home so they could hang them over their fireplace.

He said he hadn't gotten a big one yet to hang over his fireplace at the cabin, but maybe one of them would get one tomorrow. Jimmy listened to every word he said. He almost saw the deer Chuck told him about. He felt the pride of getting a big deer.

Another story was about a couple of deer that he found after he bought the property. One was killed by a large black bear that lived in the area. "A forest ranger told me the bear hasn't been seen for over a year and he thinks it either moved on or was shot by some hunter. Other people I've talked to said it was probably shot because a bear doesn't change its territory.

"The other deer was smaller, and a mountain lion killed it. No one has ever seen one around here though. I know I've never seen one. Of course, they're like all cats; they wander all over the place. I doubt that we'll see one. If you do, don't run. Just make sure your gun is loaded and take it off safety. Don't show any fear and they usually will move off. If it doesn't, then shoot it."

Lost Feather

"What do they look like?" Jimmy asked.

"They're a dark yellowish-brown color and when they are grown their total length is about 8 feet. You'll know what it is if you see one. You know what I've seen up here? I met a guy the other day that hunts deer with a bow and arrows."

"Wow!" Jimmy said.

"You should have seen his bow. It was fancy and had a sight on it. He said he hunts with a bow and arrow because it's a real challenge. He said most anyone could kill a deer with a gun, but just try it with a bow and arrow. I think he's right. That's real hunting."

Chuck stopped talking and sat there looking into the fire with Jimmy. He thought about what tomorrow would bring. He looked forward to a good hunt.

He got up and went out onto the porch and looked around the cabin. He took a deep breath of the cool, clear mountain air and looked up at the stars twinkling in the deep blue sky.

He walked back into the cabin and closed the door. "It's time for us to go to bed, Jimmy. Tomorrow we'll get up early and see if we can find us a deer."

Jimmy yawned and stretched, then slowly got up and went into his bedroom. He heard Mr. Miller moving around in the living room, and then in his bedroom. Jimmy shivered a little. It was cold without the heat from the fireplace. He got undressed and got under the covers real quick. He rolled up into a ball. He started shivering and pulled the covers over his head and breathed under the covers to get warm. He quit shivering as the bed warmed up. He stuck his head out from under the covers and breathed a deep lung full of air.

He felt good lying there in that quiet, dark room. Before long he was asleep.

Lost Feather

CHAPTER XIV

A loud banging on his door brought Jimmy upright in his bed. It took him a while to remember where he was. "Yes," he finally said.

"It's time to get up, Jimmy," Mr. Miller said, loudly. "We have to eat and get out in our deer stand before the sun comes up. Get dressed and get in here and clean up so we can eat."

"Yes, sir," Jimmy said, as he rubbed his eyes. He got out of bed and began searching for his clothes. It was still dark and he had a time finding them, not knowing the room that well. He finally found them and got dressed the best he could. He picked up his shoes and socks and hurried into the front room. There was no fire in the fireplace and it was cold. He then headed for the kitchen where the Coleman lantern burned brightly. It made a kind of a hissing noise as it glowed, which made Jimmy wonder if it was going to blow up.

Chuck noticed Jimmy's concern as he stood there looking at the lantern. "It always makes a noise like that when it's cold," he said, laughing. "Boy it sure is chilly in here."

Jimmy sat down on a chair and put his socks and shoes on. "It sure is, Mr. Miller. I didn't think it would be this cold up here. I sure am glad I brought my new coat. It's going to feel good."

"You'll probably need it and another one too, when we get out there," Mr. Miller replied. "You can take them off as the day warms up, but right at first you'll need plenty of protection against the cold. Wash yourself over there in the sink. There's plenty of cold water in the bucket by the sink. That will wake you up for sure."

Lost Feather

Jimmy went over and dipped out some water with the dipper and poured it into a pan in the sink. He put his hands into the water and pulled them out quickly. It was ice cold. He picked up some soap and washed his hands, then his face. The cold water woke him up in a hurry. The kitchen warmed up a little from the cooking stove.

Chuck had eggs and bacon on their plates. "This isn't bad for our first breakfast, is it Jimmy?" he said, winking. "We've got plenty of sandwiches your grandmother made for us. We'll take some of them with us for a snack and our dinner."

It sounded good to Jimmy. The eggs and bacon looked even better. They sat down and cleaned their plates. Jimmy got up and picked up the plates, placed them in the sink, and looked for some hot water to wash them.

"We'll wash them when we get back later on today," Chuck said. "Let's get our sandwiches packed and get out to our deer stands. Daybreak is only an hour away. We want to be in our stand long before it gets light. That way the deer won't know we're waiting for them."

Jimmy went into his bedroom and left his door open so he could see. He got his new and old coats out of his suitcase. He put his old one on first and went back out to the kitchen carrying his new one.

"Load up your pockets with sandwiches, Jimmy," Chuck said. "This mountain air really makes a person hungry. Put some in your new coat pockets, too. If we don't need them we can always bring them back and eat them later."

They both loaded up their coat pockets. Jimmy put on his new coat and had a hard time getting it buttoned up, but finally succeeded. He knew he probably didn't look too good but he was warm. He went back to his room and got his rifle and some shells. He put the shells in the right

Lost Feather

pocket of his new coat and walked back to the kitchen. Mr. Miller was ready and waiting for him.

"Take this thermos of water with you, Jimmy," he said, "I've got one, too. We'll need something to drink just as bad as we'll need something to eat."

Jimmy headed for the door as Chuck reached over and picked up a coiled rope that lay on a chair. He stuffed it into his coat pocket, walked over and picked up a flashlight, then turned off the lantern. He turned on the flashlight and shined it all around the room, giving everything a final check. He pointed it in the direction of the door and they made their way out onto the porch and down the steps. "Follow me, Jimmy," he said, as they headed off to the right. They were instantly in the woods.

Jimmy made sure he kept close as Mr. Miller led the way. The dark woods were on both sides of them. It wasn't long until they came to a good-size clearing and stopped.

"I'm going to leave you here by this tree, Jimmy," he said whispering. "Lots of deer come down to this meadow and eat in the early morning. If you're quiet and they don't see or smell you, you'll get a good shot at one of them. Remember to look for horns on the one you want to shoot. If you can't see any, even though it might be a male, he would be too young."

Jimmy nodded his head without saying anything.

"I'm going to go around this meadow here to the right, until I'm about in the middle of the meadow on the other side. Do not, I repeat, do not shoot at anything in that direction. It could be me that you shoot if you do. I won't shoot anything to my left, and you don't shoot anything to your right. If you need me for anything just come over to where I'll be hiding, OK?"

"Yes, sir," Jimmy whispered.

Lost Feather

"OK," Chuck whispered back. "Good hunting. I'll see you later. I'll give you three flashes of my light when I stop. That way you'll know exactly where I am."

Chuck moved off to Jimmy's right with his flashlight beam going before him. Jimmy watched it as it flickered on and off as he moved through the trees and underbrush. Then it disappeared. He must have turned it off. Then it appeared again. It moved along a short distance then stopped. The light then flicked on and off three times. Jimmy knew exactly where he was now. It made him feel good knowing he was close by if he needed him.

Time passed slowly as he stood there. The cold night air, that he didn't notice when he began walking, settled down around him. It wasn't long until he started to shiver. "When will it get light?" he kept asking himself. He listened as closely as he could but couldn't hear a thing. He began wondering if there were any deer in this forest; or if there was, maybe they made so much noise they scared them away.

He noticed it got light off to his left through the trees. It was the first sign of a new day. It got brighter and brighter, until he saw his breath upon the cold mountain air. It was a lot colder than he thought it would be. Then he thought what thousands of hunters probably think as they stand somewhere in the woods waiting for the sun to come up. "What am I doing here? It would be warm back at the cabin compared to this place. Why did I ever think I wanted to go hunting?" His hands felt frozen, and he laid his gun up against the tree beside him and put his hands in his coat pockets.

As it got lighter he stood there in awe at the sight before him. The reflections and shadows the sun made as it slowly climbed up through the pine trees were breathtaking. The sun eventually reached the top of the

Lost Feather

trees. With all of its brilliance it bathed the small meadow in sunlight. He was amazed at all of the brilliant colors around him.

As Jimmy's eyes moved back and forth across the meadow, he spotted some deer moving through the trees. Slowly he reached for his rifle. He picked it up and remembered he hadn't loaded it. He took three shells out of his coat pocket and loaded them into the side of the rifle. He then carefully pulled the lever forward and brought it back to load a shell into the barrel. When he looked up the deer were all gone. The noise he made loading the rifle must have scared them away.

Jimmy leaned back against the tree and looked toward the place where the deer previously were. "I'll have to be quiet," he thought. He put the safety on so he wouldn't fire it accidentally. He stood there for some time not moving a muscle. "Come on deer. Please come back," he said to himself.

Time passed and as the sun climbed higher, it got warmer. Soon he was too warm to be wearing two coats. He took off his new coat, folded it up and placed it on the ground next to the tree where he stood.

More time passed and he started thinking about the sandwiches in his coat pockets. He wanted to eat one but he didn't want to make any noise. It became a troublesome thought after a while. What should he do, eat and make noise, or be hungry and quiet? He finally decided he would eat and sat down next to the tree. He took one of the sandwiches from his new coat and looked at it. It was an egg sandwich, and he happily ate it quickly.

He stood up and looked around for deer. There were none in sight. He opened his thermos bottle and drank some water. It sure did taste good. Everything tasted good in the mountains, just like Mr. Miller said it would.

Lost Feather

Near noon, Jimmy decided to go find Mr. Miller. If there were no deer in this meadow, maybe they should go to another place.

Jimmy reached down to pick up his new coat, then stopped. He'd leave it there for now. If Mr. Miller wanted to stay, there would be no reason to carry it all the way over to where he was, and then back. "If we're going to move, I'll come back and get it," he thought.

Jimmy moved slowly through the edge of the woods. The meadow grass grew up to where the trees started. The grass was shorter near the trees than it was out in the meadow. As he moved through the grass, he kept his ears alert for any sound. He heard nothing but the swish of the grass against his pants legs.

He moved like one of his ancestors. He thought of the Indians that used to hunt these mountains just as he was doing. All they had was a bow and arrow. They must have been great hunters. "I'll be a great hunter some day," he thought. He slowed down even more and watched everything in sight.

Suddenly there was a snort behind him and off to his right. He turned and saw that a large deer stood in the trees looking at him. He froze. They stood there looking at each other for a couple moments. Jimmy saw it was a big buck. "What a beautiful picture the deer makes," he thought as it turned and walked away through the trees.

Jimmy came out of his trance, put the rifle to his shoulder and aimed. He took a deep breath, let a little air out and squeezed the trigger. Nothing happened. "The safety is on," he shouted in his head.

He quickly reached down, pushed off the safety, and again looked down the barrel of the rifle. The deer started to run through the woods.

Lost Feather

Jimmy aimed the rifle ahead of the deer a little and squeezed the trigger. "Bang!" The sound deafened him for an instant, but he saw the deer drop after a couple of jumps. Jimmy took off running the minute the deer hit the ground.

He ran up to the deer and stopped and looked at it. Then, to his amazement it jumped up and ran off. Jimmy lifted his rifle, and again it wouldn't shoot. He levered a shell into the chamber of the rifle, aimed, and fired a little ahead of the deer. The deer kept going, disappearing through some high brush.

He remembered what Mr. Miller told him last night about tracking. When you shoot a deer and it gets up and runs off, you track it until you find it. It won't go far if it has been hit. So Jimmy ran in the direction the deer went, looking as he went for some signs.

In his mind he saw himself a great Indian hunter on the trail of an animal he shot. He started seeing large drops of blood here and there.

He levered his last shell into the rifle as he ran. "I won't make the same mistake twice," he thought. Then up ahead he saw the deer standing near a large tree looking at him. Jimmy stopped, aimed the rifle again and pulled the trigger. Bark flew from the tree next to the deer. The deer turned and with two mighty leaps disappeared into the woods. "Squeeze the trigger," he thought, angry with himself.

Jimmy ran to the tree where the deer stood. He ran in the direction the deer went, looking for signs of blood. There were no signs of blood. "There must be," he thought. Then it dawned on him that it had been another deer, not the one he shot earlier.

He went back to the spot where he thought he fired. He looked around for signs of blood but there were none. He stood there not moving, hoping to hear the deer. There

Lost Feather

was not a sound. He then walked in a large circle and found no signs of blood. This was discouraging.

Time passed slowly and after some time, Jimmy gave up trying to find the trail of the deer and walked back towards the meadow. "Mr. Miller will have heard my shots and will be looking for me," he thought. He could help him trail the deer. He surely didn't want to lose that big buck.

He thought of how much meat his grandparents would have when he found that big buck. He came to a meadow and looked around to see if Mr. Miller was anywhere in sight. He couldn't see him, so he walked around the edge. This is where Mr. Miller said he'd be. As he walked, he realized that this meadow was much smaller than the one he'd been in. He stopped and looked around. Slowly it dawned on him. He was lost.

Fear gripped him at first, and he yelled Mr. Miller's name over and over, but there was no answer. He ran around the edge of the meadow and called again. He stopped and listened but only heard the soft sound of the wind blowing through the tops of the trees. He was a city boy and not used to the mountains and forest. He panicked and started running. He ran until he fell exhausted. He got his second wind, then got up and ran some more. He was too exhausted to run any further so he lay down on the ground and cried.

He stopped sobbing, then stood up and looked around. It was then he realized he lost his rifle somewhere. Again he looked all around. The sun was directly overhead and he didn't know which way to go. He remembered the sun came up on his left that morning and that would be the east. He would wait until the sun started to go down, then he would know which way was west. That way he could find his way back to the cabin.

Lost Feather

He sat down next to a large tree. His stomach told him it was time to eat. He felt his coat pocket and smiled when he felt two sandwiches. That would be enough for him. That is, if Mr. Miller found him that day. He started to take both of them out of his pocket and stopped. "What if Mr. Miller doesn't find me today?" he thought. Slowly, he put the sandwich back in his pocket. What could he do to let Mr. Miller know where he was? There had to be some way.

He thought about shooting his rifle, but remembered he lost it. Besides that, he shot all the shells he put in the rifle. The other shells were in his new coat pocket. Not only the shells, but the other sandwiches and the thermos bottle of water he brought that morning. He got angry with himself for not bringing them.

His anger soon passed as fear once again returned. He realized that he didn't have any way to let Mr. Miller know where he was. He put his head between his knees and gave a long sigh. "Things don't look too good," he thought. "What should I do," he wondered. He sat upright against the tree. He would survive like his ancestors did. He would use his wits. Indians survived many days by themselves wherever they were. He could do it. He knew he could.

He was glad he wore his old coat. It kept him warm many times. Then he remembered how cold it was that morning. He sure wished he had his new coat, too. Maybe he could find it before it got dark. If he could find his coat he could find his way back to the cabin.

Jimmy looked up and saw the sun started going down to his right. That meant it came up on his left, just like it did in the other meadow. That was the way he came into the other meadow that morning. He turned around and headed that way. He wound his way in and out of the trees, always trying to keep going in the right direction.

Lost Feather

Sometimes a ravine or a large hill appeared in front of him. He'd have to go around the hill, or down one edge of the ravine and up the other side. He knew that they were not in his path when he came from the cabin, but he didn't know what else to do.

He approached another hill and decided to climb to the top and see if he could see anything. When he got to the top, the trees were too thick for him to see any distance, so he climbed a tree and looked at the surrounding area. Nothing looked familiar.

The sun started to go down. It wouldn't be too long until it would be dark. He'd have to find a place to stay for the night. He climbed back down the tree and ran down the hill to the bottom. "Which way should I go?" he thought. The way he had been going didn't seem to lead him in the right direction. He probably went by the cabin and didn't even know it. He decided to go back the way he came for a while. If that wasn't right, he would go left and see where that led.

It got dark fast and Jimmy hadn't found a place to stay. It would be cold out in the open without any cover at all. He saw an opening to his right. He walked over to the opening in the trees and came to a sudden stop. The ground dropped away from where he stood. A small valley lay before him. He looked across the valley and saw that the ground rose above the level at which he stood.

He looked closer and saw a dark spot on the hill across from where he stood. "It must be a cave of some kind," he thought. He ran down the slight incline and across the opening to the other side of the valley. He made his way up the incline and saw that it was a small cave.

He looked inside and saw that it was large enough for him to sleep in. He started to go in, then stopped. "It could be the home of a bear or something else," he thought.

Lost Feather

He looked inside and made sure there was nothing in there. Satisfied that the cave was empty, he bent over and went inside. He saw some tracks, but he didn't know what kind of an animal made them.

He turned around and looked out the cave entrance to see if there was anything looking in. There was no sign of anything anywhere. He sat down and put his head up against the wall of the cave. He sat and looked down at the valley he just came across. "This would be a good place to stay for the night," he thought.

The sun started going down behind the mountains. He heard a shot and ran out of the cave and stood and waited. He looked in all directions but saw nothing. He went back inside. Then he heard a second shot. It echoed back and forth across the valley. Again he ran out and listened. There were no more shots. It was too dark now to do anything. He'd have to wait until morning. He sat down outside the cave and leaned back against a large rock. The stars soon came out and filled the sky like diamonds. They looked so close it seemed like he could almost touch them.

With the darkness came the cold. Jimmy started shivering again. He got up and went back inside the cave and lay down. It sure was a lot colder than it was in Mr. Miller's cabin. He rolled up in a ball, but it didn't help, he just got colder and colder. How could he get any sleep shaking like he was? "I might even freeze to death. If I froze I might never be found," he thought. He got up and stepped outside the cave only to find it colder out there. Quickly he returned to the cave and lay down again.

Sleep came to Jimmy, but it was not a restful sleep. He was awake several times through the night, and each time he shook so hard his teeth chattered. He rubbed his arms and legs real hard to get the blood circulating. It

Lost Feather

helped a little but it was only temporary. He wondered if daylight would ever come.

Lost Feather

CHAPTER XV

Mr. Miller sat in his deer stand all morning. He really wanted to get a deer, but more than that, he hoped Jimmy would get at least a good shot at a deer. But it looked like they were not going to be lucky enough to see anything that morning. It was getting late and he was hungry. He took out one of his sandwiches and ate it.

He opened his thermos bottle, and poured a cup of the black, hot coffee he'd made that morning. After he drank it he put the cap back on and set it down when he heard a shot off to his left. "Yippee," he shouted. "Jimmy must have gotten himself a deer," he thought. He picked up his coat he took off earlier and walked toward the sound of the shot. As he came close to the place where he left Jimmy he heard another shot. This one was in the woods to his left.

"That a boy, Jimmy," he said out loud. "Track him down, don't let him get away."

He turned and headed in the direction of the last shot. When he got to the place where he thought Jimmy should be he wasn't there. "He's still tracking him," he said to himself. He looked around the area for some signs where maybe the deer had been hit. Sure enough there were drops of blood on the ground. "You got him, Jimmy, you got him," he said out loud, getting excited. "You keep on his trail and I'll keep on yours. We'll meet up where that deer stops."

Then there was a third shot ahead of him. He took off running, watching the spots of blood as he ran. The spots were getting closer together and bigger as he ran. "You've got him for sure, Jimmy," he said to himself, "you've got him."

Lost Feather

After he went about a hundred yards he stopped and looked up ahead. A thick area of bushes was just ahead of him. He saw something moving inside the bushes. "Is that you, Jimmy?" he shouted. "I've been chasing you for quite a while. Did you get a big deer, Jimmy? I saw a lot of blood, so I know you hit something."

Just then a large buck came crashing out of the bushes and fell at his feet. Startled, he jumped back and hid behind the nearest tree. He peeked around the tree trunk and saw the deer was dead. He ran over to it and counted the points on its horns. "It has twelve points, Jimmy!" he shouted, "Twelve points! That's the biggest set of antlers I've seen around this part of the country. We can put this one above the fireplace. I sure would like that, wouldn't you?"

Mr. Miller turned around and looked back at the bushes. There was no movement anywhere. "Jimmy," he said over and over, as he walked around the edge of the bushes. There was no one there. He looked all around and saw no sign of Jimmy. He realized Jimmy must have lost the deer's trail. That meant he was out there somewhere looking for him. If he didn't find him quickly he'd be lost. He sure couldn't let that happen.

He shouted, "Jimmy!" over and over, but there was no answer. "Why didn't I tell Jimmy what to do if he got lost?" he thought. He started getting mad at himself for not telling him. Without realizing what he was doing, he began looking in all directions. Suddenly, he got dizzy and lost his balance. He automatically reached out with his right hand to keep from falling down. His rifle stuck in the ground and discharged. There was a muffled sound as dirt flew in all directions, peppering everything around him, especially his face and clothes. He slowly raised the rifle and looked at the barrel. The discharge had also blown

Lost Feather

back through the gun barrel and jammed the firing mechanism.

He sat down next to a tree and shook his head. Now he couldn't fire his rifle to let Jimmy know where he was. He sat there for some time and looked at his rifle and shook his head. Then he gathered his thoughts and realized what happened and what he must do.

He got up and hurried back to where the deer lay. He took out his knife and started working on it. The insides had to be taken out while it was still warm. He finally had it ready to take back to the cabin.

He pulled the deer along behind him, but tired quickly. He found a branch that would be tall enough to get the deer a couple feet off the ground. He took the coil of rope out of his coat pocket and unwound it. He tied it around the deer's neck and then threw the other end of the rope over the tree limb and pulled it up as high as he could on the tree limb. He wrapped the other end around the trunk of the tree and tied it. Up off the ground kept the insects and small animals from it, plus it could air out better. It would keep there until he got back.

He'd have to go back to the cabin and get another rifle. He looked up at the sun and realized there were only a couple more hours of daylight left. He ran towards the cabin but soon got dizzy. He stopped and sat down and rested. To be of any help to Jimmy, he had to take it easy. "I can't help either of us if I have a heart attack," he thought.

He got up, walked at a slow pace, and watched where he stepped. He realized the only way he could help Jimmy now was to keep from getting hurt. The sun started to go down behind the mountains when he arrived back at the cabin. He hurried up the steps and went inside. He rushed to his bedroom, got out his handgun and ran back

Lost Feather

outside and fired it into the air. He waited a few minutes and fired again. Night was coming on fast and he was sure Jimmy wouldn't move in the dark. His heart went out to him, knowing that he was alone and scared. He decided to wait until morning to fire his gun again.

It was a long night for Chuck. He sat in front of the fire and thought of different ways he could let Jimmy know where the cabin was. He would build a big fire in the fireplace the next morning so Jimmy could see the smoke. Then he'd fire his gun now and then so he could get a bearing on the cabin.

He thought about the deer Jimmy shot and he prepared and hung in the tree. He'd have to get it in the morning if it was still there. He sure hoped nothing would get it. The light from the fire dimmed as he sat there. He finally got up and went into the kitchen where the lantern sat on a table. It hissed at him as he looked at it.

"It sure would be great if Jimmy was here to hear you hissing," he thought. He picked it up and went to his bedroom. He undressed and started to get into bed. He stopped and knelt beside the bed. "Please, Lord, take care of Jimmy tonight. He needs your protection and guidance. Help me to find him tomorrow. And please don't let anything happen to that deer he shot. Thank you."

Chuck got up and slipped into bed. He felt better.

He tossed and turned that night, and woke up now and then to see if it was light outside. But the darkness was still there, and he lay back down and dozed off again. Then the time came when he woke up and the light streamed in his window. He looked at his watch and saw it was almost nine o'clock. He overslept. "Why didn't I set the alarm clock?" he thought, and hit himself in the head with his open hands. Things just didn't go the way he wanted them to go. He planned to be more careful from now on.

Lost Feather

He jumped out of bed and ran into the kitchen. He put his handgun on the kitchen table the night before. He grabbed the gun and ran out the front door, raised it and fired. He listened but heard nothing.

Chuck waited five minutes and fired again. That way Jimmy could follow the sound of the gunshots to find the cabin. He went back inside and started a fire in the fireplace. After he got it going he went out and fired another shot.

He continued firing his gun every five minutes. He ate breakfast and was ready to go get the deer. He went into his room and got all the shells he had for the handgun. "I'll have to fire the gun less often now," he thought, "or I'll soon run out of shells." He went outside to the shed and got a canvas tarp to put the deer on. He carried it over to the truck and put it in the back. He rushed back inside the cabin and checked everything to make sure it was O.K.

He sure didn't want the cabin burning down while he was gone. He went back outside and started the truck. He put it in gear and drove down the lane. He slowed down as he drove out through one of the meadows. He wanted to get as close as he could to where he left the deer, so he wouldn't have to carry it a long way. He learned his lesson the day before. That deer was heavy and he wasn't as young as he used to be.

Chuck drove through some brush at the end of the meadow and followed the ruts until he entered another meadow. At the other end he turned the truck around, backed it up and stopped near the edge of the grass and got out. He got the tarp out of the back of the truck and walked into the woods to the spot he left the deer. There it was, hanging just like he left it. He sure was glad to see it all in one piece.

Lost Feather

He laid the tarp under the limb and untied the rope, lowering the deer onto the tarp. Then taking hold of one end of the tarp he tugged and pulled the deer through the trees and up to where the truck was parked. He let the tailgate down, and slowly pulled the deer up and into the back of the truck. He quickly covered the deer with the tarp, jumped down onto the ground, and put the tailgate up. He sat down on the bumper and leaned back. All of that pulling and tugging tired him out.

As soon as he breathed normally he got into the truck. He heard someone shoot, far off. He put his hands on the steering wheel and leaned his head on them. There were other hunters in the woods firing their rifles. He thought about firing his gun, but decided to wait until he got back to the cabin. But now he knew Jimmy wouldn't know if he fired or some other hunter.

Then Chuck sat up and smiled. Jimmy might be at the cabin. If he was he might need help. Chuck started the truck and drove back to the cabin and parked up under a shady tree. The deer would stay cool enough in the shade so it wouldn't spoil. He got out and rushed to the cabin, opened the door, and looked in. Jimmy had not been there. He went back outside and took his gun out of his coat pocket and looked at it. He didn't hear any more shooting, so he raised his gun and fired. Then he yelled, "Where are you, Jimmy?" There was no answer.

Every fifteen minutes he fired the gun. He was quickly running out of shells. It was past noon and there was still no sign of Jimmy. With only six shells left he decided to go out and look for him. "Maybe he hurt himself and wasn't able to get back to the cabin," he thought. "Why didn't I think of that before?"

Chuck put his last six shells in the handgun and hurried back into the cabin to his bedroom. He opened the

Lost Feather

closet door and took his gun holster off the hook on the back of the door. He put it on and placed his revolver in it. He pulled a lighter coat off a hanger, put it on, and hurried back to the kitchen.

He opened the refrigerator and grabbed some sandwiches, put them in his coat pockets, and headed for the door. He was going to do his best to find Jimmy. Two nights out there in the woods could be fatal. If he didn't find him before the sun went down, he'd go down to Ward and get some help.

The afternoon passed slowly for Chuck. He yelled Jimmy's name over and over as he walked through the woods. As the evening shadows started to settle in around him he went back to the cabin. When he got there he checked to see if Jimmy had come in. There still was no sign of him anywhere. He felt a sickness down deep inside that was starting to grow, and he couldn't do a thing about. He felt awful. What if a wild animal attacked him? What if he fell and broke his foot or leg? "I'll have to get help," he thought, "I can't do it alone."

Chuck ran to his truck, started it, and headed down the lane. He got to the end of the narrow road and sped up. As the road improved he drove faster until he was flying around the corners when he got into Ward. He wanted everyone to know he was coming.

He pulled up in front of a friend's house and slid to a stop. He jumped out and ran over to the house and up onto the porch. He ran up to his friend who stood on the porch. "Pete, I need your help!"

"What's wrong, Chuck?" his friend said. "What's wrong?"

"Pete, I've got a lost boy up at my place," he said, running everything together because he was so excited. Pete couldn't understand him.

Lost Feather

"Start all over, Chuck, and this time slow it down," his friend, Pete Steel, said.

"Well, I took this boy, Jimmy Warrior, up to my place yesterday," he said more slowly. "We went hunting and he shot a good size buck. He trailed it and lost it. I found it, but Jimmy got lost trailing the deer. I searched for him all yesterday, and all today, and I can't find him. I need help. Get some men together, Pete. I've got to find that boy. I'm responsible for him."

"Let's go inside, Chuck," Pete replied. "We'll phone everyone I know who might help." They hurried inside and Pete began calling his friends. Soon there was a crowd of people around his front porch. He then called the game warden to let him know about the lost boy.

When the game warden asked the name of the lost boy Pete let Chuck talk to him. When he picked up the phone he heard Dale Walton on the other end. "This is Chuck Miller. It's Jimmy Warrior," he said.

"Oh, no," came the reply from Dale. "Have you notified his grandparents, Mr. Miller?"

"No, I haven't; I'm sorry," he replied. "I hadn't even thought about them. Would you please do that for me? Tell Mr. Wilson at the garage also."

"I'll do that," Dale said. "Don't worry, Mr. Miller, we'll find him."

There was silence on the phone; then Dale continued, "I'll see you in about a half hour. Do you have a search party organized?"

"Yes," Mr. Miller said. "Pete Steel, here in Ward, has a bunch of his friends ready to go up to my place."

"Fine," Dale said. "There's not much we can do tonight, but we can start out tomorrow bright and early. Leave someone there who knows how to get to your place

Lost Feather

and you go on ahead. I'll get there as soon as I can. Is your cabin big enough for everyone?"

"I have two bedrooms and a big front room," Chuck replied. "I've got plenty of blankets, and a lot of room on the floor."

"Good," Dale replied, "I'll see you up at your cabin," and the phone went dead. Chuck hung up and went out onto the front porch.

"That's a good size deer you have in the back of your truck, Chuck," Pete said. "In fact, it's one of the biggest I've seen around here in some time."

"Jimmy, the boy who is lost, got it yesterday about noon," Chuck said proudly. He got lost tracking the deer."

"How about leaving it here? My wife will fix it up for you and the boy," Pete said. "That boy sure will be proud of it when we find him and show him what he got. What do you think?"

"That's a great idea, Pete," Chuck said. "Thanks."

"Glad to help," he replied. "Now what do you want us to do?"

"Dale Walton, the game warden, will be up here pretty soon," Chuck said. "He wants us to go on ahead and get everything ready for the search tomorrow. He wants someone to stay here and show him how to get to my place."

Pete looked around and then back at Chuck. "I'll stay here and wait for the game warden, Chuck. You take the rest of the guys along with you. I'll help my wife get that deer ready for that young lad."

"Thanks again, Pete," Chuck said, slapping him on his back. He lowered the tailgate on the truck and waited as two men grabbed hold of the buck and carried it inside.

He closed the tailgate and said, "OK, you guys, let's go. You two can ride up front with me and the rest will

Lost Feather

have to get in the back." The two who carried the deer inside came out and got in the back, along with two other men. Chuck started the truck and turned on the headlights. Darkness came while he was on the phone. He turned on the lights and backed the truck around, then headed back up the winding road through town, headed toward his cabin. He wondered how Jimmy was getting along.

He soon slowed down, turned left, and drove down the narrow lane that led up to his cabin. It seemed to take longer to get there when it was dark. Finally, the cabin came into the beam of the headlights. He pulled up in front and stopped. Everyone followed him into the cabin where he lit the Coleman lantern. One of the men went back out to the truck and turned off the headlights.

One of the men started a fire in the fireplace as the other men made plans for the manhunt the next day. Chuck went into the kitchen and looked in the refrigerator. There wasn't much to eat. He got all of the sandwiches out and put them on a plate. He placed the plate on the table and offered one to everyone. They all refused.

They ate before they got the call to come help. "You go ahead and eat, Chuck," one of the men said. "You're going to need all the strength you can get for tomorrow. Our wives will bring some food up here tomorrow."

Chuck sat down and ate four of the sandwiches. He did not realize he was so hungry. His mind wandered as he ate, thinking about everything that happened the last two days. It started out so well. He wanted it to end the same way, but now look at the mess he'd got everyone into.

It was getting late and Dale Walton hadn't shown up yet. "Where could he be?" Chuck wondered. He got up several times and looked out through the glass to see if there was anyone outside. When he saw there was no one

Lost Feather

there, he went back and sat down at the kitchen table and listened to the guys talk.

Chuck heard the sound of a car door slam and he jumped up out of his chair. He opened the door to find Tom Warrior and Bill Wilson coming up the steps, with Dale Walton close behind. A dog ran up the steps and between his legs. It was Mary's dog, Goldie. He watched as Goldie ran into the cabin and sat down under the table in the kitchen.

Mr. Wilson came up to Chuck and said, "Goldie wouldn't be left behind, Chuck. She won't get in the way, I promise. I'll see that she stays with me all the time. I just want her to be here because she likes Jimmy a lot, and she's also good at finding things. I thought she just might be able to track Jimmy and find him for us."

"That's a good idea, Bill," Chuck replied. He thought a moment. "It can't hurt, that's for sure. If she can track a scent like I've been told, we can use her. I'm ready to try anything that might help."

He turned and looked at Tom. Tears formed in his eyes and his lips trembled. He started to say something but Tom grabbed him by the arm. "I know, Chuck, I know," he said.

Dale Walton patted Chuck on the back as he went past him and over to where the other men were. He began talking to them about the plans for the next day. He took out a map and divided the men into groups. They would each search a separate area. That way each sector would be covered. He then suggested they all get to bed. The next day could be a long one, and they would need all of their strength. Everyone agreed and it wasn't long until everyone was either in bed, or under some blankets on the floor. Chuck had a good fire going and he banked it.

Lost Feather

Morning came real early the next day. Dale Walton, the first up, made sure everyone knew what each was supposed to do. He passed out police whistles to everyone there. No guns were to be fired. There were a lot of hunters in different parts of the mountains. The lost boy wouldn't know if they were hunters firing a shot, or someone looking for him. Whistles, on the other hand, would let hunters know they were there. That way they wouldn't get shot at, and the boy would know it was someone he could contact. Whistles were used successfully on many occasions when someone was lost in the woods.

Two cars pulled up outside, and the wives of the men came into the cabin. They brought a lot of food they cooked the night before and earlier that morning. Everyone sat down and ate. When they finished, the men went outside and the women started cleaning up and planning dinner.

It started to get light in the east. It wasn't long until the men went off, two by two, headed to their assigned part of the map.

The women stood on the porch and wished them good luck for finding Jimmy that day. Some of the women went back to Ward, but a few stayed to fix meals for the men. They would be coming in, resting, and going back out the rest of the day. Each knew what had to be done. If they needed to stay another day, the women who went back to Ward would come back and relieve those who stayed today.

As they stood on the porch, Goldie ran down the steps and up to Mr. Wilson. He forgot she was there. "Come on Goldie," he said. "Let's go find Jimmy." Mr. Wilson and Chuck walked together and Goldie ran back and forth ahead of them.

Lost Feather

CHAPTER XVI

Jimmy sat up in the cave and looked around. Almost every part of his body ached. He looked out of the cave opening and saw the sky start to get light in the east. He crawled out of the cave and stood up. He was cold. He slapped his arms around his body and jumped up and down. It warmed him up a little. "Come on sun," he said out loud. "Get up high enough so I can get warm. I'm cold."

He stopped slapping his arms and put his hands in his coat pockets. His left hand felt the two sandwiches. They were flattened out from his lying on them all night. The day before, fear drove his hunger away, but now he realized how hungry he was. He pulled both of them out of his pocket and opened one. It was an egg sandwich with tomato and lettuce on it. The tomato made one side of the bread mushy. He wouldn't have eaten it before, but now it tasted good.

He started to open the other one but stopped. "I'd better save it," he thought. He didn't know what lay ahead of him that day, and he might need it later. Sadly, he put it back in his coat pocket. He patted it gently and turned his eyes toward the east. The sun was about to come over the far mountains. He sat down and watched as the light from the sun crept down the higher trees on the mountains around him.

It marched along from treetop to treetop, then slowly, it moved across the valley, bathing everything in an orange glow. He enjoyed the quiet beauty as a sliver of orange came over the rim of one of the smaller mountains. It became larger and through the morning haze in the air, soon looked like half of a large orange.

The sun rose higher and higher and the morning mist evaporated. The orange ball turned to a white ball that

Lost Feather

he could no longer look at. The warm sunrays felt good as they warmed up his hands and face. His clothes were soon nice and warm, which caused his body to relax. He did not want to get up. It felt so good to just sit there in the warm sunlight. But he knew he had to get up and look for Mr. Miller's cabin.

He heard a distant rifle shot far to his right. He jumped up and ran down the little hill and across the valley. He ran toward the sound he heard. He entered a large stand of trees, slowed down, but kept up a good pace. He wanted to find Mr. Miller as soon as he could.

He soon came to a meadow. As he started across he heard another shot to his left. He turned and headed that way. Then he heard another shot up ahead of him. He stopped and wondered what was happening. Then he knew what was going on. It was deer hunting season and there were hunters all over the woods.

The thought of all those hunters firing their rifles made him sad. He realized there was no way he would know which shot would be Mr. Miller's. "And I'll have to be careful or someone might shoot me," he thought.

He sat down to figure out what he should do now. He didn't want to get too far away from where he started. There was no way of knowing if he wandered off Mr. Miller's property or not. If he had, no one knew it, and they'd think he was still close by. He'd have to look for signs that reminded him of Mr. Miller's property.

He spotted a high point and headed for it. He was very tired when he reached the top. He looked for a place to see a large part of the forest so he could spot anyone who might come by. To his right was a higher place, so he headed in that direction. He made his way through the woods and up a very steep incline. Some very large rocks

Lost Feather

stuck out here and there. It would be no easy task getting up there.

He rested a couple of times, and finally arrived at the top and found to his surprise that he looked out over the trees in all directions except behind him. A slight valley sloped down and away from where he stood on the rocks. He couldn't see through the trees but he saw a long way down the valley and along each side of its ridges.

He lay down on one of the rocks to rest. His mind was still alert but his body was tired. He'd have to rest to regain his strength. He thought of the sandwich in his pocket but shook his head. He wouldn't eat it until he had to. Rest was what he needed. He took off his coat and laid it under his head for a pillow. It felt good lying there in the sun. His eyes grew heavy and he quickly fell asleep.

As he lay there asleep, a man came out of the woods about halfway down the valley. It was Chuck Miller. He looked up toward the rocks where Jimmy lay. Slowly his eyes scanned the rocks, then, followed the other side of the valley's rim to the bottom. "Jimmy!" he shouted, as loud as he could. His voice was getting weak and the breeze was blowing down the valley. Jimmy didn't hear his call and he slept on.

Chuck wondered which way he should go. He looked up at the rocks again and wondered if Jimmy was somewhere up there. "Surely not. He would go down the valley, not up," Chuck thought. He headed down the small valley, looking back now and then at the rocks. He reached the bottom and disappeared into the trees, as if they swallowed him up.

Then he popped out again. He looked up at the rocks once more. The sun would be setting in a few hours and he needed to cover a lot of woods before it got dark.

Lost Feather

He promised himself he would come back and check the rocks later.

It was late in the afternoon when Jimmy awoke. It seemed every bone in his body ached. He needed to find a place to stay for the night. There were no caves in the rocks where he was now. He had to find something else. He wished he knew where the cave was that he stayed in the night before.

Jimmy carefully made his way back down the steep side of the rocky incline toward the small valley below. As he rounded a large rock, he lost his footing and slid a short distance into a large bush. He was glad the bush stopped him. He started to get out of the bush but felt some thorns sticking him in his left leg and arm. He gently pulled the branches back and limped out. He pulled some of the thorns off his clothes. He checked his arm and saw a small hole where a thorn stuck him.

He looked around wondering which way he should go. He shook his head as he looked around the area. Maybe he could find some kind of shelter down the valley. He started to climb on down the slope and stopped. He sprained his left ankle when he slid into the bush and it was already starting to swell. Slowly he made his way down the hill. At the bottom he limped along the right rim of the valley. He started looking for a place to sleep, or even some kind of shelter he could get under.

Jimmy now walked with a slight jerking motion. For some reason his left leg hurt. "Maybe it's caused from my sprained ankle," he thought. He leaned up against a tree and rubbed his leg to get relief. He kept walking around the rim but the further he walked the worse the pain got. He stopped and looked around for a stick to use as a cane to help him walk. If he didn't find something soon he'd have to stay in this area all night.

Lost Feather

He looked down in the valley and saw some branches from a dead tree. One of them looked like one he could use as a crutch. Now he had to get down there. He started down the incline and then stopped. "How would I get out once I was down there?" he wondered. He changed his mind and looked around at the trees where he was. There was nothing in sight that he could use. "If I just had a knife or an ax like the one I cut wood with back home," he thought.

Jimmy limped up to a pine tree and sat down with his back against the trunk. He hadn't gone very far from the rocks, when he needed to rest. His leg hurt really bad. He rubbed it and tried to work out the pain, but it seemed to make it worse. It looked like this was where he was going to spend the night. He looked around the area for something he could use to keep himself warm, but didn't see a thing.

There was nothing but a lot of pine needles all over the ground. They were around and under all of the trees. There was a large evergreen tree near by with its lower branches close to the ground. Jimmy made his way over to the tree and raked some pine needles into a large pile near the lower branches. He would use the pine needles to make a cover. "Maybe if I could get them under and over me I'd stay warm," he thought.

The sun soon dipped behind the mountains and the darkness slowly closed in around him. Jimmy continued the best he could to gather pine needles. He gathered all the needles he could from the trees he was under, but it wasn't enough. He then gathered the pine needles from under the nearby trees, making sure not to get needles that were wet. Only the ones that were on the top were dry. He crawled around using a stick to gather the dry needles from under other trees.

Lost Feather

The work tired Jimmy, but he knew he'd have to get it ready before it got too dark to see. He worked until he had all that he thought he needed. He then made a nice thick pine needle mattress. Next he piled a large mound of needles on both sides of his pine needle mattress. All he would have to do now was pull the two piles over on top of himself. It looked like it would work.

He looked out among the trees around him and smiled. There among the branches were twinkling lights. The moon was not up yet and the stars had that part of the world all to themselves. A slight breeze passed through the pine trees like a whisper bidding him goodnight.

Jimmy crawled under the branches. He reached into his coat pocket and pulled out his last sandwich. He opened it and found it was peanut butter and jelly. He hated peanut butter, but he was hungry enough to eat anything.

He took a big bite and the peanut butter stuck to the roof of his mouth. After a lot of hard work with his tongue he got most of it loose. He swallowed as hard as he could to get it out of his mouth. He wished it to be any other kind of sandwich but peanut butter. After a few minutes he felt some strength in his body. He even seemed to warm up some.

He looked at the sandwich and shook his head. He couldn't eat it all, so he wrapped what was left in the wax paper. He saved the rest for the next day. He'd already suffered enough that day without having to eat the rest of that peanut butter and jelly sandwich. He put it back into his coat pocket and began to pull the pine needles over himself.

He worked slowly so he wouldn't disturb the pine needles he already pulled over. He soon had something that looked like a cocoon over and around himself. His head was the only part that stuck out when he finished and he

Lost Feather

slowly warmed up nicely. His leg and ankle that were hurt began to relax and the pain almost went away. He was soon asleep.

His sleep didn't last long though. The cold crept in under the evergreen tree and now seeped through the pine needles. Jimmy turned every way he could think of to get warm, but he just got colder. He thought about getting out from under the pine needles, but knew that if he did he'd really get cold. His nose and ears felt like they were frozen and his leg and ankle hurt again.

Jimmy shivered and it seemed to make him feel a little warmer for a while. But he soon shook harder and harder for longer periods of time. When he stopped, he drifted off to sleep, only to be awakened by another shivering spasm. It drained all of his strength.

Another night in the woods passed slowly for Jimmy. When morning's first light came to the eastern sky, Jimmy was wide-awake. He found his eyes would only half open. Something caused them to puff up and water a lot. Even though they were sore, he could still see.

It became lighter around him and he saw the nearby trees. It wasn't long until he saw the rim of the valley a short distance away from where he lay. He decided he would follow the valley and see where it led. "I'll have to find my way out of the woods today," he thought. He just had to. He couldn't take it much longer. Everything was going wrong and he was so hungry and scared and hurting. And the cold---it was so cold, and his strength was almost gone. He just didn't know what to do.

He pushed the pile of pine needles off and rolled out from underneath the tree. He tried to get up but fell back down. He was too weak and his leg and ankle really hurt again. He needed something to give him strength. He remembered the peanut butter and jelly sandwich and took

Lost Feather

it out of his pocket and took the wax paper off. It didn't look too inviting, but it was all he had.

Slowly he put it to his mouth, took a bite, and chewed and swallowed it quickly. It was like warm water flowing throughout his body. Something in the sandwich relaxed him and gave him strength. He felt better all over. He took another bite and then another. He still didn't like peanut butter, but he ate to help him get his strength back. When Jimmy finished he struggled to his feet. The pain in his leg was still there. He could hardly walk.

He hopped a short distance and found a long stick he tried to use as a cane. He picked it up and saw it was a little too long. He hit it against the side of a pine tree and broke off a short piece on one end. He tried it and found it was just the right length. It helped take the weight off his bad leg and ankle.

Walking used up a lot of his energy, but he wanted to get as far down the valley as he could. As he neared the end of the small valley, he sat down on a rock and rested. He heard his heart pounding in his ears. After a few minutes the pounding slowly disappeared, but now he heard a different sound. He turned his head so he could hear better and tried to figure out what it was. It was a sound that he heard before but now he had a hard time remembering what it was. Then he knew---it was the sound of running water. He heard it bubbling and splashing as it ran over some rocks not far below.

Jimmy got up and headed down the mountain. The incline leading down to where the sound came from was quite steep, and he found it hard to get down there. The nearer he got, the louder the sound. It was music to his ears. This was the second day he'd been without water. He went around a large tree and saw the stream of water below him. He hopped down the slope towards the water as fast as he

Lost Feather

could. When he reached the bank of the stream he fell on his knees. He cupped his hands and drank the water as fast as he could.

He drank all he wanted and splashed some on his face. It felt so good. He got up and hobbled over and sat on one of the large rocks beside the creek. He bent over and cupped his hands, scooped up some water and washed his face. The cold water helped him get wide-awake. His mind that was cloudy most of the day was now alert. He felt so much better.

He sat and watched the water disappear through the trees. He knew he must now follow this stream. It had to come out somewhere below where there were people. He lay back on the rock and was soon asleep.

It was late in the afternoon when he awoke. A strange sound behind him caused him to turn over to see what it was. He saw nothing. Slowly he sat up. Again he heard it. He wondered if it was someone looking for him. He started to get up and see who or what it was, when he saw a deer come out of the trees up the creek. He froze.

It was a beautiful large doe. The wind was blowing toward him and she couldn't smell him. She stopped and looked up and down the creek. Nothing moved. She lowered her head and took a drink. She raised her head and looked around and Jimmy saw movement behind her. A smaller deer came out of the trees and ran up to her. It was her fawn. It hadn't grown very big, but it was beautiful. They rubbed noses and then both took a long drink. Then it ran out into the creek.

It wanted to play, so it danced up and down in the water all around its mother. It kept on kicking and splashing, jumping up and down wanting her to play with it. But she wasn't in the mood for play right then. She was

Lost Feather

thirsty. But the fawn wouldn't quit, and soon they were both splashing and dancing around in the water.

Jimmy just sat there with a big smile on his face as he watched the deer frolicking. Then suddenly they stopped and took a long drink of water. They made a beautiful picture with the mountain stream running by them. They came out of the water and the doe ate grass that grew on the bank of the stream. The fawn nibbled the grass here and there. It then stopped and drank some water and went and nibbled on some flowers.

Their eating reminded Jimmy how hungry he was. He longed for a tall glass of milk. If he had it, he would even eat another peanut butter sandwich. It might help to wash the peanut butter off the roof of his mouth and down his throat.

He smiled. "A glass of milk and a couple of oatmeal cookies would be even better," he thought.

Then the deer and fawn raised their heads and their ears stuck straight up. Something startled them. Jimmy heard nothing, but he could tell they did. Whatever it was, they were afraid of it. They turned and bounded away through the trees. Jimmy could hardly believe his eyes. They were there one second, and gone the next. He now wondered what they heard.

He moved over near some large rocks and listened, but still heard nothing. Then he heard something crack somewhere up the hill. Something was moving down the hill towards the creek. He stood there wondering what it could be. Then he smiled. It must be a buck deer that came to watch over his family that was there a few minutes earlier.

"It has to be something very large," he thought, "to make something crack like that." Jimmy peeked around the side of the rock to see what it was. If it wasn't a deer, he

Lost Feather

had to know. He had come this far without being attacked or hurt much; he surely didn't want something to harm him now. He quickly moved back behind the rocks for protection. He thought twice about wanting to see what made the noise. Then he heard some muffled sounds and a lot of brush cracking up the hill.

He stood still wondering what to do. He swallowed hard. What if it was that big black bear Mr. Miller told him about that was in this area. It had killed a large buck.

Or it could be a mountain lion. It too had killed a deer. It had to be something large to make all of that noise.

He wanted to see what it was but was too scared to look. He just stood there listening. Whatever it was, it came down the hill fast. He heard a lot of rocks roll down the side of the hill and splash into the creek not far away. Then he froze. He knew whatever made that much noise had to be large, and it was coming fast. It was not just a small noise now.

Things cracked and popped as it came crashing through the trees. The water also made noise. It roared and splashed as small and big rocks fell into it. "Maybe it is more than one bear or mountain lion," he thought. It got closer and closer, and then it was on the other side of the rock. Jimmy backed up as tight as he could get between a rock and the tree. Something tan came around the rock and leaped at him. Jimmy tried raising his arms to protect himself, but he was too late.

Lost Feather

CHAPTER XVII

The search parties went out early that morning. They soon found Jimmy's coat and thermos bottle under the tree where he left them. That was all they found until later that morning when one of the search teams found his rifle. It was not far from where Chuck found the deer.

The men who came back in to get new area assignments at the cabin were not happy. They knew Jimmy needed to be found that day.

The women fixed dinner for the men as they came in. They all should be hungry, but most of them were too keyed up to realize how hungry they were.

Tom Warrior's partner was Dale Walton. He felt that Dale would know what was going on all the time, and Tom wanted to be there when his grandson was found. He was disappointed when they came back early from the nearby area and they did not find Jimmy. Dale didn't want Tom doing too much walking. He thought the altitude might cause some problems for him at his age.

Tom knew he wasn't as spry as he once was, so he told Dale he didn't want to hold him back. He'd stay at the cabin and take the reports as they came in from all the different areas.

Dale agreed that they needed someone to do that. He would go back out into the woods and check on the teams. That way Tom would be close by when they found Jimmy.

Tom moved a desk up near the cabin door and got himself a chair. He found a pencil and some paper, and sat down at the desk. As the men came in, he put their names down and what areas they covered. When someone went back out, he wrote their name down and where they were going. It did him a lot of good knowing where everyone

Lost Feather

was searching. He got a map and checked off the areas that were already searched. Hopefully, that would prevent their covering the same area again, or missing one.

Chuck Miller and Bill Wilson came in about one o'clock. They took an area that was farther away than most of them. When Tom told them that Jimmy was not found yet, they looked at each other and shook their heads. There was a worried look on their faces as they made plans to go out again after dinner.

As they ate, Bill tried to keep Chuck's spirits up, but he found it hard. Goldie made her way under the table and sat down next to Bill's leg. She wagged her tail now and then to let him know she was there.

Chuck smiled, got up and went over and got a bowl out of the cupboard. He looked in the trash and found some bones the women put there when they cleaned off the plates. The bones had meat and gristle on them. He put them in a bowl and brought it over and put it on the table.

He added some meat off his plate to the bowl and placed it on the floor next to Goldie.

"Eat well Goldie," he said. "You've worked harder than the two of us this morning."

"She surely did," Mr. Wilson replied. "She covered three or four times as much ground as we did. If we had the energy she has, we would have covered all of the different areas by ourselves."

Chuck agreed as he sat down at the table. His mind wandered as he tried to think of where Jimmy might be. He was somewhere they hadn't thought of yet, some place they overlooked. "Where, oh where could that be?" he thought.

They finished eating and got up to go outside. Tom asked where they planned to go. Bill shrugged his shoulders, looked at Chuck, and waited for him to tell Tom. Chuck searched his brain for an answer.

Lost Feather

"I don't know right now, Tom," Chuck finally said. "I'm trying to think of some area I may have forgotten. We'll go outside and sit on the porch for a few minutes and clear our minds. I have a feeling he's somewhere we haven't even been close to." Goldie followed them out onto the porch. She lay down at Mr. Wilson's feet when they sat down on the steps.

Tom shook his head in agreement as he watched Chuck and Bill sit down on the porch steps.

They found they were in the way of people going up and down the steps, so they got up and walked around the cabin. They walked past the back door and Chuck looked toward some trees not too far away. Then he looked at Bill.

"You know, Bill, there's a small cave just on the other side of those trees. If Jimmy came that close to the house he would have heard the noise and come on in, don't you think?"

"I would think so, Chuck," Bill said. "He would have if he'd been there today. But if he was there earlier, he might not have known he was that close to the cabin. Let's go take a look."

They walked towards the trees and Goldie trotted along beside Bill. As they came close to the spot where the cave was, Goldie began running. Chuck and Bill followed her through the trees to the opening of the cave. Goldie sat inside the cave wagging her tail with her tongue hanging out. She looked like she was laughing at them. Chuck bent down and took a better look. He reached in and pulled out a piece of wax paper. It was the paper from one of their sandwiches. Chuck looked at Bill and grinned. "He was here, Bill," he said. "This close, and didn't know it."

Bill called Goldie out of the cave and grabbed her collar. He patted Goldie on the head and told her to sit.

Lost Feather

Goldie moved swiftly around his legs and sat down by his right foot. He took the piece of wax paper from Chuck and put it up to Goldie's nose. She smelled it and looked up at Bill. "Hunt!" Mr. Wilson said, pointing into the cave. "Find Jimmy, girl. I know you can do it. Find Jimmy."

Goldie ran into the cave and sniffed around. She came out and headed down the side of the hill. She ran with her nose to the ground. She lost the trail now and then, and ran in circles until she found it again. The trail grew cold but she kept finding it.

Slowly she led them to the rocky spot where Chuck almost went the day before. As they headed up toward the rocks he said, "I know now I should have come up here yesterday, Bill. I had a feeling he was up here but I called and looked, again and again, before I left. I should have come on up here."

As they reached the top, Goldie found a place where the ground was torn up down the hill to a thorn bush. "It looks like Jimmy slid into that thorn bush," Chuck said, pointing.

They followed Goldie on up to the flat rock. She sniffed all around it and looked up at them. "I'd say that he probably lay down here to rest, Chuck," Bill said.

Chuck nodded in agreement. They turned and looked down the valley below, and wondered which way he went from there. They didn't know but they felt good knowing he stopped here to rest.

Again, Mr. Wilson gave Goldie the command, "Hunt!" She sniffed around a little then she went down the hill. At the end of the rocks she turned right. They headed in the direction of the rim that ran around the right side of the small valley that Chuck went down earlier that day. If Jimmy went down before he had, he might have just missed him. If not, he could be anywhere down there.

Lost Feather

Before they went halfway around the rim of the valley Goldie turned and ran towards a large group of blue spruce trees. With them right behind her she ran up to one of the trees that had a lot of low hanging branches. She stopped and sniffed around the branches, then disappeared under one of the branches. She scratched around then came out with another piece of wax paper in her mouth.

"How in the world did it get under there?" Bill asked.

Chuck walked over and lifted one of the branches of the tree. "Well, what do you know, Bill," he said. "Jimmy made himself a bed out of pine needles. You can see where he piled the needles up on both sides. They probably didn't keep him too warm, but it was better than nothing. That boy has more spunk than I gave him credit for."

Bill looked at Chuck and smiled. "For a boy who came out here from the big city, I'd say he's got more than his share of common sense. He probably saved his life by doing that."

"That's right, Bill," Chuck agreed. "He stayed in a cave one night and under this tree last night. I'm sure he's alive. I feel a big load lift off my shoulders. He's somewhere around here, maybe up ahead of us, Bill. Let's go find him."

Bill called Goldie to his side. "We can't let him spend another night out here, Chuck. He might not make it if we do."

He knelt down beside Goldie and patted her. "You've done a real good job so far, Goldie. Now we have to find Jimmy. You find him for us." He stood back up. "Hunt, Goldie!" he said.

She went under the tree and sniffed around for some time. Then she crawled out from under the limbs and headed down the ridge that ran along the side of the valley.

Lost Feather

She didn't lose the scent like she did earlier. They could tell she was hot on the trail now. Chuck and Bill had to walk fast to keep up with her. They felt sure that Jimmy came this way not very long ago.

Goldie came to a big tree and sniffed the ground around it. She stopped, looked up at them and turned and trotted off into the valley. She quickly got ahead of them, which caused them to have to run now and then. They came to the end of the valley just as she ran into the woods out of sight.

Chuck and Bill followed her as fast as they could. They entered the woods and saw her running up ahead of them. They ran into branches and stumbled over rocks they couldn't see. They made a lot of noise as they followed Goldie.

Rocks rolled down the hill in front of them and splashed into the creek below. Bill and Chuck followed through the trees and underbrush. Limbs cracked and they grabbed hold of branches as they slid down the hill. Goldie lost her footing and slid down the embankment and landed in the creek.

Chuck and Bill stumbled as they crashed through the underbrush trying to keep up with her. They reached the creek embankment and came to an abrupt stop. Fortunately, they didn't fall over the embankment into the creek.

They saw Goldie running along the creek bank toward one of the large boulders. Then she leaped into the air at something and disappeared behind the rock. Fear started to rise in their minds. What did she jump at behind that rock?

What were they going to do? They had brought no weapons.

"Why didn't I put on my holster and pistol?" he thought.

Lost Feather

They slowly made their way along the creek bank towards the rock. Bill whispered at Chuck, "I sure hope Goldie was not tracking some wild animal instead of Jimmy. If she did, we are going to be in a lot of trouble when we come face to face with it."

They walked up to the large rock and stopped in their tracks. There sat Jimmy with Goldie in his arms. She was licking his face and he was hugging her and grinning.

"Jimmy!" Chuck and Bill yelled at the same time.

Jimmy jumped and almost dropped Goldie. He looked up and saw Mr. Miller and Mr. Wilson stood there looking at him. He let Goldie out of his arms, got up and limped toward them. He stumbled as he reached them.

They reached out and grabbed Jimmy, then patted him on the back. Jimmy's cane lay on the ground so they helped him over to a rock where he sat down. He looked up at them and smiled.

"Boy, am I glad to see you two," he said.

"Not any more than we are to see you, Jimmy," Chuck replied.

Goldie jumped into Jimmy's lap again and looked up at him. She wanted some attention, too. Jimmy reached down and patted her, then grabbed her and hugged her real tight.

"She led us to you, Jimmy," Mr. Wilson said. "I've always been proud of Goldie, but never any more than right now. She earned her keep today."

The three of them patted Goldie to show their gratitude. Chuck looked at Jimmy. "How strong are you, Jimmy? Can you walk?"

"Not very good, Mr. Miller," he replied. "I kind of sprained my ankle and got some kind of a cramp in my leg yesterday, and it caused a lot of problems in my walking. I got so tired yesterday afternoon that I had to take a nap. It

Lost Feather

felt better this morning but the pain came back. Not as bad as it was before, but it caused me to limp when I try to walk. It was hurting real bad when I stopped here for a drink, so I sat down and rested"

Mr. Wilson took a candy bar out of his coat, took the wrapper off, and handed it to Jimmy. "Here's something for you to snack on right now, Jimmy," he said. "It will give you a little strength."

Jimmy took the candy bar and ate it in a few bites. "It surely is good to have something to eat," he said.

"We'll get you back to the cabin as soon as we can," Mr. Wilson replied. "I'd be hungry, too, if I'd been out here in the woods three days and only had two sandwiches to eat."

"How did you know that?" Jimmy asked.

"We found the wax paper from your sandwiches," Chuck said.

"Not us, really," Mr. Wilson said. "Goldie found them for us. That's how we found you, Jimmy. If you hadn't left those wax papers each place you stayed we might not have found you. They made good trail markers."

"How about that," Jimmy replied. "I sure didn't realize it at the time."

Chuck turned to Bill and asked, "Do you know the fireman's carry?"

Bill thought a moment. "I think so, Chuck. We grab each other's arms like a swing and Jimmy gets up on them. Then we can carry him like he was in a chair. Is that what you mean?"

"That's what I mean," Chuck said. "Let's try to get Jimmy out to the road downstream a short distance. It's about a half-mile down this creek. Then one of us can go get someone to bring a car. That way Jimmy won't have to walk too far. We don't know what his problem is, but we

Lost Feather

don't want it to get worse. It might just be a sprain, but it could be something else."

They grabbed each other's arms and made a cradle for Jimmy to sit in. Then they bent down and Jimmy got up and sat down on their arms. "It will feel good not to have to walk for a while," he thought.

It was difficult at first to carry Jimmy, but the two men soon got used to it. Occasionally, they stopped and rested because they, too, walked a lot lately and were tired from all the stress. It was slow but the end of their trip was not far away.

They came around a bend in the creek. Chuck said, "We'll have to climb up the bank of the creek. The road doesn't cross the creek. It runs along side it for a short distance."

As gently as possible, they carried Jimmy up the side of the creek bank and through some trees. They soon came out where Chuck said the road was located. It was only two ruts that ran through the trees. It didn't look like much of a road. They set Jimmy down near a tree and shook their hands to get the blood flowing.

"I'll go get the car," Chuck said to Bill. "If you can, just follow this road." He motioned in the direction they should go.

Without waiting for an answer, Chuck went through the trees and was soon out of sight. The road they now followed twisted and turned as it went through the trees. Mr. Wilson helped Jimmy walk the best he could. They came to a tree stump and sat down on it and rested.

"Let's sit here for a while, Jimmy," he said. "At least until I get my wind. I'm not used to this high altitude, let alone helping carry someone; not that I wouldn't carry you all the way back if I had to. It's just that I have to get my breath now and then."

Lost Feather

Goldie ran over and lay down in front of them and wagged her tail. Jimmy reached down and patted her. "I've always loved your dog, Mr. Wilson," Jimmy said. "She worked so well with Mary and me, and with the hawks. She helped us train all of our hawks. She's a wonderful dog, you know, and now she was the one who found me. I'll always love her."

Mr. Wilson looked at Goldie and then at Jimmy. "You know, Jimmy," he replied, "she loves you, too. When Dale Walton came by and told us you were lost up here in the mountains Mary asked me if I would go up with the others and try to help find you. When I walked out of the house, Goldie came out to the car with me, and she seldom ever does that. When I told her to go back inside with Mary she wouldn't go. I started to tell her again, when Mary suggested that I should bring her along. She said that Goldie would help me find you. Now what do you think about that, Jimmy?"

"Well, Mary knew what she was talking about, Mr. Wilson," Jimmy said. "I'm just glad you brought her. Boy, am I glad."

"Yes, Jimmy," Mr. Wilson said, grinning, "We all are. Even Goldie is happy she came along. Just look at her lying there smiling."

Sure enough, she looked like she was smiling.

Mr. Wilson stood up. "Let's walk a little," he said, helping Jimmy up. "The sooner we get to the cabin the quicker we can find out about that leg. I want you to get a good meal and a good night's sleep. I believe that will do you more good than anything else."

Jimmy got up and put all of his weight on Mr. Wilson's arm. He still had a bad limp. They moved along slowly in the direction Chuck went. With Mr. Wilson's help Jimmy's leg and ankle began to feel some better. The pain

Lost Feather

was still there but not as bad as it was earlier when he tried to put his weight on it.

Off in the distance they heard a car coming. Closer and closer it got until they saw it coming through the trees headed straight toward them. The car pulled up in front of them and stopped. It was the game warden's car. Jimmy saw it before at his grandparents' house. Dale Walton was driving.

Tom was the first out of the car. He ran over to Jimmy and gave him a great big hug. "I'm so glad to see you, Jimmy," he said, his voice quivering. "We were so worried."

Chuck and Dale came over to Jimmy. Dale shook his hand and asked, "Where are you hurting, Jimmy? Mr. Miller said you hurt yourself somehow and were limping pretty bad."

Jimmy rubbed the side of his left leg where it hurt. His ankle was still a little sore, too. He flinched when he touched a certain spot.

Dale saw Jimmy's face and knew it hurt. He knelt down and carefully rubbed the same area. There was a large knot there now. Dale felt the knot and gently squeezed it a couple of times. Pain from his squeezing, again showed on Jimmy's face, but he didn't say a word.

"It's not broken, Jimmy," he said, standing up. "I guess you bruised it somehow along the way. You've got a good size knot though. We'll get you back to the cabin and I'll check it out better. We need to get you cleaned up and get a good hot meal in you as soon as we can."

Tom and Chuck helped Jimmy over to the car and then into the back seat. They all got in and closed the doors. Dale started his car and took the microphone off the hook on the dashboard. He pushed a button on it and talked

Lost Feather

to another unit somewhere near by, telling them he picked up Jimmy and was headed for the Miller cabin.

He turned the car around and drove slowly back down the trail through the woods. It wasn't long until they came out onto the small lane that led to Mr. Miller's cabin. A couple more minutes and it appeared through the trees. There were a lot of people standing all around it.

Everyone smiled at Jimmy when he got out of the car. They told him they were glad that he was found. Jimmy thanked them as he limped up the steps of the cabin. Inside the cabin he sat down and looked around. He could hardly believe that many people came out and looked for him. It was strange he did not see any of them out there.

Pete came over and said, "I'm Pete Steel, Jimmy." He patted him on the shoulder. "That's my wife, Jean, in the kitchen. By the time you get cleaned up, she'll have some food cooked for you. You'd like that wouldn't you?" he asked with a smile.

"I sure would, Mr. Steel." Jimmy said, smiling back at him. "I would like that."

Tom and Jimmy went into the bathroom so he could check his leg. He wanted to see if he could find out what made it hurt. As Jimmy washed himself, they heard cars start up and leave. The people who worked so hard headed home. Chuck thanked each of them as they left. They told him they were glad they could lend a helping hand.

Tom discovered a thorn embedded in the side of Jimmy's left leg. It was swollen and turned blue around the thorn. He asked Jimmy if he remembered how he got it but he told him he didn't know.

With all that happened to him Tom was not surprised. It's hard to remember things when you're stressed and hurting. They went into the bedroom and Jimmy lay down on the bed. Tom hurried out of the

Lost Feather

bedroom and into the kitchen and asked Chuck if he had a first aid kit.

"Sure do," he said. He headed towards the bathroom with Tom following. He got the kit out of the bottom cabinet and handed it to Tom.

They hurried back to the bedroom where Jimmy sat on the side of the bed. Tom took out the small bottle of alcohol and a cotton ball. He looked at the thorn and wondered how he would get it out. He called Dale Walton in and asked him what he thought he should do.

Dale felt where the thorn was. "Ouch!" Jimmy exclaimed.

Dale pressed both of his thumbs down real hard on the flesh on each side of the swelling. Out popped a good size thorn, along with a yell from Jimmy. It left a small hole in Jimmy's leg. It bled, so Tom put some alcohol on a cotton ball and washed it off.

"Ouch!" Jimmy yelled and clenched his teeth.

"It needs to bleed," Tom said, smiling at his grandson.

"I think it has bled enough," Dale said, as he took a Band-Aid out of the first aid kit. He gently put it over the hole in Jimmy's leg. "Sorry I had to hurt you, but that thorn had to come out. That should fix you up, Jimmy. Your ankle doesn't seem to be broken, just sprained. You'll be your old self before you know it. Let's go get something to eat."

Jimmy got dressed and the three of them went back into the front room. "Tom found a thorn in Jimmy's leg," Chuck said. "Dale got it out, and I'm sure he'll be feeling better as soon as he gets some food."

Jean Steel walked over to him and motioned for Jimmy to follow her. "Come in here and eat some of this spaghetti and meatballs I fixed for you, Jimmy," she said,

Lost Feather

smiling. Dale Walton told me your grandmother said it is your favorite meal."

"Yes, ma'am, it is." Jimmy replied as he limped into the kitchen. He looked at the big plate of spaghetti in front of him. "When did Mr. Walton talk to my grandma, Mrs. Steel?"

"When Mr. Miller came in and told us you were found, Mr. Walton went out to his car and had a call put through to Mrs. Wilson," Jean said. She sat down across the table from him. "Your grandmother was there so he talked to her, too."

Tom came over and sat down at the table. He watched Jimmy, and his eyes showed the love he had for his grandson. Tom felt as if a heavy burden was lifted from his shoulders.

Jimmy started eating. He thought he could eat all of the spaghetti in front of him, but he filled up quickly. He sat back and picked up the large glass of milk beside his plate and drank it down. He put the glass down and wiped his mouth with the back of his hand. "That milk tasted great," he said.

His eyes slowly closed and his head nodded forward, then jerked backward. His stomach was full and his body was ready for some much-needed rest.

Tom got up and walked around the table where Jimmy sat. He got Jimmy to his feet and put his arm around his waist. He looked at his grandson and then at everyone at the table and smiled. Without a word they headed for the bedroom. He closed the door and gently helped Jimmy lie down on the bed, then covered him with a quilt.

Jimmy was asleep before Tom told him to sleep well. He gently tucked him in and stood and looked at him. "My heart is so full of joy, Jimmy. Just knowing you are all right," he said softly.

Lost Feather

There was a rocking chair in the corner of the room. He pulled it over to the side of the bed and sat down. He wanted to be there if he woke up and needed something. He would watch his grandson all night.

He looked out the window as the last rays of light lit up the tops of the tall pine trees. Then he saw something drifting toward the ground. It was snowflakes. Tears came to his eyes as he thought of what could have happened to his grandson if they had not found him when they did. "Thank you, Lord," he said softly. "Thank you for answering my prayers."

Lost Feather

CHAPTER XVIII

It wasn't long until Tom fell asleep in the rocking chair. Later that evening Chuck looked in on them and saw they were asleep. He covered Tom with a blanket and left without waking either of them.

Early the next morning before Dale Walton left, he looked in on them. He smiled when he saw they were still asleep. He quietly closed the door and walked into the kitchen where Chuck, Jean, and Pete Steel sat at the table.

"I've got to go," he said. "Tell Jimmy and Tom that I'll drop by their place and see them as soon as I can." He walked over to the door, opened it and looked at the ground all covered with snow. "I'm sure glad we found that boy when we did. I'll see all of you later."

"I'll walk you to your car, Dale" Chuck said. They shook hands. "Thanks again."

"You are welcome, Chuck," he said. You know it's just my job, but it's times like this that it's the best job around. Jimmy is a great kid, but you already know that."

"Yeah," Chuck said, looking down at the snow. "I sure do."

Bill Wilson walked up and Goldie trotted beside him. "I think I'll ride back with you, Dale," he said, "if it's all right with you."

"Sure," Dale said. "You and Goldie hop in. I'm glad to have your company."

Bill turned around and looked at Chuck. "It sure was great the way it all worked out like it did, Chuck." They hugged, each knowing deep inside what could have happened if Jimmy hadn't been found yesterday.

He walked around his car, opened the door and waved at the Steels, who came out onto the porch. He got

Lost Feather

in his car, started the engine and backed up. He turned the wheels and waved as he drove off.

Chuck walked back to the porch where Pete and Jean were. He looked around the outside of the cabin. "You know, everything around here looks better today than it has for some time," he said grinning. "Look at that sun coming up through those beautiful trees, turning the snow orange with its rays. I love this place. Yesterday I wondered if I'd ever feel that way about it again. If something bad happened to Jimmy, I think I would have sold the place and I would have never come back."

"But it turned out real good, Chuck," Pete said. "Just the way it should. We're going to go, too. Remember to come by and get the deer Jimmy shot. It will be ready when you get there."

"That's right, Pete. I'd forgot all about that deer," Chuck said. "Jimmy's sure going to be proud of that."

"He has a right to be proud," Pete replied. "That's a good size deer, Chuck. Everyone around here will be talking about all of this for years. We'll see you later."

They got in their car and drove away. Chuck watched them disappear through the trees; then he turned and went inside the cabin. It was so quiet. There was so much hustle and bustle the last couple of days, the quiet now seemed strange.

He went in to see if either Tom or Jimmy was awake, but they were still asleep. He closed the door as quietly as he could, but it made a clicking noise when it shut. Tom's eyes opened. He looked around to see what the noise was. He realized where he was and looked over at Jimmy, but he was still asleep. He nodded his head with pride, and love showed in his eyes for his grandson as he sat and looked at him.

Lost Feather

"The name Strong Feather Jimmy Warrior that Chuck gave you surely fits you," he thought. To be able to survive in the woods takes a lot of strength, not only physical, but also inner strength. Many people get lost in these mountains, but few survive more than a couple days in the winter. You survived three days."

"I'm proud of you," he said out loud.

Tom looked out the window. Sunlight played through the treetops. Beams of light stretched from the tops of the pine trees to the white snow on the ground. They looked like giant's playground slides. What a wonderful way to awake to a new day. He was glad to be alive. A new inner strength flowed through his body. He was old, but not too old to enjoy the beautiful life he had.

The rocking chair squeaked as he rocked back and forth and enjoyed the view from the window. Tom was so engrossed he didn't notice the squeaking, but Jimmy did. He rolled over and opened his eyes and looked around the room. He smiled when he saw his grandpa sitting and rocking. He watched Tom for a minute, then turned and looked out the window. The rays of light were so beautiful he gave a little gasp.

Tom turned quickly to see what was wrong. When he saw Jimmy looking at the view he enjoyed, he reached over and patted him on the foot and smiled.

Jimmy started to sit up but the pain in his leg stopped him, so he lay back down. "I'll have to get out of bed a little slower," he thought.

Tom got up, came over to the bed, and pulled the quilt cover off. "I saw the look on your face. Your leg still bothers you. We'll get you home as fast as we can so your grandma can put some salve on it, just like she did on my spider bite, remember? She'll soon have you feeling good again."

Lost Feather

Jimmy remembered how his grandma put salve on his grandpa, and on wounds his hawk made on his arm. Now she'd do the same for his leg. She might even show him how to fix the salve and teach him the other things she told him she would someday.

Tom got up and helped Jimmy get out of bed. They headed for the kitchen and something to eat. Chuck heard them talking in the bedroom and knew he probably woke them when he shut the door. He started cooking breakfast, and by the time Tom and Jimmy came into the kitchen the biscuits, eggs, and bacon were almost ready. The smell made Tom's and Jimmy's mouths water.

A good breakfast soon made them feel much better. Tom checked the place on Jimmy's leg again and it didn't look any better.

"We need to get him home, Chuck," Tom said. "Alice needs to get that poison out of his leg as soon as possible. Can we leave now? I'll come back up here with you later, and help straighten the cabin up."

"Sure," Chuck said. "We'll have to stop at Pete's house in Ward and pick up Jimmy's deer. Pete said it should be ready when we come by. After that, we can drive straight home."

"What deer?" Jimmy asked, puzzled.

"Oh yeah, that's right," Chuck replied. "You two don't know about the deer. Well, it's the one you shot the other day. I trailed it, hoping to find you, but I found the deer and not you. I don't know what happened to cause you to miss the trail but you missed it somehow. After I looked for you awhile I went back and fixed it and hung it in a tree.

"I left it there and went looking for you again, so I didn't get back to it until the next day. It was in the back of the truck when I went down to Ward for help. Pete and

Lost Feather

Jean offered to prepare it for us and get it ready to put in your freezer. He told me this morning that it will be ready when we get there."

"Wow!" Jimmy exclaimed.

"It had twelve points," Chuck continued, looking for some reaction from them. "That's a big deer, Jimmy. As Pete said, it's not the biggest one that came out of these woods, but it's probably the biggest one shot on this place. You can be proud of it."

Jimmy felt like shouting. Then he remembered. "I lost your rifle, Grandpa," he said sadly.

"Don't worry, Jimmy. They found it yesterday," Tom said.

"That's great, Grandpa!" Jimmy almost shouted. "I felt bad about losing it. It meant so much to me, but I must have dropped it when I got scared. I looked all over the place for it but couldn't find it."

Tom went over and picked up the rifle and Jimmy's coat. "Here's your new coat, too," he said. "Let's go see your grandma, Jimmy."

They all got up and headed for the door. Chuck opened it and let them go out first, and then he put the padlock on the door. When Jimmy and his grandpa stepped outside they saw the beautiful snow on everything. They stopped on the porch and looked at it. "I sure am glad I'm not out there in the mountains today, Grandpa."

"Yes," Tom said slowly, not moving. He knew how fortunate they all were.

With the padlock once again on the front door, Tom helped Jimmy walk to Chuck's truck and helped him get in. The warmth of the sun's rays melted most of the snow off the truck. Chuck started the motor and backed up. He turned the steering wheel and drove down the lane they

Lost Feather

came up four days earlier. Soon they were on the highway headed for Ward.

They made a quick stop in Ward at the Steel's house to pick up the deer. They saw several people who helped in the search for Jimmy. Good-byes were said again, and they soon headed down Left Hand Canyon. It wouldn't be much longer and they would all be back home.

They pulled up in front of the Warrior house and Tom was the first one out. He helped Jimmy out of the truck. Mary came running out the front door. She threw her arms around Jimmy and gave him a big hug.

"I'm so glad to see you're all right!" she exclaimed. "We were so worried about you. How do you feel?" she asked. The words came so fast he waited to answer her.

"I'm feeling good," Jimmy said, blushing a little. Mary hadn't hugged him like that before and he didn't know how to take it. "My leg hurts where I had a thorn in it. We got it out but it still hurts. My ankle hurts some, too."

Alice followed Mary out to the truck and now stood by the truck door waiting for her hug. She heard what Jimmy said, and without a word or a hug, she rushed back into the house. By the time Jimmy got up the steps and into the house she had some salve made. It was only then that she gave him a big hug. She asked Tom and Chuck to help him to his bedroom. When he sat on his bed she asked everyone to leave.

They looked at each other sadly, wanting to stay and see what she did. Tom thought he knew, but he hadn't been too rational when she doctored him for the spider bite. They all went out the door, and Tom closed it softly.

Alice asked Jimmy to take his trousers off. Jimmy hesitated. "I'm a young man now," he thought. Again she spoke, only this time she told him and he didn't hesitate. She made him lie down on the bed with his swollen leg

Lost Feather

toward the outside of the bed. She took the Band-Aid off and looked at the place where the thorn punctured the skin. It was all red and swollen. It started to change colors around the outside of the wound. Alice touched the discolored area with a flat bladed knife. Jimmy jumped. The cold of the knife against his skin caused him to groan in pain.

"It has to be opened up, Jimmy," Alice said. "We have to get that poison out of it right now; then I'll put some salve on it. The salve will draw the rest of the poison out. It's going to hurt." She took a small package from her apron pocket, unrolled it and handed Jimmy a small round stick. "Put this between your teeth," she said.

He put it in his mouth and bit down on it. Grandma said it was going to hurt; he believed her.

She took a needle from the package and with it she quickly pulled the scab off the wound. Jimmy groaned and bit the stick real hard. He looked around at his leg and saw a trickle of blood and pus start running from the opened wound. She gently squeezed it a couple of times. She took a soft cloth and wiped the blood off his leg. It wasn't long until the bleeding stopped.

Next she took the knife and dipped it into the bowl with the salve in it. She gently spread it in and around the wound. Jimmy felt the salve start to work. It was a strange, drawing kind of feeling on his skin. His grandma waited a few minutes, then, wiped off the excess salve with another clean cloth. She looked at the wound carefully and smiled at Jimmy.

"It's going to be fine, Jimmy," she said.

She repeated the operation over and over until she was sure she had gotten out as much of the poison as she could. She put a small amount of salve on the wound and

Lost Feather

placed a bandage over it. She put everything back into her bag and sat down on the side of the bed and looked at him.

"You know, Jimmy," she said. "It's time for you and me to give each other another big hug. I've prayed every minute since I heard you were lost that I'd be able to sit here and hug you again."

Jimmy sat up and they hugged each other for a long time. Slowly Alice turned loose of him and he lay back down. She pulled the quilt up that she folded earlier at the bottom of his bed, and covered him up. "Don't worry about missing school, Jimmy," she said. "You'll be well enough to go Monday."

Jimmy forgot about school. Too many things happened. "What day is it, Grandma?" he asked.

"It's Saturday," she said, smiling. "You were lost three days."

Jimmy thought for a moment. "Did you know I got a deer, Grandma?" he exclaimed.

"Yes," she replied. "I'm proud of you. They told me how big it is, too. We'll have plenty of meat this winter, thanks to you, Jimmy."

"You knew why I wanted to get a deer, didn't you, Grandma?" Jimmy asked.

"Yes, Jimmy, I knew all the time," Alice replied.

Jimmy was silent for a while. Alice looked at him. "You're wondering if I plan to teach you how I make the salve and about the other things that I said I'd teach you some day. Well, Jimmy, when you said the things you did to your grandpa when you were mad, that caused me to wonder if it was the right time. You earned the right to know, but then you lost the right when you lost your temper."

"You're young, Jimmy, and I'm not young any more, but I'll have to wait and see. It's something I cannot

Lost Feather

give to just anyone. If you're the one, we'll both know it someday. Give me a little time, and I'll know for sure if it's to be you or someone else."

Jimmy smiled up at her. His grandma always seemed to know what he thought.

"Get some sleep now, Jimmy," she continued. "The salve takes out the poison, that's true, but it also takes away the pain and helps a person to rest better. You need a lot of rest. Close your eyes." She stood up as Jimmy closed his eyes, and he was soon asleep.

Jimmy awoke the next morning by someone knocking on his door. He opened his eyes and looked around. He was in bed with his pajamas on. He didn't remember putting them on. He started to sit up. The door swung open and his grandparents came in, followed by the Wilsons. All of a sudden his bedroom was full of people. He sat up and rubbed his eyes and looked around at all of them.

"How's your leg feeling today, Jimmy? His grandma asked.

Jimmy reached down and felt it. "It feels great," he said. "There's no pain in my leg at all. It's healed."

"Not all healed, Jimmy," she replied, "Just a lot better than it was. Get up and see how it feels. Walk over to the window and back."

Jimmy got up and walked to the window, then back to the bed and sat down. He only had a slight limp. "It hurts a little bit, Grandma."

Tom walked over to the desk and picked up the feather holder. He took a beautiful black and white feather out of his shirt pocket and put it in the hole next to the white feather. Without a word, he set it back down on the desk and turned around. He smiled and winked at Jimmy.

Lost Feather

Jimmy winked back, then looked at the feathers and smiled.

Just then someone tapped on the door. Chuck Miller came in smiling at everyone in the room. His hands hid something behind his back as he walked in. "What is Mr. Miller going to do now?" Jimmy wondered.

"How is Jimmy doing today?" he asked.

They told him how Jimmy just walked to the window and back with only a slight limp. Everyone bubbled over with happiness.

Chuck motioned to someone standing out in the hall. It was his wife Jackie. She came in and handed him something. He turned and looked at Jimmy. "I have something for you," Chuck said. "I sure hope you like what I did."

He turned the plaque around so Jimmy could see. It was in the shape of a cocker spaniel dog and it had been painted a golden color like Mary's dog Goldie, and in beautiful letters were the words, "LOST FEATHER." Jimmy looked at it with his mouth open.

Jimmy smiled real big as he looked around the room at everyone. "I sure am glad Goldie found this Lost Feather," he said, pointing to himself. "I'll always be grateful to her."

Chuck handed him the plaque and smiled.

Jimmy stood up and hugged him. He walked over to where the other plaques hung on his wall. He held the new plaque under "STRONG FEATHER JIMMY WARRIOR," the first plaque Mr. Miller made for him. He turned and looked at each one in the room then started speaking softly.

"No matter how strong a person is," he said, "I now know they can get lost. I realize anyone can get lost no matter how strong they think they are. I found that I need

Lost Feather

each one of you every day. Without all of you as my friends, I would be lost every day."

Jimmy stopped and smiled, then said, "But if I ever get lost again, bring out Goldie, the greatest tracker under the sun, to find me. She'll forever have a special place in this LOST FEATHER'S heart."

The Feather Book Series

<u>Strong Feather</u>, the first in the series of the Feather Books, is a story about a young American Indian boy, Jimmy Warrior, and the problems he encounters while living in the northeastern United States. He moves to Colorado to live with his grandparents and begins coping with the challenges presented to him, while becoming very attached to a hawk. He makes several new friends in Colorado, as well as being briefly reunited with his father. The two have something in common which draws them even closer. Read about Jimmy's thoughts as an adolescent, while he tries desperately to become accustomed to his new home and cultural surroundings.

<u>Lost Feather</u>, the second in the series of the Feather Books, continues the story of Jimmy Warrior in his new home of Mercer, Colorado. He learns there are interesting things to do in a place where he thought life was just one boring day after another. Read about the hawk Jimmy and his young female friend, Mary Wilson, trained to hunt. In addition to becoming a tremendously accurate and skilled hunter, Jimmy's hawk, Lady Samson, wins several area contests. Through Jimmy's eyes, experience what life for a young boy is all about as he learns from his grandparents and friends what real love and sacrifice means.

The third book in the Feather Series, <u>Soft Feather</u>, (to be published) continues young Jimmy's adventures when he is given two homing pigeons.

The first two books, <u>Strong Feather</u> and <u>Lost Feather</u>, retail for $ 17.95 each in several national chain bookstores, as well as being available on selected Internet sites. Booksellers may order through their usual distribution channels.